The Old Coaching Inn

Daphne Neville

PublishNation
www.publishnation.co.uk

Other Titles by This Author

Prologue

The Old Coaching Inn was built in the early seventeen hundreds on a sloping stretch of road known locally as Wreckers' Hill. A granite construction with uninterrupted views of the sea it served the needs of travellers as they crossed the remote Cornish landscape. In its heyday the clatter of horses' hooves, and the rumble of cartwheels as they crossed the cobblestoned courtyard, were to the landlord of the day welcome sounds, for once the passengers had disembarked and the horses were led to the on-site stables for overnight care, the travellers would enjoy his hospitality inside the cosy Inn where the friendly atmosphere rang with laughter and loud chatter as the travellers ate, and quenched their thirst with real ale until need of sleep drew them to the guest rooms on the upper floor.

For decades the Old Coaching Inn thrived throughout the year but gradually the railway superseded the horse and carriage and by the mid-eighteen hundreds it was possible to travel from London to Penzance by train. For several years the establishment struggled to survive but then along came the motor car and holidaymakers visited Cornwall in their droves giving the tavern a new lease of life. But the revival was short lived, for in the mid-nineteen sixties everything changed yet again and the future once more looked bleak. A newly constructed road five miles inland meant very little traffic had need to drive along the narrow country lanes and over the hill where the Old Coaching Inn stood. Porthgwyns, the nearest village, was five miles away and no houses stood between it and the Inn. The sandy beach at Quignog Cove over which the hostelry looked, although attractive, was extremely difficult to access on foot and offered none of the amenities that visitors to Cornwall expected in the twentieth century.

The family who had owned the Inn for generations and who had endured hardship during the early days of the railway, sold the premises shortly before the new road was finalised to avoid a second period of suffering. The subsequent licensees tried hard to make a living but eventually they too accepted defeat, sold up and bought a cottage in Porthgwyns. After that the Inn had several owners; the last was Jacob Smythe, a businessman who, enticed by the notion of running a public house by the sea bought the premises in 1977. But he soon found the tavern was not a viable proposition because the law having changed ten years before making drink-driving a criminal offence meant very few people crossed its threshold. Realising he was beaten he applied for and received planning permission to turn the business into a private dwelling but long before the work was completed he fell into dispute with the builders; the work ceased and he abandoned the project, returned up-country never to set foot in Cornwall again.

Over the ensuing years, the Old Coaching Inn stood empty. Ivy crept along the old stone walls, and brambles, grass, bindweed, nettles and wild gorse spread across the courtyard hiding in its wake every cobblestone and the trough where horses once drank. The gardens behind the building became a wilderness and the stables fell into disrepair. Slates slipped from the pitched roof of the main building and the old front door, battered by winter storms, hung from its hinges and creaked mournfully. The only aspect unchanged by time was the continuous motion of the sea as it tumbled and splashed around the base of the steep cliffs that surrounded the deserted sandy beach.

Chapter One

Charles Marcus Everson, known by family and friends as Charlie, woke early on the last full day of his stay in Cornwall and groaned. It was early-May, two whole weeks had gone and he was no nearer finding his future than he had been when he had first arrived. During his stay he had checked the internet daily for businesses for sale but so far nothing had taken his fancy and it didn't help that he was unsure how he wanted to spend the latter part of his life. Should he opt for a pub, a guest house, a shop, a small-holding? Or should he just buy a house and supplement his bank balance by writing or painting, or even growing and selling garden produce?

Charlie slipped from his bed, crossed the room and pulled back the plain blue curtains. The sun was shining across the decking in the hotel garden and a few of the guests were outside drinking tea and coffee in the May sunshine. Charlie took a shower, dressed, slipped on his lightweight jacket and went outside to join them.

"Any luck with your search?" Cissy Hosking, a cheery young waitress with whom he saw eye to eye, asked as she placed a teapot, hot water jug, cup, saucer and a jug of milk on the table where he was seated.

Charlie shook his head. "Regrettably not and as you know I had planned to go home tomorrow. Now I'm not so sure. On the other hand, perhaps fate is telling me that Cornwall isn't the right place for me after all."

Cissy tutted. "Oh no, don't give up, Mr Everton. People would be delighted to be in your situation, myself included.

Anyway, if you opt for something and it doesn't suit you can always sell it and move on to something else."

"True," Charlie agreed, "very true."

Charlie was in a very enviable position, for during the previous month he had won three and a half million pounds on the National Lottery. The money was now safely deposited with his bank and he was keen to put it to good use. He was forty-seven years of age, had been a widower since he was forty-three and his ambitions were few. He'd married young and never had a real career but had worked in shops and factories to earn money to provide for his wife and two children. With Rachel, his wife, gone long before her time due to illness, and his children, now grown up and having flown the nest, he lived alone in a rented house and his time was his own. Two days after learning of his good fortune he had handed in his notice at the supermarket where he worked having decided to move away and start a new life elsewhere. Cornwall was his first choice because he knew it was a county much loved by his late wife who with her family had enjoyed many holidays there during her childhood. It was also, Charlie believed, the county in which his maternal grandmother had been born and bred. However, Charlie never knew either of his grandparents on his mother's side of the family because both had died before he was born. But he firmly believed that his maternal grandmother had left Cornwall for Buckinghamshire after she married his grandfather. For that reason he was proud to claim he had a little Cornish blood.

After breakfast Charlie decided to go for a long walk to collect his thoughts and get some fresh air and much-needed exercise. He put on his most comfortable trainers and set off on a route he had not walked before, along the coastal path in an easterly direction. Despite it being a beautiful day he met no-one along the cliff path and so he sang in order to keep himself company and spoke to gulls gathered on rocks and a rabbit as it scuttled through the undergrowth. After three miles, his ankles felt the effects of walking along the rugged path, so when he glimpsed a road through a gap in a hedge, he crossed the corner of a field where sheep grazed, climbed over a five bar gate and then continued along the road in the same direction.

The narrow lane appeared to be little used. The old tarmac was littered with potholes and the overgrown hedgerows on either side gave the impression they were seldom trimmed. The grass verges were crammed with a mass of cow parsley, red campion, bluebells, and perfectly rounded dandelion clocks awaiting a puff of wind to break up the soft white balls and scatter the seeds. Charlie, paused, took in a deep breath, closed his eyes and relished the warm sun on his face; the location was idyllic...peaceful; as he listened to the sound of birdsong and the gentle splashing of the sea against the cliffs below, it was hard to imagine crowds of people, traffic jams and the hustle and bustle of urban life.

A mile further on and having encountered no vehicles, Charlie reasoned he ought to turn and make his way back to the hotel for he was walking uphill, the heat was making him thirsty and he longed to sit down in the shade with a pint of cold beer. But something urged him on. *I'll just carry on to the top and then I really will turn back.*

So that he could take in his surroundings and catch his breath, Charlie slowed his pace as he neared the bend at the top of the steep hill. On his left, seven tall conifers, slightly bent by the prevailing winds, stood in a straight line and stretched up towards the cloudless blue sky. On his right, waves gently splashed onto the sandy beach of a small cove. It was as he passed the last tree, marvelling at its height, that the Old Coaching Inn came into view. Charlie paused momentarily and then slowly walked towards it. His body experienced a strange tingling sensation, he felt light-headed and when he saw the estate agents' board indicating the property was to be sold at auction, his heart skipped a beat. Intrigued by its neglected appearance and isolated location he felt compelled to take a closer look and so crossed the area in front of the building where unbeknown to him cobblestones lay hidden beneath tufts of grass, wild gorse, nettles, brambles and ivy. Around the building, long grass was flattened where prospective purchasers and inquisitive persons had beaten a well-worn path. The windows were intact but filthy and in places the wood had rotted away. The door of the main entrance hung from its hinges and beyond it the rooms looked dark and gloomy. Some slates were missing from the roof and one of the chimneys had part-tumbled down.

On the left-hand side of the house behind the seven trees, the floor of an outbuilding which he assumed to be a stable block was littered with rubbish and long decayed straw. The back garden was overgrown and beyond a mass of brambles and nettles, apple blossom bloomed on trees in a neglected orchard. Yet, there was something magical about the place. It had character. It had charm and it was in desperate need of tender loving care.

As Charlie leaned back on the curved, wall edge of an old well, folded his arms and looked up to the sky, his green eyes twinkled with happiness and a huge grin crossed his face, for he knew that after two weeks of searching he had found his dream.

Chapter Two

On returning to the hotel, Charlie saw Cissy sitting on a bench outside the kitchen taking a tea break. Had she been alone he would have asked her what she knew about the Old Coaching Inn for he was puzzled as to why he had seen no mention of it before. Certainly it was not a viable business at present but it might have been once and could be again. Not that Charlie wanted to run it as a business. Not straight away, anyway. He saw it as a home where he might in the future do bed and breakfast for just a few weeks in the summer if he felt the need. Because Cissy was with two other girls he waved and instead of quizzing her, commented on the weather, went into the hotel by the main entrance and up to his room. With an hour to spare before the dining room opened for evening meals, he opened up his laptop and looked on-line for the agents handling the auction. To his surprise he found the Inn's location was on Wreckers Hill. Enthralled by the name he made a mental note to learn something of its history in the future should the Inn on Wreckers Hill ever become his home.

Eager for more information, Charlie was first in the dining room when it opened at six-thirty and because it was quiet he was able to question Cissy when she came in with freshly washed glasses to put on a shelf.

"The Coaching Old Inn, yes I know it. It's a right tip now but won't be for much longer. It's reckoned to be a forgone conclusion as to who will buy the place. Apparently Mickey Potts has had his eyes on it for years. He wants to turn it into a health farm. At least his missus does and she wears the trousers in that house."

Charlie's heart sank. "But surely it's not big enough to be a health farm."

"No, not as it is, but she wants to have what's there now as sort of oldie worlde accommodation and then build a huge complex in the grounds at the back. You know, a swimming pool, spa, a gym and stuff like that." Cissy chuckled. "She intends to call it The Old and the New or something like that."

"But that's criminal as it would mean destroying the orchard if they built out the back."

"Is there an orchard there then? I know there are trees because I went up there back in late March and had a quick look round. The trees had no leaves on then of course so I didn't know what they were."

"Well they're definitely fruit of some sort because they're currently covered in blossom. You ought to pop up there again, Cissy before the blossom falls because it's a magnificent sight."

"I'll do that then next time I have the day off. I've just remembered though that there's a field out the back somewhere that belongs to the Inn so perhaps Tracey is thinking of building on that in which case the orchard would be safe."

"Oh, I didn't know that so I suppose it makes their case even stronger then," Charlie felt downcast, "Would I be right in thinking that Mr and Mrs Potts have plenty of money?"

Cissy wrinkled her nose. "Not sure about that. I mean they might be intending to get a loan or perhaps they've recently had a good win on the Lottery too."

"Hmm. So what line of work are they in at present?"

"They're farmers, at least Mickey is. I don't think his missus gets her hands dirty. She's more the sort to waft around in high heels and I've never seen her without make-up."

"I see, so not quite a family affair then."

"Good heavens no. Far from it. I don't think Mickey knows a great deal about farming either but Sam says he's learning fast and is a good boss."

"Sam?"

"Sam Nixon. According to my dad, Sam's been working on that farm since he left school and what he doesn't know about agriculture isn't worth knowing. When the Potts bought the farm they kept him on and I've often heard Mickey say he's worth his weight in gold."

"So where is their farm?"

"Out at Treverry Cross which is a mile or so outside the village of Little Treverry. It's called Bracken Farm and has about six hundred acres."

Charlie scowled. "So why don't they start a health farm on their own land?"

Cissy shrugged her shoulders. "Don't know the answer to that but it might be because their land is not near the sea whereas the Old Coaching Inn has fantastic views and its own beach. Not that you can get down there very easily. In fact you'd probably need to abseil."

"Or maybe it's just that they can't get planning permission to build on their land. Green belt and all that."

"Could be. I've no idea although my gran might know."

Charlie's shoulders slumped. "Well whatever it looks like I'll have competition and if that's the case it'll go for a high price."

Cissy looked surprised. "You mean to say you're interested in the old dum...dum...place?"

"Yes, you might call me an old softy but I've fallen in love with it, but whether or not I'll get it remains to be seen. I can certainly afford it but if your Mr and Mrs Potts get wind of my good fortune they may well push the price up so that I pay over the odds."

"Then we must make sure that they don't find out," said Cissy with a cheeky wink. "If I'm honest I'm not too keen on the pair. They're not locals and have only been in the area for a few years. Some folks like them but they're not my type of people. They're too pushy and I probably know more about them than most. My mum does a bit of work for them, you see. You know, cleaning and stuff like that."

"Hmm, now that is interesting."

"Although to be fair she gets on alright with Mickey. Well, everyone gets on alright with Mickey, it's Tracey she's not too keen on. Mum reckons she's a bit of an airhead despite the fact she likes to let it be known that she went to a good school."

"I see, and it's just occurred to me that someone must be the Inn's current owner. Do you know who?"

Cissy shook his head. "No, not really. That is to say I don't know the people by name. But according to local gossip it's a joint inheritance from the bloke who tried to make a go of it back in the nineteen-seventies and then left it to rot. Mum told me about him years ago and if I remember correctly his name was Jacob something or other. Apparently because he couldn't make a go of it as a pub he decided to turn it from a business into a residence but then he fell out with the builders before it was done and moved back up-country in a huff. I'm told he was a crusty old bachelor and pretty well off, so when he died recently his entire estate went to various nieces and nephews and I suppose it's them selling it because they want the cash to share out."

"Hmm, that makes sense especially if they're young and live up-country."

Cissy glanced around to make sure they were alone and then spoke in a lowered voice. "Have you told anyone about your win other than me? Down here, I mean, not at your home."

Charlie shook his head. "No, actually I haven't."

"There's no problem then. I like you, Mr Everton, you remind me of my mum and so your secret is safe with me."

"Your mum!" spluttered Charlie. "In what way do I remind you of your mum?"

Cissy giggled. "You both have the same colour hair and lots of curls, freckles too, but I reckon it's the dimples in your cheeks. Mum has them as well and for that reason she always looks happy even when she's not."

Charlie smiled. "Well if I'm lucky enough to buy the Old Inn and I get to come and live down here then I shall look forward to meeting her especially if she's as charming as you."

"Well if you like a drink you're bound to see her as she works at the Harbour Lights."

"A pub I assume."

"Yes and it's a really good one. It's run by Greg and Grace. Greg runs the bar and Grace does the cooking. Her food is fantastic as she's a fully qualified chef."

"Is it here in Porthgwyns?"

"Yes, and believe it or not, it overlooks the harbour."

"Well if things go to plan I'll make the Harbour Lights my local."

Cissy looked up as several people came into the dining room. "Oh, getting busy now. I'd better do some work while you decide what you want to eat." She walked briskly off to the kitchen.

Charlie, realising he was very hungry after his walk, picked up the menu with a strong feeling of hope.

Chapter Three

The auction was scheduled to take place at a hotel in Truro in early June, and so with a week or so to spare, Charlie returned home so that he could discuss his plans with his family and friends. To his delight all were in favour and his sister, Laura said that, should he be able to buy it then, once the building and repair work was done she would come to Cornwall for a working holiday and help him with the finishing touches.

Charlie returned to Cornwall the day before the auction and stayed at the same hotel in Porthgwyns as on his previous visit. It was Cissy's day off when he arrived but when she saw him the following morning as he entered the dining room for breakfast she welcomed him back and said she'd have her fingers crossed for him throughout the morning.

Charlie left Porthgwyns just after ten and drove to Truro; on arrival he was dismayed to see the hotel car park full and vehicles parked nose-to-tail along the adjoining road. Hoping most were holiday makers and residents of the street he drove down another road and parked in front of a row of terraced houses. With only ten minutes to spare before the auction began he walked quickly back to the hotel and when inside followed directions along a deeply carpeted hallway to the conference room. Inside he was dismayed even further for there were at least forty people seated in rows waiting for the auction to begin. As he took a seat, Charlie consoled himself that most were probably after some of the other five properties to be sold that morning.

The Old Coaching Inn was the third Lot to be auctioned. As the second Lot was knocked down to its purchaser, Charlie said a little prayer and prepared to bid. Five people other than himself were in the running but as the price rose three dropped out within the first minute. The remaining bidders were a middle-aged couple who he assumed to be Mr and Mrs Potts and an older man alone with a careworn face and shoulder length obviously dyed hair. The bidding continued and Charlie heaved a sigh of relief when the lone bidder shook his head and dropped out leaving just himself and Mr and Mrs Potts. With the sound of his heart thumping in his head, Charlie cast a quick glance at the farmer who was wiping his brow with a red and white spotted handkerchief; his wife was on the edge of her chair egging him on, a look of sheer determination on her face. The bidding continued until Mr Potts with shoulders slumped finally shook his head thus causing his wife to thump his arm and run from the room clearly vexed with her left hand over her face. Charlie, much relieved felt his heart rate decrease. Thrilled to have won, he wiped his clammy hands on his trousers and then left his chair to speak with a member of the team handling the sale.

Exhilarated by his win and the fact he now had a focus in life, Charlie left the hotel with a spring in his step and to celebrate went to a pub for a slap up meal. He then returned to the hotel in Porthgwyns where he stayed for one more night. On hearing of his success, Cissy squealed with delight and wished him the very best of luck.

The following morning, Charlie returned home to Buckinghamshire where he gave notice for his rented home. He then sold items of furniture he didn't want and packed up everything else to be delivered to the Old Coaching Inn when the sale was completed.

Three weeks later, Charlie was informed by his solicitor that the purchase should be finalised by the end of the week and so he contacted a removal firm to book their services for the following Monday. Over the weekend he said goodbye to friends and neighbours many of whom he had known for as long as he cared to remember. He then cleaned the house that had been his home for twenty-six years from top to bottom.

On Monday morning the removal van arrived promptly at eight-thirty and by midday Charlie's possessions were all safely inside the lorry. After it was driven away, Charlie locked up his house and gave the keys to a neighbour who had agreed to return them to their landlord. He then climbed into his car, waved goodbye to his former home and set off for Cornwall.

Charlie and the removal van arrived at the Old Coaching Inn within minutes of each other and the removal men, hoping to get back to the office yard between midnight and one, placed the furniture in the driest part of the stable block for storage until it would be needed. By half past seven the lorry was empty and so after bidding the removal men farewell, Charlie went to his usual hotel in Porthgwyns where he had a room booked.

The following morning at breakfast, Cissy, delighted to see him back, gave him the names and addresses of tradesmen she knew. He then invited them along to give estimates as to the cost of renovations.

Meanwhile, because the Inn was not fit to live in and because Charlie wanted to be on site, he bought a six berth caravan and had it positioned in the grounds at the back of the building. In it he had electricity installed and water was available from an outside tap. Happy that everything needed was at hand, he then left the hotel for the last time and took up residency on Wreckers Hill.

The following day, in need of groceries Charlie went shopping. While in a supermarket he stopped in the drinks aisle and contemplated whether to buy wine, cider or both. As he was reading the label on a wine bottle, Mickey Potts approached him. He offered his hand to shake and smiled broadly. "Good afternoon, Mr Everton. Lovely to meet you at last. I don't know whether or not you remember me but I was at the auction for your place."

"Of course, I remember you, and your good lady wife."

The two men shook hands.

"I trust you're settling in well."

"Very well, thank you. The house isn't fit to live in of course so I've bought a caravan for the time being and I'm rather liking it."

"I heard you'd done that. A bit of camping's nice this time of year but not so good in the winter when the old wind howls."

"I'm sure you're right but the builders are due to start soon so hopefully the house will be habitable long before the bad weather comes. Might be a problem if it's not though because the kids want to come down for Christmas."

"You have children. I didn't realise that."

"Yes, I have two, a son and a daughter. Both are grown up: Dan's a music teacher and Flo is at uni."

"And you're a widower, I believe?"

"Yes, sadly I lost my wife four years ago to illness."

"I'm sorry to hear that, Mr Everton. Four years is a long time to be on your own. Assuming you are still on your own, that is."

"Yes, I am but I'm used to it now."

"Maybe, but everyone needs a soulmate, someone to love, someone to share their problems with. As I like to say, where there is love there is happiness."

"That's a nice thought and thank you for your condolences but please call me Charlie. Everyone else does."

"Of course, Charlie, and as you probably know, I'm Mickey."

Charlie having decided it was more thirst quenching, picked up a case of cider and placed it in his trolley.

"Ah, well done, you've got my favourite there," Mickey pointed to the same drink in his trolley.

"Well, I'm a great believer in supporting homemade products especially cider now I live in the West Country."

"Yes, yes of course," but the smile vanished from Mickey's face and he looked uncomfortable. "Well actually you mentioning living in the West Country reminds me why I've come over to speak to you." He took in a deep breath, "You see, it's Tracey. She had her heart set on owning your place. Wants to start up a health farm or some such nonsense and she's gutted I lost the auction. And as if that's not enough she's still going on about her phone. She's lost it, you see. Been missing a while, in fact I'm pretty sure she lost it on the day of the auction. You'd think she'd be over it by now but she's still moaning despite the fact I bought her a new one which is even better and more up-to-date than the other. But no she's still not happy. Says it's because she's lost all her contact numbers. Women, eh? Anyway, to try and cheer her up I'm prepared to sell off some of my land and offer you fifty grand more than what you paid for the Inn. How does that grab you?"

Charlie was taken aback because even when taking into consideration what he had so far laid out it was a very good offer. He bit his bottom lip. "I'm really sorry to disappoint you, Mickey, and I'm sorry that your wife lost her phone but the Inn is not for sale. I love my new home and all the money in the world would not entice me to leave it."

Mickey patted Charlie's back. "I guessed you'd say that and I quite understand but at least I tried." He looked relieved. "Meanwhile, I reckon you've been a widower long enough and so I hope you find a nice lass down here to keep you company. In fact, I'll keep my ears to the ground for you because you don't want to be on your own in a lonely place like Wreckers Hill. It can get quite spooky up there especially when the old mist rolls in."

"Thank you." Charlie wanted to object but thought better of it.

"You're welcome. Anyway, best get off now. Always plenty to do on the farm."

Two days later, Charlie received a crate of cider with a card from Mickey saying that if he changed his mind the offer still stood. His email address was included and he had drawn a smiley face with a sun hat on its head beside his name.

A team of tradesmen began work in early August and by the end of September parts of the Old Coaching Inn were ready for use, mainly downstairs where Tom a plumber had given priority to renovating a downstairs toilet and creating a shower room so that Charlie had somewhere to perform his ablutions other than in the cramped conditions of the caravan. The building also had a new roof and the chimney was repaired but because the property was Grade Two listed the windows could not be replaced unless like-for-like. Because of the Inn's exposed position, Charlie would have preferred double glazed windows to minimise heat loss but instead had the originals repaired by Pat, a talented chippy who specialised in restoration work. Likewise, the door once it had been sanded and new hinges fitted was as good as new. Inside, several floorboards badly damaged by damp and woodworm had to be replaced. Some of the ceilings in the upstairs rooms had to be ripped out and replastered due to rain damage from the leaking roof. New units were fitted in the kitchen, the bathroom refurbished and four of the six bedrooms were in the throes of being made en suite.

"You should be able to move in before the bad weather comes," said Tom, the plumber, when Charlie took him a mug of coffee.

"That's the plan as my two kids and my sister are coming down for Christmas so they can help me move in properly. That's if I haven't already done it by then."

"Smashing. I bet it'll be a Christmas to remember."

"I hope so. I know they're all longing to see the place."

To keep himself occupied while the work was being done, Charlie laboriously weeded between the cobblestones in the forecourt. He asked one of the tradesmen to drill holes in the bottom of the granite trough where the horses once drank, then filled it with compost and planted spring flowering bulbs. Out the back he made plans for a vegetable plot, cleared brambles and nettles from the orchard and strimmed the grass around the trees. He liked the idea of having a large greenhouse and definitely a summerhouse and a lawn. He'd have the well restored too and perhaps create a pond. The sky really was the limit.

Chapter Four

By the end of October, renovation of the house was completed and so Charlie sold his caravan, moved indoors and began decorating. Work, however, continued outside; the stable block, empty after the removal of the furniture, was the last in line for a makeover. The end nearest the lane behind the conifer trees was to be converted into garages, the middle section a log-cum-tool shed and the far end nearest the orchard was to be kept as stables and restored to look much as it would have done in the Inn's heyday. Charlie was undecided what to do with the field he owned beyond the orchard. Having a horse or two was one option, for even though he'd never ridden one in his life, the notion of horses grazing on his own land appealed greatly. Meanwhile, for the boundary at the front of the Inn, three foot high, galvanised steel railings were on order to be erected along the edge of the cobblestones and two sets of granite stone gateposts, already built by Alex a local tradesman who specialised in stonework, awaited double gates on order to match the railings.

In the middle of November the weather turned wet and it rained continually for ten days. But on the very last day the sun came out and everywhere dried up. Charlie was delighted for it was the day the railing sections and gates were due to be installed. They arrived mid-morning and Charlie watched as they were unloaded and put in place. When the work was completed he closed both sets of gates, took several pictures on his phone and forwarded them to family and friends. Overawed by the transformation he went to bed that night a very happy man.

In early December, Charlie's sister, Laura, arrived for a month's stay to help him settle in and prepare for Christmas. She brought with her, Ben a four year old Golden Labrador and enough luggage Charlie considered to keep her clothed for a year.

"It's not all clothing, Charlie," she chided him. "One bag contains food, including a Christmas cake I made back in October, another is full of presents and the rucksack contains Ben's stuff. Only the two cases have my clothes in them and I needed two because I've brought plenty of winter woollies with me just in case the weather turns cold."

"Humph, you've only just got here and you're bossing me around already."

Laura laughed and gave him a tight hug. "That's because I've missed you, you numpty. You've gone from being twenty minutes away to five hours away. I've actually been quite lonely lately; with you and hubby both gone I've less people to talk to."

Laura was happy to spend a month in Cornwall for her husband of twenty-eight years was away with the Army and not due home on leave until Easter. The couple had a daughter but she was married and lived abroad hence their meetings were few and far between.

After everything was taken from Laura's car, the siblings carried the two cases upstairs for Charlie was eager to show his sister the bedrooms and the panoramic views from the windows of both the sea and the Cornish landscape.

"It's much bigger than I expected," Laura stepped onto the landing and glanced down the long corridor, "and much grander than it looked on the pics you sent to me."

"It is rather large but then that's ideal for if I ever decide to do bed and breakfast in the future. I must admit I frequently got lost when it was little more than a building site but I'm used to it now and know every nook and cranny."

They walked along the corridor and went inside each room. The three bedrooms on the front of the house were doubles and en suite; on the back there were four rooms, one double en suite, two singles without facilities and a large luxury bathroom.

"So which one is mine?" Laura asked as they came to the end where a small window overlooked the stable block.

"Whichever you like. I purposely didn't select one for you because I knew you'd like to choose for yourself."

"Thanks, in that case I'll opt for this one in the middle with sea views." Laura dropped her case by the window and bounced on the bed to test its comfort.

Charlie placed the other case by the wardrobe. "I think you've made a good choice. I'm in the room next to you with duel aspect."

"Yes, I saw some of your things in there and I must say I'm impressed, Charlie. You obviously have great domestic skills because all the rooms are neat and tidy. In fact it doesn't look like you'll need my help at all."

"I have to confess I've been working flat out to get it ready for your arrival because I wanted you to see it at its best."

She jumped off the bed and slipped her arm through his. "Well you succeeded which means we will be able to spend lots and lots of quality time together catching up with things."

Back downstairs, Laura toured the ground floor rooms; the large kitchen looked out towards the stable block, an Aga stood inside an inglenook fireplace and various kitchen utensils hung from the wooden beams. A large stripped pine table stood in the centre of the flagstone floor with eight matching chairs tucked beneath it. The dining room was equally large as also was the sitting room which had originally housed the bar; like the kitchen an inglenook fireplace dominated the room. As Laura gazed around the furnishings her eyes filled with tears. "Oh, Charlie, this room is beautiful. How Rachel would have loved it."

"I think that every time I come in here. She was mad about open fires and I always felt she was cheated because our home back in Bucks only had central heating," Charlie moved forwards and lovingly patted the huge granite lintel, "Alex, one of the builders who specialises in stone work cleaned every stone up and redid the pointing. I love it and as you say, Rachel would have too."

Laura squeezed her brother's hand. "Well your Alex has done a marvellous job and as for Rachel, I'm sure she is here with you in spirit."

"I hope so and at least I have her ashes over there so she can see the fire." Charlie pointed to the sideboard where the urn containing Rachel's ashes stood between two vases of carnations, her favourite flowers.

"Bless you, you're such an old softie."

"Would you like to see the cellar?" Charlie was keen to avoid getting emotional and wanted to lighten the mood.

"You have a cellar?"

Charlie nodded. "Of course and it's huge. Half the size of the building in fact."

The entrance to the cellar was from a utility room accessed through the kitchen. Charlie opened a dark stained door and flicked on a switch; two florescent light strips illuminated the vast area below accessible via a curved stone staircase.

"Hmm, creepy and cold yet at the same time fascinating," whispered Laura, as they slowly walked down the stone steps. "I don't think I'd want to be down here on my own though."

"Me neither and for that reason I've done nothing about all this junk. It was here when I bought the place, you see, although to be honest I suppose it's not all junk as there might be a few nice things amongst it."

Laura cast her eyes over old tea chests, barrels, bar stools, tables, boxes of drinking vessels and dusty cobwebs dangling from the beams. "So I see. Stuff from when it was an up and running inn no doubt. I should imagine that pub memorabilia is quite collectable."

"Could well be. It's my intention to sort through it one day and then when it's all gone to do the cellar up but for now this is a no-go area."

"What would you use this for if it was cleared?"

"A good question to which I don't have an answer. I certainly don't need the space as the house is more than big enough for little old me."

"Perhaps you might remarry one day and have more children." Laura hoped that would be the case.

Charlie, knowing his sister was eager to see him settled again, ignored the comment. "I suppose its future depends on whether or not I take in paying guests in the fullness of time. If I did perhaps I could make it a games room. You know, a pool table, a dartboard and stuff like that."

"Yes, I suppose you could. Anyway, if you do want to clear it I can always give you a hand while I'm here. I'd like to make myself useful."

"That might be a good idea. Dan and Flo could help too. With many hands we should be able to clear it in no time and it wouldn't seem creepy with four of us down here either."

Laura looked up at the spiders' webs hanging from wooden beams that ran along the ceiling. "I suppose this would have been used to store barrels of ale in days gone by."

"Probably, although someone suggested it might have been used as accommodation for servants, coachmen and stable hands in its early days because there's evidence of it having been partitioned off at some point."

"Really! Be interesting to see it empty then to see where the partitions would have been."

"That's just what I said when whoever it was mentioned it."

"So have you looked to see if there's anything in the tea chests?" A quick glance told Laura there were at least a dozen.

Charlie shook his head. "We checked a few but they were empty so I assume they all are."

"We?"

"Yeah, Tom and me. Tom's the plumber who would you believe did all the plumbing. He does other building type jobs too. You'll meet him tomorrow when he comes to finish off the loo in the garage section of the stable block. He's a good bloke and so is Pat. Pat's a chippy but he's done here now and so is Alex who did the stonework."

"Alex being the chap who did up the fireplace."

"That's right and he built the four lovely granite gateposts too and got me the birdbath. It's quite fascinating to watch the birds splashing around in it but I need to top up the water every day especially when the magpies, doves and pigeons have been in it."

"I can imagine. Anyway, if we do clear this lot out you'll be able to have a huge bonfire."

"Yes, might even be worth saving it all for November the fifth and then have a bonfire night party in the field. Although that might be a bit daft as it's nearly a year away."

"Maybe but I like the idea and if you went ahead with it you could invite your neighbours along."

Charlie laughed. "But I don't think I have any neighbours. I expect there might be a house or two tucked away up an old track here and there but from what I've seen there appears to be no buildings between here and the village where I stayed in the hotel and that's five miles away."

Laura shuddered. "Ugh, I don't think I'd like that especially in the winter when it's dark at half past four. I think I'd be scared."

"Scared. But why and of what?"

"I don't know it's just an automatic reaction I suppose. You know, fear of the dark. I mean if you were to hear strange noises up here it'd be impossible to track them down because you'd be unable to see anything, and if visibility is poor the old imagination starts playing tricks."

"Yeah, maybe but I'm not the sort to get spooked."

They walked back up the stairs to the utility room and Charlie bolted the door. "Do you feel safe living in a town then?"

"Yes, because there are streetlamps everywhere so it's never really dark."

"Well, if it's any consolation I've had flood lights installed out the front which light up the cobbled area. They're sensitive to movement so should any bogeymen or ghoulies and ghosties come round then we'll know."

"You're mocking me," said Laura, "I remember that look in your eyes from when we were children."

Chapter Five

In the evening, Charlie and Laura sat down beside a roaring fire in the sitting room and chatted over a glass or two of wine; by midnight Laura was struggling to keep her eyes open. "I need to go to bed, Charlie. Getting up early this morning and the drive down here is starting to catch up with me."

"I'm not surprised and I must admit I'm feeling tired too."

Laura yawned. "Must be all the housework you did this morning."

"Or the wine," Charlie glanced down at the Golden Labrador as he picked up the empty glasses. "Would you like Ben in the room with you for company? I don't mind if you do."

"Oh no, we mustn't spoil him. He doesn't sleep in our room at home and he'll be perfectly alright down here in the warm," she stooped and stroked his golden fur, "He loves a real fire and always makes a bee-line for the one in our local pub, don't you my darling?"

Liking the fuss, Ben lifted his head as his wagging tail thumped rhythmically against the hearth rug.

Charlie took the empty glasses through to the kitchen, switched off the lights and made sure the doors were locked, the siblings then made their way upstairs. At the top on the landing they wished each other goodnight and went their separate ways. Charlie, who had risen early in order to make sure everything was ready for his sister's arrival, fell asleep within minutes of his head hitting the pillow but despite her tiredness, Laura lay awake for a while listening to the wind whistling down the chimney to the fireplace in her room and unfamiliar countryside noises seldom heard in the towns and cities. As she drifted between awakeness and sleep her thoughts turned to Charlie who she hoped would meet someone soon, preferably in Cornwall, so that he had a soulmate and someone to love and care for him. For at present she was concerned for his welfare and hated the idea of him living alone, especially in such a large isolated house. Eventually she drifted off to sleep but within an hour was woken suddenly and Ben was barking loudly. Feeling wide awake she sat up. The clattering of horse's hooves was audible in the lane. Quickly she climbed from her bed and headed for the door. As she stepped onto the landing, Charlie emerged from his room.

"Why's Ben barking?" Charlie leaned over the balustrade; persistent barks and the sound of scratching came up from the sitting room.

"It's alright, Ben," shouted Laura, "Everything's okay, boy." On hearing her voice, the Labrador instantly stopped barking and gently whined.

"You'll think I'm mad, Charlie, but I heard horses clomping along the lane."

"What! You're kidding. I didn't hear anything. It was Ben that woke me."

"I'm not, honestly and I know it wasn't a dream."

"Makes sense I suppose because if it was a dream Ben wouldn't have barked, would he?"

Having quietened Ben, they walked along the landing to the window at the end. Charlie opened it and a blast of cold air blew the curtain back; he pushed it to one side and then hung his head out. He looked towards the lane. All was quiet: the only sound the rumble of the nearby sea and the only movement the branches of the conifer trees, their dark eerie shapes illuminated in the glow from the landing light. There was no sign of a horse nor any other indication of life.

"Despite what you say I reckon you must have dreamt it, Laura, and Ben probably barked because he heard an owl hoot or something like that. I mean being a townie like you he's not familiar with the sounds of wildlife and the countryside."

"Well that was my first thought but then I realised I could still hear it after I woke and sat up in bed although the noise was getting quieter as though fading in the distance."

Charlie laughed. "In which case there really must have been a horse trotting by. I mean it's possible, isn't it? I'm sure several people in the countryside would own a horse or two. I'm even thinking about it myself."

"Yes, but he or she would have to be an insomniac to be out riding at half past one in the morning. Daft as well because it's really dark out there and horses don't have headlights, do they?"

"No, and notion of such is very silly." Charlie closed the window.

"I must have dreamt it then and the sound was in my head."

"Like when a tune gets stuck there."

"Something like that," Laura felt a little comforted, "Anyway, if there had been anyone out there the security lights would have come on, wouldn't they?"

"I doubt it, I don't think the sensors would pick up movement as far away as the lane. Anyway, fancy a cup of tea? I don't know about you but I'm wide awake now."

Laura tied the sash of her dressing gown. "Good idea and I'll check Ben's okay at the same time."

Next morning the wind had decreased to a gentle breeze and as soon as it was light, Charlie went outside to see if there were any signs of a horse having been in the lane. As he walked across the cobblestones and opened the lower gates, Laura called out from her bedroom window. "What are you looking for?"

"I don't really know. Something that might indicate your horse was here, I suppose."

Laura laughed. "Well, I can't see as you'll find anything unless it's a lump of manure for your roses."

"I don't have any roses. Not yet anyway." He walked between the gates and glanced back and forth along the lane. "Oh, this is silly. I give up. Are you coming down for breakfast now?"

"Yes, I'm starving so I'll have a shower later."

By mid-morning the sun was shining brightly and so Charlie and Laura went Christmas shopping in Truro. On the way back they passed a garden centre and so called in to see if they had any holly wreaths. They did and so they bought two; one for the back door which led into the kitchen, the other for the main front entrance even though it was seldom used. Laura also bought a poinsettia and a bowl of hyacinths and Charlie bought four stone owls. As soon as they arrived back at the Inn he stood the owls on each of the four granite gateposts and then stepped out into the lane to study the effect.

"Yes," he clapped his hands together in delight, "I think they're the perfect finishing touch. Alex made the tops flat so that I could put something on them. I had thought of getting eagles or granite balls but I think I prefer owls."

"I agree and they look really nice, fantastic in fact but surely if you just stand them there like that someone will pinch them," reasoned Laura.

"Yes, you're probably right even though very few people ever go past here and of course they're heavy so not the sort of thing anyone would want to carry far. To make sure they stay put though I'll get Tom to cement them on. He can do it when he fixes the name plate on the gate post but that won't be for a week or so yet because I only ordered it three days ago."

Leaving the owls on the gate posts the two siblings took the rest of the shopping from the car and went indoors.

"So are you keeping the name The Old Coaching Inn?" Laura asked, as she put dairy products inside the fridge.

Charlie shook his head. "No, I was going to but then Tom said I might get a few people wandering in thinking it was a pub even though I've got gates and railings now, so I've opted instead for Seven Pines."

"Oh, I like that."

"So do I. Back in May the trees were the first thing I saw when I came round the corner so I felt they should be honoured in the name."

"Hmm, please don't think I'm being awkward, Charlie, but are they pines? I mean, I would have thought they were conifers."

"Conifers, firs, pines, it's all the same to me, Laura. Anyway, Seven Conifers doesn't have the same ring to it and nor does Seven Firs."

"Yes, I know but…"

Charlie wagged his figure, "…that's enough Mrs Pernickety Pants. It's Seven Pines, end of."

"Aw, you haven't called me that for years," chuckled Laura.

As darkness fell Charlie went into the sitting room where Laura was wrapping Christmas presents. He drew the curtains, then knelt down in front of the hearth and took a box of matches from a copper pot. "It's just a thought but shall we pop in to the Harbour Lights tonight? I've not been there yet but Cissy's mum works there and Ciss tells me it's very nice. Good atmosphere and all that. They do decent food too so we could get something to eat as well. Save cooking. What do you think?"

Laura pulled a piece of sticky tape from its reel. "Good idea but where is the pub and who is Cissy?"

"It's about five miles away in a lovely village called Porthgwyns. You know, the hotel I stayed in while looking for somewhere to buy?" Laura nodded. "Well that's where the pub is and Cissy works at the hotel. She's a waitress and a smashing girl. Very helpful. We got on really well in fact she helped endear me to this area."

"Really! What sort of age?"

"Who?"

"Cissy."

"Nineteen, twenty, something like that."

"Oh." Laura couldn't hide her disappointment.

Charlie laughed. "I suppose you were hoping she'd be a future partner for me."

"Well, yes, I was actually. I don't like the thought of you out here on your own especially now we're in the depths of winter and the nights draw in so early. I don't like the fact mysterious horses go clopping by in the middle of the night either."

"Yes, that was a bit odd, I must admit, but don't worry about me, I'll be fine." He flexed his muscles.

"Humph."

"Anyway, back to tonight. I suggest we take a taxi so neither of us have to drive because I know you'll want a glass of wine or whatever as much as I will."

"Only one glass! Gosh, Charlie have you turned into a lightweight?"

"You know what I mean." He returned the matches to the pot and stood up. "I won't bother lighting the fire then if we're going out soon."

"I agree, it's more than warm enough in here anyway with the central heating on," Laura having wrapped the last of the presents gathered up the offcuts of paper, "So who runs the pub?"

"I don't know. That is I know of them but I've never met them. Cissy told me a while back that it's run by a married couple called Greg and Grace. I don't know their surname but Greg apparently runs the bar and Grace, a chef of some note, runs the kitchen and if it's busy she helps out on the bar when she's finished cooking."

Later as they took their coats from the pegs in the hallway, Laura seemed puzzled. "Have you seen my scarf, Charlie? I definitely had it this morning because I wore it when we went shopping."

"Don't know. What's it look like?"

"A white silk square with a fringe and a repeat pattern of holly leaves and berries. I bought it in a charity shop back home and thought it would be appropriate since it's nearly Christmas."

Charlie looked around as though expecting the scarf to float by. "Can't say that I have. Might it be in your room?"

"I doubt it because I usually keep it with my coat and I hung my coat in the hall. Oh well never mind, I must have lost it while out shopping. Probably when we stopped for a coffee in the supermarket café. I unbuttoned my coat then and being silky the scarf must have slipped onto the floor. Remind me next time we go into town to pop in and ask if anyone has handed it in."

"I will but you might even have dropped it outside somewhere when we got back. In which case I suggest we have a good look round in the morning when it's light."

Chapter Six

Porthgwyns was once a flourishing fishing village but over the years the number of registered boats had diminished as younger men from the village opted for a more reliable source of income than that chosen by their forefathers. Hence, where fishing vessels had once moored inside the harbour walls, small yachts and pleasure boats had taken their places.

It was dark when the taxi dropped Charlie and Laura outside the front entrance of the Harbour Lights. As the car drove away, Charlie suggested they take a walk along the harbour wall where Christmas lights danced in the gentle south westerly breeze. Laura agreed; at the end of the wall they sat down on a bench which faced the village, where a sea of twinkling lights from houses and cottages lined the narrow hillside streets.

"What an idyllic spot," murmured Laura, "and the village is much bigger than I expected it to be. It's almost a small town."

"Yes, it is. There are several shops and so forth which I'm told do quite well as the place is very popular with tourists."

"I'm not surprised by that," Laura cast her eyes towards the silhouette of buildings overlooking the harbour. "I can certainly see why you chose to spend the rest of your life in this area, Charlie. I might even try and persuade hubby to do the same when he comes out of the Army."

They saw no-one as they sat and drank in the beauty of the village. A few cars passed by and a helicopter circled overhead. In the harbour, sea water slashed against the hulls of small boats and a cat walked by without even glancing in their direction. They would have stayed for longer but as the church clock in the distance struck eight a few spots of rain fell. Eager to get indoors in case the rain became heavier, they left the bench and made their way back along the harbour wall.

Outside the Harbour Lights, a two storey, detached building, towered a large Christmas tree; the glow from its colourful lights reflected on the wet surface of empty picnic benches and the surrounding paved area. A dark green board displaying the name of the pub stretched across the sea-facing whitewashed wall, its gold lettering illuminated by two spotlights tucked beneath the guttering. And from the ground floor windows, a welcoming, warm glow shone through raindrops trickled down the glass panes.

Laura wiped her feet on the porch mat and pushed strands of wet hair from her face. "Are there any other pubs here? I mean it's quite a large village for just one."

"I believe there's another and of course hotel bars are open to the public too but I've not been to any bars other than the hotel where I stayed."

"Why ever not? I mean you've been down here since the summer."

Charlie opened the door leading into the bar and waved his hand for Laura to step inside. "I know but I suppose I didn't really fancy coming out on my own and I always seemed to have lots to do anyway."

The pub was fairly busy with between twenty and thirty people gathered around tables and sitting on stools at the bar. In an adjoining room, young men played pool and some older men played darts. Charlie recognised a few faces but most were strangers to him.

"May I buy you and this charming young lady a drink?" Charlie turned to see Mickey Potts approaching from behind as he and Laura stopped beside a free table.

"You may if you wish but it'll not sway my mind as regards selling the Inn." Charlie unzipped his wet jacket.

"Dash it," roared Mickey, slapping his thigh, "you damn up-country folks are too clever by half and can read me like a book."

"Well you're hardly being subtle." Charlie tried not to laugh as he took Laura's coat and hung it with his own on a peg by the door.

"Only joking. I know nothing will change your mind and if I'm honest I can't blame you. I drove by the Inn this afternoon and was very impressed. You've done a great job, Charlie. The gates and railings look fantastic and I love the owls."

"Thank you. I'm really pleased with them. The owls aren't fixed down yet though. Tom's going to do that when he puts up the name plate."

"Ideal. Anyway, the offer of a drink still stands as it was to show there's no hard feeling."

"In which case thank you very much and we accept. Two glasses of merlot please and we'll be sitting here." As Mickey left for the bar, Charlie pulled out a chair and sat down.

"I take it that's the chap who you beat at the auction." Laura sat down opposite her brother. "Yes, he's a good bloke. When he heard about Rachel he said he was sorry because everyone needs a soulmate and I really think he meant it."

"And I wholeheartedly agree with him."

Charlie chuckled. "I reckon he's a bit of a romantic too because he also said, where there is love there is happiness or something soppy like that."

"It's not soppy," tutted Laura, "and I'm liking him more by the minute."

"Good, but I'm still not going to sell him my house."

Laura laughed. "I should hope not but I'd like to think you and he will become friends because I'm sure he'd be good company."

"I hope so. In fact I'm certain he'll play a big part in my life down here. I don't know how or why but I just feel it in my bones."

"So who is that dolled up woman over there giving us the evil eye?"

Charlie followed the nod of his sister's head to a heavily made-up, blonde haired female sitting on a stool at the bar. "Ah, now that is Mickey's wife, Tracey. She's the one I told you about who wanted to turn my house into a health farm. Well actually she still does. I've never seen her smile, not that I've seen much of her anyway. I get the impression that she doesn't like me though. You know, if looks could kill and all that."

"That explains the sourpuss expression then. Poor Mickey, he deserves better than that."

"I agree and I really hope she's not making his life a misery just because they didn't win the auction."

"So do I, but I suppose she'll get over it in time and if she's serious about a health farm another property will come up somewhere."

"Your drinks," Mickey placed the two glasses on the table in front of them. "Good health to you both," he nodded to Laura, "So how do you like the Old Inn?"

"Very much. I feel it oozes history and has a good aura about it. As you said just now, Charlie's done a good job."

"I can't take all the credit, it was the lads who worked on the place that made it what it is now. They came up with some good ideas too."

"Ah yes, you had the best tradesmen in the area," Mickey lowered his head and his voice, "Before I forget, you and your boyfriend haven't heard any strange noises or seen any weird goings on in the night, have you?"

"Noises and weird goings on in the night," Laura's face dropped, "What on earth do you mean?"

Charlie spoke before Mickey had a chance to reply. "I'm not Laura's boyfriend, I'm her brother."

"Little brother," Laura added.

"Really! Oh, that's a shame. I was hoping you'd been quick off the mark and found a partner already," Mickey looked at Laura, "I've told him he shouldn't be up there on his own. Far too lonely."

"There you and I have something in common, Mickey because those are my sentiments too."

Mickey beamed. "Actually I've been thinking about it these past few weeks and I reckon Crazy Chris might be a good match for you, Charlie. She's about your age, got a nice face, good figure, never been wed as far as I know and she collects compasses."

"What for mathematical purposes?"

"No, the ones that tell you which way to go. She's into country stuff, riding, hiking and so forth."

"She sounds ideal," laughed Laura, "So is she local and does she come in here at all?"

Charlie kicked Laura under the table. "That's enough you two, let's change the subject because I want to know what you mean, Mickey by noises and weird things?"

Mickey sat down at their table and quickly glanced over his shoulder. "I'm referring to the ghostly thing that lurks around your place. I just hope you've not yet been bothered by it, that's all."

Charlie thought Mickey was pulling his leg. "Really, a ghostly thing. Can't say as we've seen it have we, Laura?"

"No," Laura took a sip of her wine, "but if what you say is true, Mickey, then that should add a few extra thousand to the value of Charlie's place because everyone loves a resident ghost."

"A friendly ghost, yes," agreed Charlie, "but a bad tempered poltergeist, no way."

"A poltergeist," Mickey looked confused.

"Yes," said Laura, "you know, they're a type of ghost, spirit or whatever and they make a lot of noise, move things around and are a real pain in the neck. As Charlie said, he wouldn't want to encounter one of them and neither would I."

Mickey laughed. "Oh, I'm with you now."

"Good, so does this ghostly thing you mentioned have a name and what does it look like?" Laura asked.

"I've no idea what he's called but he's male and apparently rides a horse and haunts the lane outside the Old Coaching Inn. I'm surprised no-one's mentioned him to you yet, Charlie, because you've been here for several months now."

Charlie noted that Mickey was trying to keep a straight face. "No, they haven't and if they had I'd tell them not to be so daft. Ghostly thing indeed. Whatever next."

Sitting on a stool at the bar enjoying a pint with Tom the plumber, was Pat the carpenter who had worked on the Old Inn. "You're not trying to spin that old yarn again, are you, Mick?"

"It's not an old yarn. I know it sounds daft but it's true because I've seen him. He was up the top of Wreckers Hill on his horse. Quite a magnificent sight if I remember correctly."

Laura felt impish. "If he was on a horse, then the horse must be a ghostly thing too."

"Good heavens. You know, I'd never thought of that before."

"You surprise me there," said Charlie, "So where were you when you saw this chap and his horse?"

Mickey's eyes flashed. "I was out in a boat fishing at the time with some mates and I saw him as plain as day."

"Bet your mates didn't see him, did they?" Tom chuckled.

"Actually, no, they didn't, soppy ha'p'orths."

"No surprise there then." Tom finished his pint and picked up a fresh one bought for him by Pat.

"It's because they were too busy nattering about fishing. On the other hand they probably didn't see him because they're not receptive like me." With eyes closed, Mickey dramatically brushed his fingertips across his forehead.

"Stuff and nonsense," scoffed Pat.

Mickey opened one eye. "It's not nonsense, Patrick, and I reckon because the ghostly thing was on a horse he's likely to be a highwayman or something like that. I mean back in its heyday lots of folks, some well-breeched, must have stayed at the Inn so there was pickings to be had."

Charlie decided to humour the farmer. "You could well be right. No doubt there were a few dishonest folks around here in days gone by and as you say some of the Inn's well-breeched clientele would have had a few valuables about their person."

"And there are plenty of dishonest folks around today as well," said Pat, "and some of them tell porkies."

Mickey stood up; his laughter filled the bar. He slapped Charlie on the back, "Just pulling your leg," With a nod and a grin, he finished his pint and returned to his scowling wife who was shaking her head in a disapproving manner.

"He's a character, isn't he?" Charlie found it difficult to sip his wine as his mouth was set in a broad grin, "The ghost of a highwayman indeed. I'll give him ten out of ten for imagination though."

"Yes, I agree, but it's a bit unnerving, isn't it? What he said about the ghostly thing, I mean. Especially when I heard a horse in the lane last night."

Charlie's face dropped. "Good heavens. That never even crossed my mind."

"Really, you are slipping, Charlie. As much as I think it's nonsense it was my first thought when he mentioned it even though I didn't let it show and I'm pretty sure he was joking anyway."

"Hmm, so if it really was a horse you heard then I wouldn't be surprised to find that it was Mickey himself out there trying to put the wind up us. I daresay he has a horse or two on the farm."

"But surely he wouldn't be that blatant."

"If he's a desperate man then I think he might and the look on the face of his wife tells me she's still nagging." Charlie glanced towards Tracey whose face was like thunder.

A little later when Charlie went to the bar he noticed business cards for Laurence James Howard, a landscape gardener and designer. He picked one up and looked at the barmaid. "Is he any good?"

Her smile brought out dimples. "The best."

Charlie frowned. "Are you Ruby? Cissy's mum."

"Yes, I am, and you must be Mr Everton the new owner of the Old Coaching Inn?"

"I am, but to avoid it being mistaken for a business I'm renaming it Seven Pines."

"Yes, Tom told me. Or was it Pat. It might even have been Alex. Well, whatever I think it's a good idea."

"Probably Tom because he suggested it. Anyway, how did you know who I am?"

"The dimples. Cissy told me you had dimples like me and you also have curly hair and a few freckles."

Charlie laughed. "That's how I guessed who you were too but I think the similarity ends there."

"I agree, although I'm quite envious of your eyelashes. I reckon they're longer than mine and I'm wearing mascara."

"It's a family trait. My sister has long eyelashes too." He nodded to where Laura sat beside the fire.

"Ah, lucky lady. I didn't realise she was your sister though."

"Yep, my big sister and she's here to keep an eye on me 'til the new year."

"That's nice. I mean, it must get a bit lonely up there on Wreckers Hill."

"I quite like the solitude," he pointed to the business cards. "Is it alright if I take one of these?"

"Of course. Cissy would be dead chuffed if she thought you might have Laurence do your gardens."

"She knows him then?"

Ruby chuckled. "Yes, he's her uncle and my brother."

"That's a good enough recommendation for me then." He put the card in his pocket.

"You'll not be disappointed with his work. Laurence loves gardening as did our father. In fact it was Dad who planted the conifers at your place for the then owner Jacob Smythe. Not that I remember because it was several years before I was born. I've watched them grow over the years and feel close to Dad when I see them. Poor Dad. He never made old bones and died ten years ago following a heart attack."

"I'm sorry to hear that."

"Thank you and thank you for naming the Inn after the trees. He'd be dead chuffed to know that. I wonder if conifers are pines though. Still it doesn't matter, does it?"

Charlie's face dropped. "Hmm, that's what Laura said. Never mind though and before I forget I'd better get what I came up for, so may I have two large glasses of merlot and please put a drink in for yourself as well."

"That's very kind, Mr Everton. Thank you."

"You're welcome but please call me Charlie."

As Charlie returned to his seat, a man walked into the pub who he recognised as the person who at the auction had put in several bids for the Inn. Charlie caught Mickey's eye and beckoned him over. "I recognise that chap at the bar wearing a leather jacket? He was bidding for my place. Any idea who he is?"

"That's Jiffy, he's our local celebrity. Used to be in a band back in the sixties but I think they called them groups back then. My mum used to be a fan when she was a teenager and collected all their albums. I've got them now as sadly she's no longer with us but I've put them in the loft because I've nothing to play them on."

"Didn't your mother still have her record player then?" Charlie asked.

"No, that packed up years ago."

"Jiffy," said Laura, "Not his real name surely."

"No, his real name is Jeffrey but very few people call him that. His surname is Lemon, you see."

"Hmm, it sort of makes sense, I suppose."

"So what was the group called?" Charlie asked.

"Gooseberry Pie. They broke up years ago but I remember Mum playing the records I mentioned when I was a kid and they were quite good. Jiffy was the drummer."

Charlie watched as the newcomer took a seat on a stool at the bar and ordered a drink from landlord, Greg. "So does he live locally?"

"Yes, got a great luxury place a few miles down the coast up on the cliffs. Must be worth a fortune."

"I wonder why he wanted my place then."

"I thought that when I saw him at the auction. I mean, a chap can only live in one place at once, can't he?"

"Is he married?" Laura observed no ring on Jiffy's finger.

"Not any more. If I remember he's had two wives. I'm not sure what happened to the first one but the second moved on a few years back. I've heard her new bloke's into heavy metal."

"Any children?" Charlie was equally inquisitive.

"Just one daughter as far as I know."

"Well thanks for that," said Charlie, "I'm keen to get to know who everyone is."

Mickey turned to leave. "My pleasure and I hope you sleep well tonight."

The rain had stopped when the siblings left the pub and Mickey was outside arguing with another man in the smoker's den over an unpaid wager.

"It looks like Mickey likes a bit of a flutter," said Charlie as they stepped into the taxi."

"Yes, as well as spinning far-fetched yarns."

After three glasses of wine, Laura vowed she'd sleep like a log and no amount of noises in the night would wake her. She was annoyed therefore when in the dead of night, she was woken by the neighing of a horse and the sound of hooves galloping by as on the previous night. This time, however, Charlie heard it too and once again so did Ben. Laura and Charlie sprang from their beds, grabbed their dressing gowns and ran outside. Ben, let out of the sitting room to stop him barking, followed. To their surprise, the lane was in darkness and all was quiet.

Laura laughed. "Well do you believe me now?"

Charlie smiled as they returned indoors. "I suppose I'll have to but that was no ghost. I reckon it was Mickey Potts trying to scare us."

"I agree one hundred percent, but what an ass. I mean, surely he doesn't think you're that gullible."

Charlie locked the back door. "Who knows? Anyway, remind me tomorrow to see if we can find out whether there are horses at Bracken Farm. If there are we'll know for sure who the phantom rider is."

Chapter Seven

Jeffrey (Jiffy) Lemon stood deep in thought inside the huge conservatory on the sea-facing side of his large house watching the waves tumbling onto the rocks far below. On a table behind him, his first wife, Amelia smiled up from the open pages of a photograph album. Most of the pictures in the book were of Gooseberry Pie taken by Amelia in the months following the number one hit that made them a household name. The picture of Amelia, however, was taken by Danny Jarrams another member of the group and Jiffy adored it, for it captured her true natural beauty, good, caring nature and reminded him how precious she had been to him and how much he missed her.

When Gooseberry Pie first got together Jiffy was just a lad of twenty, the group never expected to achieve fame or even make a record. It was just a bit of fun and a way of impressing the local girls. It was pure luck that they were spotted in their village youth club by someone in the music industry who was trawling the country looking for talent and thought they had potential. He signed them up and the rest thought Jiffy, was history.

It was shortly before the group became famous that Jiffy was introduced to Amelia. A model – tall, elegant and beautiful. They married a year later but it was not for another five years that their daughter was born. Amelia at first was reluctant to have children in case it spoiled her figure but after her sister's son was born she changed her mind. Motherhood suited her well and she seemed happier than he had ever known her to be. But happiness seldom lasts for ever. When she was just thirty-five tragedy struck.

She was diagnosed with cancer and was dead within the year.

Jiffy sighed and sat down beside the potted olive tree his daughter had given to him for his seventieth birthday and turned his thoughts to days gone by. Halcyon days when it seemed life couldn't get any better. Days that brought fame and fortune and a lifestyle that as a boy he could only have dreamed of. But a lot of water had flowed under the bridge since then. Now he was alone for his second wife had recently gone her own way and the only close family he had left was his beloved daughter, Elderflower.

He reached across to the table, blew Amelia a kiss and closed the album. As he stood to return the book to its shelf he thought of Charlie Everton. Jiffy regretted not having won the auction for the Old Coaching Inn as, having it done up would have been a gratifying project. But it seemed that Charlie had done a good job and he was glad he had pulled out when he did especially when he learned later that Charlie had in recent years also lost a spouse. Nevertheless, it was a shame. The Old Inn had stables and were he to have bought the place he would have had them restored to their former glory and kept a couple of horses. His one ambition in life yet to be fulfilled.

For lunch, Charlie booked a table at the hotel where he had stayed while looking for a property in Cornwall but before they left he and Laura searched the cobbled area and around the stables in case Laura had dropped her scarf outside when they returned from shopping the previous day. Laura even looked out in the lane but to no avail. Convinced she must have dropped it in the supermarket café, they abandoned the search.

Charlie said he'd drive to the hotel but as they walked towards his car, he glanced at the back door and frowned. "Why have you swapped the holly wreaths round, Laura?"

"Why have I what?"

Charlie pointed to the door. "The wreath on the back door has a yellow ribbon and yellow berries but I thought you put the yellow on the front and the red on the back."

"I did." Laura walked round to the front of the house where to her astonishment she saw the red ribboned wreath on the door. "Am I going mad, Charlie? I'm sure I put them as you said."

"You did, no question, because we said how nice the yellow matched the mahonia in tubs either side of the front door."

Laura scratched her head. "Then someone must have swapped them round. But who?"

"And why?" Charlie was equally nonplussed.

"Mickey perhaps?"

Charlie laughed. "Yes, of course, it has to be him. I suppose he's hoping we'll think it was done by a poltergeist. What a numpty." Charlie reached for the wreath on the back door, "Let's swap them back and then get off because I'm hungry."

They arrived at the hotel just before one and to Charlie's delight, Cissy was in the dining room folding paper napkins.

"Cissy," she looked up on hearing her name, "allow me to introduce you to Laura, my big sister."

Cissy crossed the room and smiling sweetly proffered her hand. "Hi, pleased to meet you."

"Likewise."

"I met your mother the other day," said Charlie, "and I can see what you mean by the likeness."

"Yes, she told me you'd been in the pub. What did you think of it?"

"Very impressed and I daresay I'll be a frequent visitor over the next few weeks now I have big sister here."

Laura lightly punched his arm. "Humph. That makes it sound like I'm always drinking."

"And...?" Charlie smiled impishly. "Anyway, Ciss, I'm glad you're working today because you might be able to tell us something. That is, do you know of anywhere around here where they have horses?" Charlie had decided to be subtle with his questions as he didn't want to be accused of making wild allegations against Mickey Potts.

"As in for riding?" Cissy asked, as she showed them to a table by a window which overlooked the hotel gardens.

"Well, yes."

"I see. Well, there are riding stables out at Treverry Cross but they're the only ones as far as I know and I've lived here all my life."

"Treverry Cross. Where's that?" Laura sat down.

"It's about two miles west of here and near the village of Little Treverry."

"Lovely name," said Laura, "Is there a Big Treverry too?"

Cissy laughed. "No, just Little."

"Treverry Cross, I've heard the name before," Charlie tried to mask his excitement, "Doesn't Mickey Potts live out that way?"

"That's right, yes. Bracken Farm is just down the lane from the stables."

"Well, thanks for that, Cissy."

"You're welcome. We've leaflets for the stables and other places if you'd like any." Cissy waved her hand towards a table in the corner where leaflets for local attractions lay in piles on a white cloth.

"Thank you, I'll go and get one now." Laura left the table.

Charlie picked up a menu. "And now we'd better decide what to eat."

"Okay," said Cissy, "I'll pop back in a few minutes to take your order."

"Are we going to pursue the phantom horse thing further?" Laura asked as she returned to the table and tucked the stable leaflet and several others in her handbag.

Charlie shrugged his shoulders. "I can't really see much point. I mean, if Mickey wants to borrow a horse just to try and scare us, well, it's his problem rather than ours. Having said that, I'd love to catch him red-handed and I wonder if it might be worth installing CCTV."

"Could be and it might be a good idea anyway for security purposes. As regards Mickey though I should imagine by the time you had it done he'd be tired of trying. Especially with it having little or no effect. I mean you made it quite obvious that you're not gullible."

"I think you're right. I actually feel quite sorry for him. Tracey must be really putting on the pressure if the poor bloke feels he has to get out of a nice warm bed in the middle of the night just to try and spook us."

Inside the kitchen at Bracken Farm, Tracey Potts sat at the table searching on her laptop for a new outfit. Not that she needed one; she was going nowhere special but she thought it might help to cheer her up.

"What do you think of this dress?" Tracey asked Ruby who had returned to the kitchen having just finished her cleaning jobs.

Ruby looked over Tracey's shoulder. "Very nice. I like blue, it's my favourite colour."

"So do I. I also like it in pink. The red's quite nice too. Oh dear, as if I haven't got enough problems."

Ruby returned the cleaning tools to the cupboard beneath the sink and then washed her hands.

Tracey smiled sweetly. "Fancy a coffee before you go?"

"I'd love to, Trace, but I don't have time. I'm working in the pub this lunchtime from one 'til four so I'd better get off." Ruby reached for her coat hanging on the back door.

"Oh that's a shame, it's nice to have someone to chat to. Mickey's no fun when it comes to fashion and so forth. Whatever I show him he says he likes it without even looking at it properly."

Ruby chuckled. "Yes, my Steve's much the same. Not that I buy clothes very often."

"Yeah, I don't suppose many men are interested in what their wives wear. It's a bit unfair though because I have to listen to Mickey talking about farm stuff even though I don't know what he's on about. Do you know, Ruby, he asked my thoughts about a new tractor the other day. I mean, come on, what was I supposed to say to that?"

Ruby smothered a smile. "I don't know, which reminds me, I keep meaning to ask but did you ever find your old phone?"

"No, which is a nuisance. I keep expecting it to turn up now I've got a new one. You know, sod's law and all that. It still might though and I hope it does because all my contact details are on it."

"I doubt it'll be much good if it's been outside all this time though."

"Damn, I hadn't thought of that."

Ruby took her car keys from her pocket. "All the same, I hope it turns up for your sake. I keep my eyes peeled when dusting and so forth but have had no luck yet. Anyway, must be off, Trace. See you on Thursday."

"Yeah, bye Ruby and thanks."

After their lunch at the hotel in Porthgwyns, Charlie and Laura returned to Seven Pines. The postman had been and several white envelopes lay on the doormat. Charlie opened them. All were Christmas cards, most from friends up-country and one local from Mickey and Tracey Potts. It was clearly written by Mickey who had drawn a smiley face with a holly wreath on its head. Charlie chuckled, amused by the farmer's artwork and then hung all the new cards alongside others on a string running across a beam in the kitchen.

Before they removed their coats they decided to go for a walk for both felt they had eaten too much. Because Laura had yet to see the field beyond the orchard that belonged to her brother they decided to go in that direction and take Ben with them.

Access to the field was along an earth based track which ran between a wild hedge and an ivy laden drystone wall and was wide enough to accommodate a vehicle. Although overgrown, the track was accessible because Charlie had strimmed a narrow pathway through the greenery on several occasions.

The field, uncultivated through lack of use over many decades, was badly overgrown with brambles, clumps of dead nettles, dried thistles, sporadic sycamore saplings and elderberry bushes. What little grass there was, was almost lost beneath dandelion leaves.

"Goodness me," gasped Laura as Charlie opened a gate and she stepped into the field, "What a view. I can understand why Tracey Potts liked the idea of a health farm up here, you can see for miles."

"Yes, had Tracey got her way she'd have had the best of both worlds. Sea views in the accommodation block on the front and panoramic views of the countryside in the spa and whatever treatment building at the back."

"She'd have had her work cut out though. I never dreamt it'd be as wild as this. You'll need heavy equipment to knock it into any sort of shape."

"That's what Tom said. As for Tracey, I don't think the plan was for her to do any work in this field. From what I've heard, work's not really her thing."

"No of course not. That was a silly thing to have said."

"My main concern now is what to do with it. I mean, I like the idea of a horse or two but knowing they need a lot of care and attention and the fact I have no equestrian knowledge, I think it might be foolhardy to go down that road."

Laura took a few cautious steps between a huge thistle and an ivy clad clump of brambles. "I suppose when you've got it cleared and it's back to grass you could always get a goat. I believe they eat most things and it would certainly keep the grass and weeds down."

"A goat. I know even less about goats than I do horses. In fact, come to think of it I'm not really an animal person especially when it comes to care and stuff like that so I think it might be best if I used the field to grow things instead."

"How about a wild flower meadow? Once established it wouldn't need much care and it'd be fantastic for wildlife and the environment."

Charlie stopped walking and cast his eyes over the field. "Of course. Why didn't I think of that? Well done, Laura, that's the obvious solution."

"I'm glad you agree. I have a small area of my garden at home filled with wild flowers and I love it. Needless to say it's miniscule compared with the size of this. If I were you I wouldn't have just wild flowers though. I think you ought to plant a few trees around the edges and keep some of the brambles too so you have blackberries."

"Oh definitely. When we get back I'll ring Tom and see if he knows someone who can clear it."

"And once that's done you can get Laurence whatever his name is to create the meadow."

"Yes, Ruby's brother. Another, brilliant idea, Laura."

After walking around the field between the tangled vegetation they returned to the house. While Laura lit the fire in the sitting room, Charlie rang Tom.

Having had a good lunch the siblings weren't very hungry and so in the evening Charlie made cauliflower and stilton soup.

"According to the weather forecast it looks as though we're in for another stormy old night," said Laura, as she sat down at the kitchen table and Charlie served the soup, "might even be some thunder. I hope not though or Ben will start whining. Poor darling hates thunder and lightning as much as he hates fireworks."

"Can't say that I'm keen on thunder either but if you're worried about Ben why not have him in your room tonight."

"Laura sighed. "I think I might do that if you don't mind."

"Of course I don't mind."

Ben, with tail wagging excitedly, escorted Laura to her room just before midnight. Charlie stayed up a little longer reading about wildflower meadows on his laptop. When he finally retired to his room he looked from his window. Way out over the sea, flashes of lightning sporadically lit up the night sky followed by distant rumbles of thunder. Charlie watched mesmerised as the irregular bursts of light flickered making the outside world looked eerie, bleak and desolate, until his eyes began to prickle and yawns were more frequent than the thunder. Happy to retire for the night he reached up to pull the curtains together but as his hands grasped the soft silk fabric he saw a dark figure out in the lane. He relaxed his grasp and waited for the next flash but when it came there was no-one there. Thinking it must have been a trick of the light, he drew the curtains and climbed into bed. Having had a few glasses of brandy as a nightcap he was asleep within minutes.

Several hours later the storm was right overhead. Laura was woken by Ben whining. To comfort him she allowed him to climb onto the bed. Without bothering to look outside she lay listening to the rain lashing against the window and then drifted back to sleep and Ben did likewise. Charlie on the other hand slept right through it and when he awoke and pulled back his bedroom curtains the following morning, he was devastated to see one of the seven conifer trees was nothing more than a jagged stump. He expressed his dismay when he met Laura downstairs for breakfast.

"I can't believe the wind has blown one down. I love those trees. Admittedly they're only cupressus macrocarpa and they're getting a bit tatty round the bottom, but they're a big part of the house and so much nicer than trees that shed their leaves in winter. It's such a shame too as we're constantly being told we need to be planting more to save the planet and all that." Charlie sat down heavily on the chair and rested his elbow on the table in a dejected manner.

"I like firs, pines and evergreens too but I also like to see the silhouette of leafless trees in the winter especially at dusk if there's a pretty sunset." Laura dropped two slices of bread in the toaster, "Anyway, let's hope the poor tree is not dead and sends up new growth from the stump."

"Well if it doesn't I'll have to rename the house Six Pines which is sad because seven is my lucky number."

Laura amused by her brother's sulky face attempted to refrain from smiling. "Which one has blown down?"

"The one nearest the house which is better than being in the middle I suppose."

"Yes, it is because you still have a row," Laura took two plates from the cupboard, "So how do you know they're cupressus macrocarpa, Charlie?"

"It was mentioned on the auction details."

Laura laughed. "I see, for a minute then I thought you might be a closet horticulturalist."

"Not when it comes to trees but I do know my vegetables."

"You take after Dad for that. Going back to the tree though, I'm surprised it's blown down because the wind wasn't very strong last night. Not when I woke anyway. It was raining and quite heavily too but there was no sound of wind in the chimney like there was the other night."

"Really? I slept like a log and didn't hear anything at all."

"I don't think I would have woken were it not for Ben whining."

Charlie took the butter dish from a shelf on the dresser and placed it on the table, "Do you want marmalade?"

"Yes please, I fancy something sweet this morning." Laura placed two slices of toast on a plate and passed them to her brother. "So I assume if the trees were mentioned on the property details and Jacob Smythe had the trees planted that you own that bit of land."

"Yes, I do," Charlie looked up from the cupboard where he searched amongst jars for a new pot of marmalade, "which means it'll be up to me to dispose of it, I suppose."

"It will but look on the bright side and think of all the logs you'll have next winter once you've cut all the wood up and dried it out."

"Good point. Pine smells nice too."

"But they're conifers so do they smell nice?" Laura placed bread in the toaster for herself.

"Let's not go down that road again."

"Only teasing."

"I'll have to hire a chain saw, won't I? It'll take forever otherwise." Charlie sat down and poured two mugs of tea from the pot on the table.

While she waited for her toast, Laura looked from the window. "Has the bit that's blown off blocked the road do you think? I mean, it was a very big tree, wasn't it?"

"Good point. I'll pop out and see when I've finished my breakfast. No rush though as very little traffic goes by here."

Shortly after as Laura loaded up the dishwasher, Charlie took his jacket from a peg by the back door and slipped his arms into its sleeves; the wind was not very strong and the rain was little more than drizzle. After crossing the cobbled area and opening the lower gates he looked out into the lane and was relieved to see that the tree had toppled sideways: only its top part was lying on the road so he'd be able to clear the offending branches and greenery with the aid of a hand saw. In order to weigh up the situation he moved in closer but when within a few yards of the debris, he stopped, aghast. Beneath the tree lay the body of a man, his lower half crushed by the weight of a thick heavy branch. Charlie's pace slowed as he approached the scene. His mouth gaped open in horror. He recognised the man. It was Mickey Potts.

Chapter Eight

In a state of shock, Charlie slowly advanced feeling it was his duty to try and establish whether or not Mickey was still alive although he was certain just by looking at the colour of his face that life had long been extinguished. With a lack of enthusiasm, he stepped over broken foliage intending to feel for a pulse but as he leaned over the motionless farmer he saw that both wrists were trapped beneath the tree. Determined not to concede defeat, Charlie lowered his shaking hand to feel for a pulse on Mickey's neck but the farmer's eyes were wide open and overcome with nausea Charlie pulled back his hands. As he stood he noticed peeping out from beneath the heavy branch what appeared to be the curved edge of a holly wreath possibly taken from one of the Inn's doors. Saddened there was nothing more he could do, he stepped out onto the lane and returned indoors to ring for the emergency services. As he approached the back of the house he looked at the door. As anticipated the red ribboned holly wreath was not there.

The police were the first to arrive and their initial assumption was that the tree was the cause of Mickey's death. The fire brigade arrived soon after, closely followed by an ambulance. Charlie who had waited at the scene was asked a few questions and then ordered to stand back. To keep out of the way he went inside the gateway nearest the trees where stood Laura, clearly anxious. From there they could hear what was said and both were surprised when the chief fire officer told a police officer that the tree had been struck by lightning and it was possible that the deceased had been sheltering underneath it from the rain.

As the tree was finally lifted, Charlie spotted a piece of white fabric quite near to Mickey's body. He stepped out into the lane so that he could take a closer look but a police officer would not let him pass. Concerned that it might be Laura's scarf, Charlie was keen to explain his interest and so told the officer that if the object was a silk scarf with a repeat holly pattern then it belonged to his sister who had recently lost it. As the police officer thanked him and walked away to report Charlie's observation to his superiors, it began to rain and so Charlie and Laura returned indoors. Ten minutes later as they sat at the kitchen table drinking coffee the doorbell rang. Charlie leapt to his feet. On the doorstep stood a police officer. Charlie hurried him in out of the rain.

Laura rose as the officer pulled a handkerchief from his pocket and dried his spectacles. "Would you like a coffee...um...um?"

"Ian Reynolds, Detective Inspector and yes, please I'd love a coffee."

While Laura re-boiled the kettle the DI asked if she was the sister of Charlie who had lost a scarf. She said she was. He then asked her to describe it in detail after which he confirmed it fitted the description of the item found near to the deceased. Laura was surprised for she and Charlie had thoroughly searched the cobbled area and the lane.

"Also not far from the deceased," continued the inspector, "we found a small battery powered amplifier along with recording equipment tucked behind the trees still standing. Do you know anything about these items?"

"You found what!" Laura gave the inspector his coffee and then sat down, her mind in a muddle.

"A battery powered amplifier and recording equipment," repeated the DI thinking they had not heard.

Charlie shook his head. "Good heavens, so it looks as though he might not have a horse after all."

"That's what I'm thinking," agreed Laura, "and if it was a recording that would explain why the horse neighed on both occasions."

The DI cast a confused glance at the siblings. "A horse. Mr Potts didn't come out here on a horse. He drove. We found his car parked some way back down the hill."

"No we didn't mean that," said Laura, "What we're trying to say is…No, it's too daft, you'll think us very silly."

"Well if you care to explain I'll be the judge of that."

Charlie, suddenly feeling hot, removed his thick woollen jumper. "Well in a nutshell, Mickey was in competition with me at the auction for this place. He wanted it so that his wife could turn it into a health farm. Needless to say I won and we think he's been trying to scare me into selling by telling wild stories about the ghost of a highwayman or some such nonsense."

"That's right," said Laura, "You see the night before he told us the silly story while we were in the pub, we'd heard a horse outside in the early hours. At least I did and Charlie was woken by Ben barking."

"It happened again another night as well," Charlie added, "but on that occasion we both heard it and after looking at the facts and discovering Mickey's farm is near riding stables at Treverry Cross we concluded it must have been him riding by on a horse which we found quite amusing."

"So you see," said Laura, "as daft as it sounds, it looks as though it wasn't Mickey riding a horse at all but was in fact a recording of a horse. Well, we don't know for sure. It all depends what's on the equipment, I suppose, but it sounds logical because when we looked out of the upstairs window the first time it happened and ran out into the lane the second, we saw nothing and that would be because on both occasions Mickey must have been hiding under the trees."

The DI looked over the top of his spectacles. "But surely no-one in their right mind would sell their home simply because they thought there might be a ghost or whatever in the lane outside. I most certainly wouldn't."

"We agree and the notion is ridiculous anyway," said Charlie, "but then we don't know what else Mickey might have had up his sleeve. I mean, I can't believe having already gone to such lengths that he'd have left it at that."

"I see...I think. Anyway, it'll be interesting to find out if you're right. When Forensics get here I'll get them to have a listen. Fortunately the equipment is intact and escaped damage from the rain because it's quite dry under the trees." He stood up, "I must get back outside. Thank you for the coffee. Please don't go anywhere because once Mr Potts has been removed we'll be wanting to take statements from you both."

Charlie stood also. "Before you go, Officer, are you able to tell me if there was a wreath entwined with a red ribbon on Mickey's chest? I couldn't see properly from where I stood."

"The DI frowned. "Yes, there was but I'd rather you didn't mention that to anyone at this stage. In fact please don't discuss anything you've witnessed at all until I say."

"Of course, but the reason I asked about the wreath was because it was taken from our back door."

"Really. Well thank you for that piece of information."

"And the other day," said Laura, "We found the wreaths on the back and front doors had been swapped around. Both have different coloured ribbons, you see."

A little later at Bracken Farm, Detective Inspector Ian Reynolds and another police officer arrived to break the news to Tracey Potts. She was in the kitchen wearing a bathrobe with a towel wrapped round her wet hair making tea when she heard a car pull up in the farmyard.

"Mrs Potts?" the detective inspector asked as she answered the door.

"Yes."

"I'm Detective Inspector Ian Reynolds and this is Police Sergeant Sally Truman." They both flashed their ID cards.

"Oh, is there something wrong?"

"It's about Mr Potts. May we come in?"

"Yes, yes, of course, but Mickey's not here. I assume he's out with the animals. He often is when I get up." She stepped aside to let the officers in and glanced at the clock, "Although he's usually in by now for a cup of tea. I expect he's talking to the lads. Likes a natter does our Mickey."

The officers looked at each other but neither spoke.

"Would you like a cup of tea or shall we wait 'til Mickey comes in? He shouldn't be long. Or I could ring his mobile and hurry him up." Tracey glanced at her phone lying on the arm of a chair.

"That's very kind but no tea thank you and forget about ringing your husband."

"Oh, alright, but please take a seat," Tracey waved her hand to a leather sofa, "So what has Mickey done? Not speeding again surely."

"Please sit down, Mrs Potts." Detective Inspector Reynolds nodded towards an armchair opposite the sofa in front of a window overlooking the farmyard.

Tracey tightened the sash of her bathrobe and then slowly lowered herself into the chair.

"I'm sorry to have to tell you, Mrs Potts, but there's been an accident."

"Involving Mickey? Is he alright?"

"I'm afraid not. Mr Potts was found dead this morning beneath a fallen tree outside the Old Coaching Inn on Wreckers Hill."

"Seven Pines," corrected the police sergeant, "Mr Everton told me he's changed the name."

"A tree," mumbled Tracey, "He was found beneath a fallen tree. But...but... how? I mean why? I thought...that is..." Tracey pointed over her shoulder to the window, "I assumed he was out on the farm somewhere. It doesn't make sense and why was he at the Inn, Seven Pines or whatever they call it now?"

"We don't know but it's possible he was sheltering from the rain when the tree was struck by lightning."

"Sheltering from the rain. Struck by lightning," Tracey's face was devoid of colour. Fearing she might pass out, the police sergeant jumped up to get her a glass of water.

"We don't know why he was there and hope maybe you can help us on that point. You see, beneath the trees not far away from him was a battery powered amplifier and recording equipment. Our team have examined the recorder on site and inside was a tape of a horse trotting along a solid surface."

"There was a what!" Tracey buried her face in her hands, "Oh Mickey, Mickey, you silly, silly man." She rubbed her eyes and then sighed deeply, "He must have been trying to frighten Charlie Everton so that he'd sell and we could buy the place. He said he might but I thought he was joking. I had my heart set on it, you see, when it went to auction but the price reached was beyond our means. At the time we didn't know that Mr Everton had access to a substantial amount of money," Tracey took several gulps of water.

Detective Inspector Reynolds nodded. "Yes, Mr Everton said something along those lines but I find it hard to believe that Mr Potts could possibly expect such a childish plan to have the desired effect."

Tracey smiled through her tears. "But Mickey was childish in many respects, bless him. He was an only child and had a doting mother who didn't want him to grow up. It took her quite a while to accept me and let him leave home and were it not for his dad putting his foot down I reckon she'd have moved in with us after we got married so she could continue to look after him. In the end she was okay with me though and I was saddened when she died. And now Mickey's gone too."

"Did you not hear your husband leave the house during the night?" Police Sergeant Sally Truman asked.

Tracey shook her head. "No, we have separate rooms. You see, Mickey snores and I fidget so we've slept apart for three years now."

"So you didn't hear the back door close or even his car drive away?"

"No, he always parks over by the big barn so I wouldn't have heard and as for the door, neither back nor front squeak so it'd be easy to slip out without being heard and Mickey obviously wouldn't want me to know what he was up to, would he?"

"According to Mr Everton, he and his sister have heard a horse in the middle of the night twice before and so we assume it was your husband on those occasions too."

"Oh dear, if what you say is true then it must have been. If only I'd known I'd have stopped him." She bit her bottom lip, "I knew he'd spun Mr Everton and his sister that silly yarn about the ghost of a highwayman or some such nonsense. He didn't make it up though. He was told it by the chap we bought the farm from, you see. Of course, Mickey being Mickey he believed every word of it. He was very gullible and naïve, bless him. I never dreamt the reason he dug up the old story and told it to Mr Everton and his sister was so he could scare them. I suppose I ought to apologise to them."

Tracey pulled a tissue from her pocket and dabbed the tears brimming in her eyes.

"Were you aware that Mr Potts had recording equipment?" asked the DI.

Tracey shook her head. "Not really. I mean, he had all sorts of gadgets and liked listening to music. He kept most of his stuff in the office and I seldom went in there. Sam probably knows what's in the room better than me."

"Sam?"

"Sam Nixon. He's one of our farm hands and an excellent one too. He was already working here when we bought the farm and he taught Mickey everything he knows. Really nice chap. Lives out at Little Treverry. The office is where they keep all farm related stuff." The towel covering Tracey's hair slipped and so she pulled it off and placed it on the arm of the chair.

"Is there anyone who could come and stay with you?" DI Reynolds asked.

Tracey glanced at a Welsh dresser where the photograph of a young woman smiled from a brass frame. "Becky, my daughter. She lives in Plymouth. I'm sure she'd come and stay for a while."

"Good, if you can provide us with her contact details we'll get one of our officers up there to visit her."

"Of course."

The police sergeant wrote down the name, address and telephone number recited by Tracey.

"And then when you're ready," said Detective Inspector Reynolds, "we'd like you to formally identify the body."

Tracey looked aghast. "Must I? I mean, he's not all crushed and in a bad way, is he?"

"The tree fell on the lower half of his body. His face is unmarked and that's all you'll be required to see."

Tracey heaved a sigh of relief. "Thank goodness for that."

On hearing the news, Becky Potts, who was self-employed and had her own mobile hairdressing business, cancelled her appointments for the following week. She then rang her boyfriend to tell him the news and drove straight down to Cornwall. That evening mother and daughter sat reminiscing about the man they had both loved and lost.

The following morning, Charlie and Laura sat at the table in the kitchen of Seven Pines eating breakfast and discussing the tragic death of Mickey Potts and the consequences thereof as they had done for much of the previous day. When the subject was exhausted their thoughts turned to more practical issues.

"I think I must look into the hiring of a chainsaw today. I don't know about you, Laura, but I'd like to see the tree gone as soon as possible to help blot out the image of poor Mickey trapped beneath it."

Laura lovingly stroked her brother's hand. "I think it might be better still if you hired a man with a chainsaw and let him deal with it. I don't like the idea of you doing it especially with you being the one who found him."

"Yes, you're right. I'll look on the internet after breakfast. I'm sure there must be someone in the area."

"Or better still why don't you give Pat or Tom a ring? They must know all the local tradesmen."

As Charlie stood to make them each another mug of tea, they heard a car pull up in the lane outside the gates. Two car doors squeaked open and then slammed shut followed by the clanging of a gate opening.

"Visitors," Charlie pulled aside the curtain and looked out of the window, "It's the police. I wonder what they want. We gave them our statements yesterday."

Laura opened the back door for them before they had a chance to ring the bell.

"Tea?" Charlie held up the kettle, "We're just having another."

"Yes please, thank you. White, no sugar for either of us."

Charlie made the tea and they all sat down around the table.

"So what brings you here this morning?" Laura asked.

Detective Inspector Reynolds cleared his throat. "There has been a development in the death of Mr Potts. The post mortem results concluded that death was caused by a wound on the back of his head not related to a fall and that he was dead before he was crushed beneath the tree. Time of death is estimated at between one and two but according to the Met office lightning in this area was not directly above until between three and three fifteen. His death therefore is now being treated as suspicious and officers will be here shortly to search the area outside your home for the blunt instrument which we believe will have caused the wound."

Charlie and Laura both sat open-mouthed.

"Are you implying he might have been murdered?" Charlie asked after a minute's silence.

"At this stage we're keeping our options open but yes, there is a strong possibility that that will be the case."

"But that's terrible," said Laura, "I mean, who would have done such a thing and why?"

"That is what we hope to establish." As the inspector spoke more vehicles pulled up outside. "That'll be the team," said Police Sergeant Sally Truman, "I'll go and brief them, sir."

"Okay, I'll be there shortly."

"Take your tea with you, Sergeant," said Laura.

"Thank you. I'll bring the mug back later."

As she left the kitchen, Charlie stood up and peeped out of the window. "Goodness knows what they hope to find. I mean, if he has a wound to his head, could he not have tripped, fallen or whatever and done it then?"

"We think it unlikely as nothing was found beneath the body or in the immediate vicinity. Meaning had he fallen backwards and hit his head on something solid then that something would have been present when he was found."

"But he might have had a fall before he went under the tree," reasoned Laura, "You know, he might have stumbled backwards, hit his head on the road and then staggered off to stand under the tree when the rain started."

"At this stage anything's possible," the detective drained his mug and then stood up. "Anyway, thanks for the tea. We'll keep you posted of course and I'd appreciate it if neither of you left the premises today as we shall be interviewing you again later regardless of whether or not we find the object that caused the fatal blow. Meanwhile the area outside your property will be marked as a crime scene so you are forbidden to enter the area we'll be taping off."

"Of course we'll stay put," Charlie felt light-headed, "we weren't planning to go anywhere anyway. In fact I was going to look into hiring someone to cut up the poor tree but that can wait, I suppose."

"The tree must be left alone for now, but we'll let you know when you can dispose of it."

As the detective left the kitchen, Laura collected up the dirty mugs and placed them in the dishwasher. "I can't believe what we've just heard, Charlie."

"Me neither and I can't see what they expect to find out there," Charlie looked from the kitchen window but was unable to see anything of the search.

Laura nodded towards the open door leading into the hallway. "Might be able to see better upstairs."

"Of course."

With haste the siblings dashed up the stairs and sat on the window seat in Charlie's room where they had an uninterrupted view of the lane along which several officers could be seen searching the grass verges on both sides of the road. Other officers were securing the area around the tree and along the boundary of the house with police tape. For twenty minutes the search seemed fruitless and then suddenly they heard an officer call out while pointing to something in the undergrowth. Charlie and Laura both stood but were unable to see what the something was. A member of the SOCO team approached the officer and lifted up one of the stone owls from the gateposts. Charlie gasped, "What! I hadn't even noticed one was missing."

Laura sat again down. "Neither had I."

Realising it was causing a great deal of interest, Charlie and Laura decided to go out to the lane to see if it was what the police had been looking for. A police officer held them back at the gates and forbade them to enter the lane but even from where they stood they could see dark stains on the snowy white stone.

An hour later the search came to an end and the owl was taken away for forensic examination. Charlie and Laura, both shocked, were asked to return indoors where their fingerprints were taken.

"So what can you tell me about the owl?" asked the DI, "When did you last handle it?"

"I only bought it and the other three from the garden centre a few days ago," said Charlie, "so the fingerprints of both of us are bound to be on it. I'm intending that all four are securely fastened to the gateposts, you see, but haven't had it done yet because we thought it made more sense to do it when Tom comes to fix the new nameplate on. He can do both jobs at the same time if you see what I mean."

After questioning the siblings extensively and taking fresh statements the police left them in peace but again asked them not to leave the area. The detective, however, had already concluded in his mind that Charlie had no motive to kill Mr Potts and neither had his sister. In fact from information received it seemed that it was Mr Potts who wanted to dispose of Mr Everton rather than the other way round. There was very little to go on at the scene but they would look further into the comment made by Charlie Everton, regarding the fact they had heard Mr Potts arguing with another man outside the Harbour Lights a day or two before his untimely death.

Chapter Nine

In the evening, Charlie and Laura sat by the fire mulling over the events of the past two days and especially the latest turn-up.

"What I can't get my head round is why someone killed poor old Mickey," said Charlie, "I mean, it certainly can't be because they caught him out by the trees with the silly tapes. Likewise I can't believe anyone disliked him enough to want him dead because he seemed to get on well with everyone."

Laura agreed, "I only met him the once but I liked him enormously and he certainly made me laugh with his ghost story nonsense."

"So can you make any sense of it, Laura?"

"No, and even if his death was to do with him wanting you to sell, no-one would expect him to be up here in the middle of the night, would they?"

Charlie shook his head. "Exactly, so how did someone know he'd be here?"

"I suppose Tracey must have known what he was up to but then she would have been in favour anyway, wouldn't she?"

Charlie poured a second glass of wine and topped up Laura's too. "Yes, but I got the impression from the police that Tracey knew nothing about it. That sergeant, Sally I think her name was, said Tracey was shocked when she heard he was out here and even more shocked when she heard about the fallen tree. Of course when she told us that, it was assumed his death was accidental. Poor Tracey, I should imagine now she knows he was murdered she's even more shocked."

Laura picked up her full glass of wine. "Thank you. Perhaps then it was Tracey who killed him and she pretended to be shocked. I mean, even if she didn't know what he was up to she could still have followed him when he crept out in the early hours."

"True but why on earth would she do that?"

"I don't know and it's a daft idea anyway. I mean, can you imagine not-a-hair-out-of-place-Tracey coming out here in the early hours with a fresh wind blowing and thunderstorms forecast? Not to mention the strong chance of rain."

"No, I can't but someone did and I should love to know who," As Charlie sat an image flashed across his mind, "Oh, for heaven's sake, I've just remembered something, Laura. Before I got into bed on the night Mickey was killed I stood by my window watching lightning flash out at sea. The storm was miles away but the lightning still lit the sky and during one flash I thought I saw someone out in the lane. I watched for the next flash but there was no-one there and so I assumed it was a trick of the light."

Laura stood her glass down on the hearth. "That's creepy because over the last few days I've felt someone has been watching us. I've not said anything though because I've nothing to back it up other than my intuition."

"Really? So when did you get these feelings?"

"Twice that I recall. The first time was when we came back after Christmas shopping and you were putting the owls on the gateposts. I thought I saw someone out of the corner of my eye but when I looked round there was no-one there. The second time was when we were walking back from your field. I thought I saw someone lurking outside the stable block but again when we got there, there was no-one around and the gates were all closed."

Charlie stood up. "Come and show me where you think they were?"

"But it's dark outside."

"Not a problem. The security lights will light up the stable block area and we'll take a torch to look in the lane."

Laura reluctantly stood wishing she'd kept her mouth shut. "Okay."

Charlie took a powerful torch from a peg in the hallway and together they walked out into the lane. It was a chilly, dark, moonless night with a fresh breeze blowing from the south west.

"So where do you reckon the figure you saw was?" Charlie flashed his torch back and forth.

Laura pointed up the lane beyond the curtilage of the Inn's grounds in the opposite direction to the entrance by the conifer trees. "Over there somewhere, near that tree whatever type it is."

"It's hawthorn. Come on, let's go and have a look."

"Why. Whoever it was isn't going to be there now." Laura wishing she had worn a coat folded her arms tightly in an attempt to get warm.

"No, but I still want to have a look."

They walked along the road to the hawthorn and found it was by a gateway leading into a field.

"Hmm, as I suspected, a good place to hide," said Charlie, "so maybe you're right and there was someone here and look, there are tyre tracks in the mud."

"But that's probably because a farmer or whoever owns the field drove in there recently."

"Could be I suppose."

"It's got to be the case," said Laura, "I know I thought I saw someone but let's be realistic. I mean, who could it be?"

"No idea. Let's go and check out the stable block."

Relieved to be nearer returning indoors, Laura happily followed.

"Right, whereabouts?" Charlie asked as they approached the stables and the security lights came back on.

"This end where you keep your car. I felt there was someone on this corner."

"So if there was he or she could easily have dashed behind the building and then disappeared amongst the trees."

"I suppose so, yes."

Charlie switched on his torch and walked around the side of the building towards the back. Laura waited by the garage door, her eyes flashing around hoping not to see anything untoward.

"Hmm, that's interesting," she heard her brother say.

"What's interesting?"

Charlie appeared back in the flood lights holding an empty cigarette packet. "What do you make of this?"

Laura shrugged her shoulders. "Anyone could have dropped it. Pat, Alex, Tom or any of the police officers who've been all over the place these past few days."

"No, it wouldn't have been Pat, Alex or Tom because I know for a fact that none of them smoke and I doubt police officers would while on duty."

"I bet they do."

"Well, there's one way to find out. I'll give DI Reynolds a ring in the morning and put him in the picture. He said to let him know if we remembered anything that might be of use."

Back indoors Charlie took a plastic bag from a drawer in the kitchen and dropped the cigarette packet inside. Laura went straight to the sitting room, warmed her hands by the fire and then picked up her glass of wine. Happy to be back in the warm she smiled as her brother entered the room. "Just thinking about the Mickey case and there's something else we've yet to fathom out, that being how on earth did my scarf get out there in the lane?"

Charlie sat down. "Goodness knows unless it blew there as I suggested to the police. I think it unlikely though. We looked all around outside to see if you'd dropped it and you checked the lane as well but there was no sign of it."

Laura looked alarmed. "Which means someone may have got hold of it with every intention of trying to frame you or us."

A log on the fire slipped precariously towards the front of the grate. Charlie poked it back into place and put another log on the fire. "But why, Laura?"

"Oh, I don't know. I'm into history: detective work's not my thing."

"It's not mine either but you could be onto something if someone's been watching our movements."

Laura shuddered. "That's a horrible thought."

"I agree but I don't think we should ignore it."

"Okay, so put your thinking cap on, Charlie, and try and remember if you've upset anyone since you've been down here? Someone who might want to get you into trouble."

Charlie rubbed his face with both hands. "As far as I can see I've not upset anyone other than the Potts but I think deep down Mickey was quite glad to have lost the auction because the impression I got was that he thought a health farm was a crackpot idea. Anyway I can't see anyone killing the poor man just to get me into trouble."

Laura frowned. "I'm trying to remember who sat near us when we went for a coffee the other day but not really knowing anyone here, no familiar faces spring to mind."

"Why are you trying to work that one out? I mean surely you don't really think someone deliberately took the scarf in the café in order to frame us."

"I do. Either that or it slipped under the table when I unbuttoned my coat and they picked it up after we left."

"You could well be right. The trouble is I don't recall seeing anyone I knew either and if someone took it on purpose intending to use it to frame us, it means that the

72

death of Mickey Potts was cold-blooded murder and that it was premeditated."

The colour drained from Laura's face. "And the Christmas wreath he had with him, which we assumed he intended to prank us with, was not on his chest by accident but was placed there by whoever killed him as a twisted mark of condolence."

Inside Bracken Farm, Tracey Potts sat at the kitchen table and wept. "I can't believe your dad went to such lengths to keep me happy and got himself killed in the process. What on earth was he thinking? Yes, I loved the idea of a health farm but I loved your dad more."

Becky stood, put her arms around her mother's shoulders and hugged her tightly. "I know you did. Poor Dad. I can't believe he's dead. It was bad enough thinking he was killed by a falling tree but to know he was murdered is just horrible. Whoever can have done it, Mum and why? It doesn't make sense."

Tracey wiped her eyes. "Well, I've thought about it a great deal, in fact it's all I've thought about and it seems to me that the person responsible has to be that Charlie bloke. You know, Charlie Everton, the chap who beat us at the auction. It happened on his doorstep so he's got to be the main suspect. I mean who else would be up there on a miserable night in December?"

Becky sat back down. "But why would he do it, Mum? He hardly knew Dad. It makes no sense."

"Probably not, but think about it. Your dad was trying to scare him and his sister away with that silly recording and what I reckon happened is that they must have realised what he was up to and crept out and caught him red-handed. I mean, according to the cops he'd done it a couple of times before so it might have really annoyed them. I know it would have annoyed me. Scared me too. Especially out there in a lonely spot like that." Tracey shuddered.

"But if they had gone out and found him, I think it more likely they'd have all had a good laugh together. I mean, come on, Mum, it's hardly a motive for murder, is it? What's more, Mr Everton and his sister have gained absolutely nothing by Dad dying. In fact quite the opposite. They have the attention of the media and the police and I'm sure they'd be a lot happier without either. If you ask me, Dad would have been the one with the motive and not the other way round."

"That's what the police say."

"Well, there you are then."

"But I'm told his sister's scarf was found near Mickey's body. You've got to admit that's a bit suspicious and don't forget the fingerprints of both of them were on the owl thing as well," persisted Tracey.

"Well it's hardly surprising their prints were on the owl as they only bought it a few days beforehand and as for the scarf, with the wind we've had lately it could quite easily have blown there from somewhere or other."

Tracey wasn't listening. "Poor Mickey, he tried to butter them up you know. He bought them both drinks in the pub the other day and sent a case of cider to the house a while back. He even sent them a Christmas card with one of his soppy smiley faces on it."

"And I'm sure they appreciated it. I really think you ought to stop making wild accusations, Mum, and let the police handle it."

"But if it wasn't them, then who was it, Becks? I mean someone did it and I need to know who." She slammed her fist down on the table and knocked over her empty coffee mug.

"You're getting overwrought, Mum. Try and keep calm."

The tears started to flow again. "I can't keep calm, Becky. Your dad's gone and I can't cope without him. I know nothing about the damn farm. I don't even know the difference between corn and hay even though your dad's explained it umpteen times. What am I going to do? I mean, I can't run this place. It's just not my thing and I hate getting mucky."

"I'll stay with you while we sort something out. Meanwhile the chaps Dad employs are very good and I'm sure they'll be only too willing to do that bit extra."

"Yes, I suppose so. Sam taught your dad everything he knows about farming and the two got on really well. The others all liked him too. Your dad made them laugh. He made me laugh. He made everyone laugh and even though we had the occasional disagreement I always loved him dearly. He was such a good-hearted peace-loving man and everyone loved him. I suppose he was right with his old phrase that where there is love there is happiness because there was lots of happiness here and now it's gone."

"And where there is love there is life," sighed Becky, "I know, he must have quoted those phrases to me a hundred times especially when I was a stroppy teenager who hated everyone and everything."

Tracey wiped her eyes and smiled. "You were a bit of a handful but your dad always said you'd turn out alright and you have."

"Thank you," Becky leaned back in her chair, glad to see her mother had moved on from thoughts of running the farm and Charlie Everton and his sister being guilty of murder. "Have you heard any more about the fact Dad was heard arguing with someone outside the Harbour Lights about an unpaid wager or something like that?"

Tracey forced a smile. "Yes, the police asked me about that."

"And?"

"The chap he was arguing with would've been Jim Pascoe. You know, he lives down by the harbour. Big chap in his mid to late fifties. Used to be a fisherman but now drives a lorry for a haulage firm."

"Can't say as I know him but then I don't live here, do I?"

"No, I keep forgetting that."

"So what was it about?"

A smile crossed Tracey's lips. "Well, as you know your dad liked to follow the tennis and apparently Jim does too and it appears they had a bit of a disagreement as to who'd win a semi-final match somewhere or other. In the end your dad said so-and-so would win and he bet five hundred quid on it. Jim told him he was daft and said the other bloke would win. They agreed and shook hands on the deal."

"I see, so was it Wimbledon?"

"No, no it was Australia, America or somewhere like that."

"So, what happened, who won?"

"Jim's man. You see, the chap your dad backed slipped and badly twisted his ankle in the second set and after the doctor was called he was deemed unfit to play, meaning Dad's bloke lost. Jim was cock-a-hoop until Dad said he wouldn't pay up. Your dad reckoned because Jim's chap's win was a fluke it wasn't fair and I'm inclined to agree with him. This was months ago and they've been arguing about it ever since but to be fair, it's usually in good humour and after they've had a few beers."

Chapter Ten

The following morning, Tom arrived to fix the name plate on one of the gateposts. As he took tools from the back of his van he asked about the owls. Charlie said he'd decided to leave them for the time being as the police still held one as evidence and he thought it would be better to wait and have all four put in place at the same time. Laura disagreed and suggested as a compromise two owls be put on one set of gateposts and the others could be done later. To keep the peace Charlie reluctantly agreed and so the upper gateposts furthest away from the crime scene were duly crowned with a pair of birds. When the name plate was securely fitted on the front of a lower gate post, Tom joined Charlie in the kitchen for coffee. After removing his jacket he sat down at the table. "Rum do about poor old Mickey, isn't it?"

"It is, he seemed a good sort and although I hardly knew him I'll definitely miss him."

"Yes, I'll miss him too and the world will be a sadder place without him. We often had a game of darts in the Harbour Lights. He nearly always won as well. He was a right deadeye Dick," Tom took a biscuit from the plate Charlie had placed on the table, "He had a smashing singing voice you know and sang with the local male voice choir."

"Really, tenor or bass?"

"Tenor and they often chose him to do the solo bits so they'll miss him too."

"I should like to have heard him. I reckon a good male voice choir takes a bit of beating." Charlie placed two mugs of coffee on the table and then sat down. "Sounds like he was a good bloke all round. He was certainly always courteous to me and he made me smile even when he was trying to persuade me to sell this place to him."

"Yes, I've heard rumours about that but to be honest I think you'll find he was secretly relieved you refused to sell because he hated the notion of the health farm. He thought it was a crazy idea but had to show he was making an effort just to appease Trace."

"I'm glad you've told me that because that's the impression I got too and was only saying the same to Laura last night."

Tom thoughtfully took a sip of his coffee. "Although having said that, I was talking to my next door neighbour the other day and she said when she was at the hairdressers last week she overheard Tracey saying she reckoned that before long you'd get fed up living here and sell the place to Mickey. She said it was a waste of space you being here on your own and the place could be put to much better use."

Laura who had been upstairs changing her bed linen overheard what was said as she entered the kitchen, "Nothing like a bit of wishful thinking, eh, Tom?"

"Maybe but I think you'll find it was a bit more than wishful thinking with Trace. She reckoned it was written in the stars, you see. Apparently she'd reads her horoscope daily and that morning it told her, not to give up hope because her dreams would soon come true."

"There's one born every minute," laughed Laura.

Charlie frowned. "Have you heard about what Mickey had been doing up here, Tom?"

"No, although I have wondered why he was up here in the early hours and my mates have said the same. Of course there are all sorts of theories but none of them make any sense."

"And the real reason makes no sense either. You see, the police found all kinds of recording equipment under the trees not far from Mickey's body. On it were horses galloping, neighing and so forth. We assume he had it because he wanted to convince us that the tale he span us about the ghost of a highwayman or whatever wasn't something he'd made up."

"You mean he was trying to put the wind up you?"

"Yes."

Tom tutted. "Dear, oh dear. I remember him going on about it in the pub that night and I must admit I did wonder why he'd dug it up."

"Of course you were there, yes. I remember now and wasn't it you who ticked him off for telling porkies?"

"No, I think it was Pat but whatever we share the same opinion."

Laura having made coffee for herself sat down at the table with the two men. "Charlie failed to mention that Mickey must have put his silly plan into action before the night he died because on a couple of occasions we were woken by the sound of a horse in the lane, little knowing it was a recording."

Tom chuckled. "Is that right? Goodness me, what a Muppet."

"Yes, and sadly we fell for it," admitted Charlie.

"But we didn't for one minute think it was anything ghostly," said Laura, "we just assumed it was Mickey on a real horse, meaning Mickey's not the only Muppet around here."

"If Trace had known what he was up to she'd have had a good laugh," said Tom, "admittedly she's been a bit grumpy of late but if you get her on a good day she's wonderful company because she has a great sense of humour, especially when she's in the pub and has had a drink. That's when she starts telling jokes and unlike me she can always remember the punchline."

"Is that right?" said Charlie, "Poor soul, she doesn't have much to laugh about now though, does she? I can't say that I liked the woman but she doesn't deserve this. Especially just before Christmas."

79

Tom nodded. "I agree. It's said she was very dependent on Mickey and he worshipped the ground she walked on."

Later, as daylight faded, Charlie stood up and drew the sitting room curtains. "Fancy going to the pub tonight, Laura? I ask because I'm sure I saw a notice on the wall when we were there saying that Wednesday was Quiz Night and I rather fancy using the old grey matter."

Laura looked up from the book she was reading. "Yes, why not. It'd be nice to get out and see a few people, we might even find out if there have been any developments in the Mickey Potts case."

Charlie sat back down. "Yes, but I somehow doubt it."

"Be more optimistic, Charlie. I mean for all we know the village might have some amateur sleuths and they'll be able to enlighten us. Ruby for instance. I bet she has her finger on the pulse especially working in the pub. She worked for Mickey and Tracey too so probably knows them as well as, if not better, than anyone."

"I expect she still does. Work for them, that is. Well, at least for Tracey anyway. As for village folk I'm sure most will have an opinion. Some might even have a suspect in mind but I bet they won't have any evidence to back up their theories."

Laura closed her book and placed it on a footstool. "And if they have I doubt they'll be right anyway."

They ordered a taxi for seven o'clock even though Charlie had checked on-line and they knew the quiz didn't start until eight-thirty. He wanted them to arrive early in case the pub was busy and there was a shortage of seats. To their delight there were several tables to choose from on their arrival so they sat in a corner where they were able to look down the length of the bar and see people as they came and went.

Shortly before eight as they were enjoying a glass of wine, a tall woman, dressed in black, slightly overweight and with short curly grey hair walked into the pub and sat down on a stool at the bar. To the surprise of Charlie and Laura she wore a dog collar.

"Good evening, Vicar," said Ruby, "your usual?"

"Yes please, Ruby." She cast her eyes around the bar, "Your mum not here yet? She's usually here well before me."

As Ruby poured the vicar a small sherry she glanced at the clock. "No, but I expect she'll be here any minute. She'd never miss Quiz Night."

"Thank goodness. I'd be rubbish without her but don't tell her that."

As she spoke, a petite lady, no more than five foot two who looked to be in her sixties and who was wearing a turquoise track suit, entered the bar. "Sorry I'm late, Joy," she puffed, "Got a damn puncture so had to patch it up and then pedal here at twice my normal speed and now my legs are a bit wobbly."

The vicar pulled out a stool and helped the latest arrival to sit.

"You should be more careful, Mum," scolded Ruby, from behind the bar, "You're not as young as you used to be."

"Nor are any of us, Ruby. Nor are any of us."

"Yeah true I suppose but you know what I mean. Anyway, half a Guinness?"

"No, a pint, please love. I'm feeling thirsty and pour one for Joy too. Her glass is nearly empty."

By eight-thirty the bar was busy and all tables were taken.

"I feel quite nervous," admitted Charlie, as he watched Landlord Greg hand out sheets of paper. "There are quite a few people in some of the teams. I hope we don't come last."

"So do I but then there are only two in that team – Ruby's mum and the vicar so we should at least be able to do as well as them."

As the questions were read out, Charlie watched team members enthusiastically scribbling down answers. There seemed to be very little chewing of pens or tapping fingers against teeth.

"I reckon this lot come here every week," he hissed to Laura, as they both tried to recall the name of a tune, "They all look very determined."

To their relief they came a respectable fifth and the winners were Vicar Joy and Ruby's mum, Joan. After the prizes had been given out, Charlie and Laura congratulated the two winners and introduced themselves.

Joan shook hands with both vigorously: her grip surprisingly firm. "Ah, so you're the new owner of the Old Inn. I've heard about you from our Ruby and our Cissy as well. How are you settling in?"

"Fine, fine," said Charlie, "especially now big sister's here to keep me company."

"It's a big place to be living in on your own," said the vicar as she shook hands with the siblings, "rather you than me."

"I agree, lonely too," Joan added, "I like to have neighbours. Nothing like a bit of gossip."

"Well, I'm happy up there. In fact I love the peace and quiet although the death of poor old Mickey Potts has rather put a damper on things these past few days."

Joan sighed. "Yes, strange that. Mickey was a nice bloke even if his missus was a bit of a floozy."

The vicar tutted.

"Do you live in Porthgwyns?" Laura asked.

"Yes, and have done all my life as did my parents before me. Cornish born, Cornish bred and all that."

"Really! You must know a little of the Inn's history then," said Charlie.

"Yes, I know a fair bit and I have some old pictures too. Pop along for a coffee sometime and I'll show them to you."

"We'd like that very much," enthused Laura, "I'm a historian so that'll be right up my street."

"So, whereabouts do you live, Joan?" Charlie asked.

"In Higher Road. It's just up past the post office. My humble dwelling is called Cuttlefish Cottage." Joan opened up her handbag, "I'll write down my phone number for you then you can ring me when you want to call to make sure I'm in. Not that I go far these days."

Vicar Joy tutted. "I wouldn't say that, Joan you're out most days pedalling around on your old bike."

"And do you live in the village too, Vicar?" Charlie asked.

"I do, yes, but I'm a relative newcomer and have only been here for a year. I'm on the opposite side of the village to Joan. In the vicarage, which would you believe is quite near the church?"

"But it's not the big rambling old place with huge gardens," said Joan, "that's the old vicarage."

"No, no, mine's a modest house a few doors away," said the vicar, "The church sold the old vicarage a while back because it needed extensive work done to it and it's currently being done up and turned into a guest house."

Joan nodded towards the door. "They had an auction there after the old vicar died and before the place was sold. That's where I got my bike. It's a beauty and much better than my old one."

Chapter Eleven

On Thursday morning, Ruby went to work at Bracken Farm. She was a little apprehensive and unsure what state of mind she might find Tracey in but hoped that Becky's presence would have a calming effect on the widow. To her relief when she arrived Tracey was putting on her jacket. "It's a nice morning so I'm just popping out for a while, Ruby. I need to clear my head and so I'm going for a leisurely stroll over the fields. I haven't been out since Mickey died, you see and I need some fresh air." She glanced towards the window, "Becky's not here at the moment, she's out in the fields with the lads cutting cauli and has taken a packed lunch with her so she won't be back before four. Anyway, I'll leave you to it but if I'm not home before you've finished I'll see you next time you're here."

"Of course, I understand and you have my deepest sympathy. He was a good bloke was Mickey and he'll be sorely missed by everyone."

"Thank you." Tracey looked on the verge of tears. She turned as she approached the door. "Please help yourself to coffee and there's a lemon drizzle cake in the tin on top of the fridge. Becky made it and it's very nice."

"Thank you."

Tracey closed the door behind her as she stepped out onto the path; Ruby watched from the window as she pulled on a pair of gloves and walked across the farmyard towards the fields.

A strong perfume hung in the air and so Ruby went into the hallway to find its source. The sitting room door was open, she stepped inside, vases filled with flowers from well-wishers stood on the mantelpiece, the sideboard and the table along with an abundance of condolence cards. Ruby read the inscriptions; most were from local people. Deep in thought she went into the kitchen and took cleaning items from the cupboard beneath the sink. Without the usual spring in her step she then made her way upstairs to the bedrooms because Thursday was the day she always changed the beds.

In the doorway of Mickey's room she paused. His king size bed was unmade and looked as he must have left it on the night he had gone to the Old Inn. His reading book and glasses were on the table beneath his bedside lamp and his blue and white striped pyjamas lay neatly across his pillows. Ruby felt her eyes begin to water. It didn't seem right to be in the room so soon after his death. It didn't seem right to be in the house. She took in a deep breath. The job had to be done even though there was no-one to sleep in the room. She stripped the bed and put the bedding into the dirty linen basket on the landing along with the pyjamas. She then put on fresh linen and dusted the hard surfaces. On top of a tall chest of drawers stood a framed photograph of Mickey in his late teens. Ruby picked it up; he was a good looking man when he died but in his younger days he was extremely handsome. She finished the room and then walked along the landing to the room next door where Tracey slept. Tracey's room was untidy; clothes were strewn across the floor; a mug half filled with cold strong coffee sat on her bedside cabinet along with an overflowing ashtray and a bottle of sleeping pills. Face down on her pillows laid an old teddy bear that Tracey had owned since childhood. Ruby placed the mug and ashtray by the door in order to take them down to the kitchen, she then changed the bed, tidied up and placed the bear beneath the duvet after first straightening the hand knitted jumper he wore bearing his name, Raymond. Ruby then went to the room at the end of the landing, Becky's choice for her stay.

Once the bedrooms were all clean and tidy, she went to the cupboard beneath the stairs to collect the vacuum cleaner. After cleaning the carpet in Mickey's room she quietly closed the door, made her way to Tracey's room and pushed the cleaner's plug into the socket beside the wardrobe. When vacuuming beneath the bed the cleaner made a sudden screeching sound. Ruby cursed. The noise indicated that something was trapped in the brush. Surprised because she knew nothing was stored under the bed, she switched off the machine and knelt down to have a look. Stuck in the end of the pipe was an item of clothing. Ruby pulled it out. It was a jacket. Tracey's jacket and there were patches of dried blood on its front and one of the sleeves.

Ruby dropped the garment in revulsion, leapt backwards and hit her elbow on the door. To whom did the blood belong? Why was the jacket tucked beneath the bed? Was it to hide it? Ruby panicked. She needed advice. She needed to phone the police but Tracey might be back at any moment and she didn't want the widow to catch her on the phone. "I'll do it when I get home," she muttered to herself and with knees trembling she kicked the jacket back beneath the bed and finished vacuuming the floor. Feeling too shaken to clean the carpets in Becky's room and on the landing, she ran down the stairs and pushed the cleaner back inside the cupboard. Trying to keep calm, she then returned to Tracey's room and again pulled out the jacket. With shaking fingers she laid it out on the floor and using her phone took several pictures of the bloodstains. Satisfied with the clarity of her work, she then pushed the garment back beneath the bed and eager to leave the room, closed the door and stepped out onto the landing.

"I must act normal, I must act normal. But what shall I do now? I don't finish 'til twelve so I can't go home yet because if I did Tracey might suspect something. Coffee, yes, I'll make a coffee."

Ruby stumbled clumsily down the stairs, along the hallway and into the kitchen. She picked up the kettle and water splashed her clothing as she filled it with unsteady hands. "I must stop shaking. Oh my God this is awful."

Somehow she managed to make a coffee and sat down at the kitchen table to drink it. She looked at the clock. It was a quarter to twelve. "Just fifteen more minutes and then I can go. Oh please get held up Tracey and don't get back before I leave."

On top of the work surface were several items which needed washing including the dirty mug and ashtray she had taken from Tracey's room. Ruby looked in the dishwasher. It was empty so not worth putting on for a few mugs, dishes and plates. "I'll wash them. I usually do anyway. Must act normal."

Ruby washed the dishes without breaking any. She then dried them, put them away and returned the clean ashtray to Tracey's room. Back downstairs she looked at the clock. It was one minute to twelve.

"Thank God," she cried as she reached for her coat. Quickly she put it on, pulled the car keys from her pocket and left the house. She looked around. No sign of Tracey. She put the keys in the ignition and drove across the farmyard. As she turned into the lane she saw Tracey walking across the field. Ruby tooted and forced a smile. Tracey waved. Ruby heaved a great sigh of relief and drove home at twice her normal speed.

Chapter Twelve

As Charlie and Laura sat watching the early evening news, the house phone rang. Expecting it to be a nuisance call, Charlie half-heartedly went out to the hallway to answer it. To his surprise, Cissy was the caller. Charlie listened to what she had to say and then returned to the sitting room in a state of shock to convey the news to his sister. He sat down. "You're never going to believe this, Laura, but Tracey Potts has been arrested for the murder of Mickey."

"What!" Laura placed the glass of wine she had half way to her lips onto the coffee table by her armchair.

"That was Cissy on the phone. Apparently her mum found a blood stained jacket under Tracey's bed when she was doing the room this morning. Tracey wasn't there, thank goodness; she'd gone for a walk. She hadn't returned when Ruby finished at twelve and so Ruby was able to get away quickly without seeing her and as soon as she got home she rang the police."

"And has she been charged?"

"Cissy doesn't know any more than what I've told you. I suppose they can't do much more than question her until they have evidence."

Laura picked up the remote control and switched off the television. "I suppose then they'll be waiting for Forensics to see if the blood matches that of Mickey. How awful."

"Yes, I expect so. We'll just have to wait and see what they come up with."

"Of course even if the blood is a match it doesn't mean she killed him though, does it? She could have been wearing it when he cut his hand or something like that."

Charlie shook his head. "But if that were to be the case, why would she hide the jacket under the bed? That's very suspicious if you ask me."

"Perhaps it got kicked under there by accident. I mean, if she's guilty surely the first thing she would have done was dispose of it as it's incriminating evidence."

"But dispose of it, where? She'd be reluctant to put it in the rubbish in case the bins were searched by the police. Likewise, she'd not risk drawing attention to it by burning it. After all, next of kin are usually the first to be questioned in a murder case and she'd be aware that the police would be unlikely to look under her bed without just cause. So it might have seemed the best option until she felt it was safe to get rid of it permanently. As it is, it looks as though she must have forgotten about it."

Laura drummed her fingers on the side of her wine glass. "I think there has to be a simple explanation, after all we agreed the other day that my scarf being there indicated the murder was possibly premeditated and if that was the case then it couldn't have been Tracey. I mean, why would she follow him all the way out here when she could have bumped him off at the farm?"

"Because on the farm she'd be a suspect whereas out here anyone could have done it."

"Yes, but on the farm she could have made it look like an accident."

"No way, not in this day and age, Laura. Forensics are pretty good at smelling rats; they'd suss out a staged accident in no time."

"What about the wreath then? I mean surely Tracey wouldn't be callous enough to place it on his body like that."

"Maybe she didn't. He might just have been holding it because he was in the throes of swapping them over again and that's why it was with him."

"Rubbish," Laura stood up and refilled her wine glass, "He wouldn't take it out under the trees if he was just swapping them over."

"Perhaps he had some other trick up his sleeve then."

"Such as?"

"Oh, I don't know, Laura."

Laura topped up Charlie's glass. "Okay, so does Tracey smoke?"

"What! How on earth should I know that?"

"No idea, but remember you found a cigarette packet behind the stable block." Laura replaced the cork in the wine bottle and sat down.

"Yes and the police said it could have been dropped by anyone and probably blew there."

"But they're hanging on to it for the time being just in case, aren't they?"

Charlie sighed deeply. "Yes, Laura, and I'm sure they'll check to see if it matches Tracey's DNA. If it does then that'll be evidence against her but even if it doesn't, it won't prove that she's innocent."

"Well I reckon she is innocent," Laura was belligerent.

Charlie, surprised by his sister's quarrelsome tone, raised his eyebrows, "Maybe and time will tell but I know where my money goes."

Over the next few days, the revelation that the murder of Mickey Potts might possibly have been committed by his wife was the main topic of conversation and everywhere Charlie and Laura went they were greeted by all who recognised them as the folks from Seven Pines or the Old Inn as locals still called it. The spurious offers of friendship were of course a means of extracting any little detail that might be unknown to their friends and neighbours so they could relish their newfound knowledge and gloat as they passed it on.

"I must admit I'm tempted to throw in a few porkies," confessed Charlie, as he and Laura sat in a coffee shop shortly after being accosted by an employee of the local hairdressing salon who was renowned for her wagging tongue.

"Oh dear, it must be a family trait then because I've thought of doing the same. Although to be perfectly honest I can't see why there's so much interest in us. I mean, we hardly knew Mickey, and Tracey even less so. And as far as a motive is concerned, there surely has to be a reason for her taking Mickey's life, if she did, which I doubt, and it certainly can't be because she was outraged to find him trying to frighten you into selling, because that's ridiculous."

"I agree and he was doing it for her anyway. At least we assume he was. I suppose it's possible that he had an ulterior motive."

Laura broke the Eccles cake on her plate in two. "Could be the case. Anyway, has she confessed, do you know?"

"Not sure. I've heard nothing from anyone in authority and I doubt village gossip is to be relied on. Having said that, I should imagine the blood stained jacket is pretty solid evidence and the blood must have been Mickey's otherwise they'd have released her by now."

"But surely as I said when we first heard, the blood could be from an accident. You know, something happened on the farm. He cut his hand maybe and she bathed and dressed it for him while wearing the jacket."

"True, but then as we've already said, why hide it under the bed? I mean, surely most women would have chucked it in the washing machine to get the stains out before they dried."

"Hmm, I certainly would have done because blood is a pain to remove from anything."

The police after being informed by Forensics that all available evidence at the murder scene had been collected, called at Seven Pines to tell Charlie that he was free to dispose of the tree in whatever manner he chose. After they left, Charlie rang the number of a chainsaw specialist and arranged for the tree to be cut up and the jagged stump to be sawn down to ground level. The contractor arrived three days later in a tractor with a trailer. After cutting the tree into rings, the rings were winched onto the trailer and transported into the courtyard where they were split into manageable pieces. Charlie and Laura then stacked them in the log shed in order for them to dry out.

Laura, who felt pretty certain the stump of the tree would never sprout new growth and even if it did the new growth would be ugly, the following day said she was popping out for a while. When she returned she called Charlie out to her car saying she had something for him. With its pot in the boot part of her hatchback and its top stretched out across the back seat was a cupressus macrocarpa tree.

A huge smile crossed Charlie's face. "Thanks Laura that's really sweet of you but we can't plant it where the other one was because of the stump and it'd take heavy machinery to get it out."

"I agree but I see no reason why you can't plant it at the other end of the row. I've checked and there's more than enough room."

"Of course, it's the obvious solution," he leaned over and kissed his sister's cheek, "And as there's no time like the present, I'll dig a hole for it now."

Together they removed the tree from the car. Charlie then went to the log shed where he kept his gardening tools. Laura made cups of tea and when the hole was dug she helped Charlie manoeuvre the tree into place and get it straight. When done they looked back to admire their handiwork.

"Well at least the locals won't be able to call it six pines now," said Laura.

Charlie laughed. "No but I bet some bright spark will call it six and a half pines on account of its size."

Chapter Thirteen

At the beginning of the Christmas holiday, Charlie's son, Daniel, who taught music at a school in Reading, arrived at the Inn. With him was his sister, Florence who he had picked up en route following her university breaking up for the festive season.

The siblings on receiving a tour of the house expressed words of approval and chose their rooms from the four unoccupied. Florence opted for an en suite overlooking the upper gates and shrubbery at the far end of the property which also had sea views. Daniel chose a smaller room without facilities at the back of the house because of its far reaching outlook over the countryside. After they had unpacked they joined their father and aunt around the kitchen table for tea, and a chocolate cake which Laura had made especially for the occasion.

"Christmas is going to be fantastic here," enthused Florence, casting a glance at the beams overhead, "because this house is just...well, so Christmassy."

"Trust you to think that," said Daniel, "but then you always were a Christmas nut. Although I must admit I can see where you're coming from. This house reeks of history but feels modern at the same time."

Charlie beamed with pride. "I'm glad it meets with your approval."

"Oh, it does," gushed Florence, "and I give it ten out of ten."

"Likewise," Daniel finished his cake and held up his plate for more.

"Someone's hungry," Laura cut him an even larger second slice.

"We didn't have any lunch, did we, Flo?"

"No, the reason being you wouldn't stop because you were so eager to get here and hear the latest news about the poor farmer who popped his clogs."

"Partly true but I also wanted to get here before it was dark."

"Fibber. That was never an issue because you left Reading at eight this morning. It's not even dark now and we've been here for an hour."

Daniel looked sheepish. "So have there been any new developments?" He looked at his father and aunt.

Charlie shook his head. "We've heard no more since you rang the other day, have we, Laura?"

"No and we don't even know whether Tracey, his wife, has been charged or not."

"Anyway, I suggest we go to the pub tonight and we might find out more then," Charlie took a second slice of cake while there was still some left.

"Sounds like a good idea," enthused Daniel, "I'm looking forward to meeting some of the people you've told me about."

It was decided that rather than go to the Harbour Lights for just a drink they would also go for a meal so that Florence and Daniel could sample the delights of Landlady Grace's culinary skills. They booked a taxi for six-thirty and a table for seven.

After they had finished their food they returned to the bar and sat around a table in the corner. As Daniel placed drinks, just purchased, on their table, two men arrived and sat down on stools at the bar. Florence's eyes lit up. Both were tanned despite it being mid-winter, were extremely handsome and dressed in expensive designer clothes. As they ordered their drinks all heads turned in their direction.

"I don't suppose you know where Mr and Mrs Potts are, do you?" The asker pushed back a loose dark curl which had fallen over his eye, "We've been up to their farm twice today and on both occasions no-one was in."

A hushed silence fell over the bar.

Ruby felt her face flush. "Ah, yes...um...do you know them then?"

"No, but when we told our neighbours we were coming to Cornwall for Christmas they said if we were anywhere near Porthgwyns to look them up. The Potts are old friends of theirs apparently. They used to live near each other years ago or something like that."

"Oh, I see, well in that case if you don't actually know Mickey and Tracey Potts it makes telling you where they are a bit easier." Ruby then went on to tell of the latest news with the help of others sitting in the bar. After they had digested information received, the two men introduced themselves as brothers, Edward and Richard Rudd down from Oxford. Both, in their mid-forties stood just short of six feet in height and were slim in build. Edward was bespectacled and wore his light brown hair short; it was Richard who owned the loose dark curls.

"So, out of curiosity, if Mr and Mrs Potts aren't here to oversee things, what'll happen to the farm?" Edward asked, "I mean, if they have livestock the animals will need to be cared for."

Ruby, who knew more than most about the ins and outs of Bracken Farm answered. "The farm has four fulltime employees and Mickey and Tracey also have a daughter, Becky. She's a hairdresser and lives somewhere in the Plymouth area. She came down after her father's death to keep her mum company and help the lads run the place but went back home yesterday because they've finished cutting cauli now for this week. She and her chap will be back tomorrow though to keep an eye on the place while they decide what to do while Tracey is in...err...away."

"I reckon they'll put tenant farmers in," said Greg the landlord.

"I hope they do," said Tom, who was in for a drink with his wife, "that way they can keep the lads on. Sam Nixon's worked on that farm since he left school and I'd hate to think of him out of a job."

Ruby nodded. "You're right. I've heard Mickey say on many occasions that he doesn't know what he'd have done without him."

Tom finished his pint, nodded to Greg to refill his glass and indicated his wife would have another one too. "It's a pity Sam couldn't raise the money when the farm came up for sale. I know he was desperate to buy it but Mickey and Tracey stepped in before he'd even had a chance to put his house on the market and approach the bank for a business loan."

"Is that right?" said Greg, "What rotten luck. Not that I've ever met the bloke. In fact I wouldn't know him from Adam."

"Sam doesn't drink, that's why. He's the early to bed early to rise type."

"Oh dear, don't want too many like that," Greg chuckled as he handed Tom a fresh pint.

"Going back to the farm, they'll have to keep it going somehow," said Ruby, "I mean, Becky can't sell the place, can she? Because it isn't hers to sell."

"True, but then Tracey might ask her to sell it on her behalf as it's going to be a while before she's free to go back there," said Tom, "In fact, I doubt she'll want to live there ever again because from what I've heard she has zero interest in it as a farm anyway."

"It'd be the ideal chance for her to turn it into a health farm though now Mickey's gone," said Ruby, "but I doubt she will because she said the location isn't right."

"Don't know why, I reckon it's a lovely spot." Tom handed Greg a ten pound note.

"Well whatever, I think now she's been charged it'll be a good few years before she's footloose and fancy free again," said Ruby, "So she'll have plenty of time to think about it."

"Assuming she's found guilty," said Greg, "remember in this country a person is innocent until proven guilty."

"Oh, she's guilty alright," said Tom, "I've heard her prints were all over the recording equipment even though she claims to know nothing about it."

"And they found a few conifer needles stuck to the fabric of her jacket," said Libby, Tom's wife.

"Has she been charged then?" Charlie was surprised.

"Yes," said Ruby.

"I didn't know. When was that then?"

"This morning," said Tom, "so the news hasn't reached everyone's ears yet. I didn't even know 'til I got here this evening."

"The thing that's baffling me though is why," said Ruby, "I mean, what on earth could have been her motive? I never picked up on any animosity between the two of them. Okay they had the odd tiff but who doesn't. Most of the time they seemed to get on really well even though they were chalk and cheese."

"Well we'll have to wait and see," said Tom, "It'll all come out in the wash."

"Does anyone know if she'll be at the funeral tomorrow?" Greg asked.

All shook their heads.

"Would she be allowed?" Edward who had listened with interest spoke with doubt.

"Probably with a police escort," said Tom, "Having said that because she's accused of his murder, I'm not so sure. I mean, it'd be a bit odd, wouldn't it?"

"And I very much doubt Becky would want her there?" Ruby having recently spoken to Becky at the farm knew she was deeply hurt and had vowed to not even visit her mother.

"What time is the funeral?" Charlie asked.

"Half twelve at the church," said Ruby, "and he's to be buried there too. Tracey let it be known she wanted him cremated but Becky overruled her mother saying her dad told her when they first bought the farm that he'd like to be buried in Porthgwyns because of the view over the harbour and the sea."

Edward frowned. "Nice thought but when you're gone you're gone so he'll not be able to enjoy the view."

"Well if Mickey's belief in ghosts is right he won't be six feet under, he'll be floating around the farm and maybe even riding his tractor." Tom chuckled at the thought.

His wife nudged him in the ribs. "Behave. It's not right to mock the dead."

"I'm not mocking him and were he here he'd whole-heartedly agree."

"Did Mr Potts believe in ghosts then?" Richard looked amused.

"Oh let's not go down that road," groaned Charlie.

Greg looked at the brothers. "Let's just say yes and leave it at that."

Jiffy Lemon listened to the talk with interest and then addressed the new arrivals. "You two lads wouldn't by any chance be the owners of that impressive luxury yacht moored offshore would you?"

Edward beamed with pride. "Yes, that's ours, the *Golden Sunset*. Had it a few years now."

"First time in Cornwall then?" Ruby asked.

"No, as a matter of fact we were in the county last summer but a bit further along the coast. We've just called in here because of our neighbours, but I don't know about you, Rich but I rather like this pub so we may well stay in the area for the festive season instead of moving round to St. Ives. Might be tricky going round Land's End anyway if the weather changes."

"I'm more than happy to do that," Richard cast his eyes over the people in the bar, "So, are you all locals?"

Several nodded.

Florence eager to speak to the brothers raised her hand. "We're not. Well, not all of us. I suppose Dad's a local now that he lives here."

"Not in the village though," Charlie added, "I live five miles along the coast, east of here."

"Is there another village there then?"

Jiffy chuckled. "No, this young man is now the owner of a charming old coaching inn. He pipped me at the post when it came up for auction."

"Really, so where did you live before that?"

"Buckinghamshire," said Charlie.

"Ah, we were nearly neighbours then. As I said earlier, we live just over the border from your erstwhile home, in Oxfordshire."

It was after eleven when the family left the Harbour Lights. As they waited outside for their taxi, Daniel pointed out the colourful illuminations on the *Golden Sunset* twinkling in the darkness offshore.

"I didn't see that when we arrived," said Charlie.

"That's because we dashed straight inside when we got out of the taxi because it was beginning to rain," Laura reminded him.

"Yes, of course, Silly me."

Florence's eyes were focused on the yacht. "Wow! Look at that. I think this Christmas is going to be one to remember."

The following day dawned bright and sunny but because it was cold everyone at Seven Pines opted to have porridge for breakfast hence the milk supply was quickly depleted.

Charlie picked up the near empty container. "Anyone fancy popping over to Porthgwyns to get some more otherwise there will be very little tea or coffee until we go shopping this afternoon."

Florence jumped up from her seat. "I'll go. I want to see how big that yacht looks in daylight."

"But Porthgwyns is five miles away," laughed Dan, "and you don't have a car."

Flo's shoulders slumped. "Is it really that far? It didn't seem it in the taxi."

"Afraid so," said Charlie.

"In which case you'd better give me a lift, Dan. Come on."

Dan reached for his car keys. "Happy to do so as I'd like to take another look at that boat as well."

"There's a small shop that sells milk down near the harbour," said Charlie, "but don't be gone too long. Remember your aunt and I have a funeral to attend later and I'm sure we'll be wanting a coffee before we go."

"I thought you weren't going." Florence sat down on the floor lacing up her shoes.

"We weren't but after hearing people talk about it last night in the pub we've changed our mind. After all the poor man died up here trying to prank us and so I feel we ought to go and show there are no hard feelings."

By late morning the sun which had welcomed the day was hidden behind threatening grey clouds. Not liking the look of the sky, Charlie searched the cupboard under the stairs for his large black umbrella and tucked it beneath his arm.

"Will you two be alright while we're gone?" he asked.

"Dad, I'm twenty and Dan's twenty-five so I think we're old enough to look after ourselves."

Laura picked up her handbag. "That's as maybe but you'll always be children to your dad. I know what it's like. I still think of Susie as my baby even though she's married, a mother and has been out in Canada for three years."

Saint Michael's Church was full and every seat taken when Charlie and Laura arrived so they joined the group of people standing at the back alongside a tub of wet umbrellas. There was a lot of hushed chatter amongst the congregation as the organ played sorrowful music and Charlie wished he had the ability to identify people by the back of their head in order to establish who was there. At half past twelve everyone stood and Vicar Joy entered the building through the arched doorway followed by Mickey Potts' coffin on the shoulders of his four loyal employees. Behind were family members: Becky wiping away tears as she clung onto the arm of her boyfriend, Mickey's two brothers, their wives, and a cousin he'd not seen for six years. Tracey was not amongst the mourners nor were any members of her family.

The service was short. Just one hymn, prayers, a reading by Vicar Joy and a eulogy presented by Sam Nixon, Mickey's instructor on all things to do with the farm. At no point was Tracey's name mentioned.

After the service mourners gathered outside in the rain for the interment. Charlie and Laura stood well back huddled beneath the black umbrella watching as Mickey was lowered into the ground.

Afterwards people headed for the Harbour Lights where Becky had arranged a buffet. She had considered asking people back to the farm but decided it would not be appropriate as pictures of her parents hung from the walls and their possessions filled every room. Charlie and Laura, feeling they were outsiders, gave the pub visit a miss and drove home deep in thought.

Chapter Fourteen

The rain continued all night but by morning had fizzled out to little more than a light drizzle. A thick mist hung in the still air, visibility was poor and from Seven Pines it was not possible to see out into the lane.

"The weather's not very Christmassy," complained Florence as she took her place around the kitchen table. "I was hoping for snow or at least a heavy frost."

Daniel looked up from his mobile phone. "But it's not Christmas yet."

"No, but it soon will be and so the weather needs to buck its ideas up to get us in the right mood."

"Well if it'll help get you in the mood, I can tell you we've a Christmas tree being delivered this morning," said Charlie, "In fact it should be here pretty soon."

"A real one?" Florence's eyes lit up.

"Yes, a six footer. Tom, who did a lot of the plumbing work here is dropping it off."

"Wow, brilliant, Dad. It'll look gorgeous in your big room." Florence blew a kiss across the table. "That's just what I need right now so thank you."

"Don't thank me, thank your Auntie Laura, it was her idea. I said we were all too old for a tree."

"Exactly," said Laura, "and I told your father you can never be too old for a Christmas tree."

"Absolutely," Florence blew a kiss to her aunt.

The tree arrived just before eleven and then Daniel with help from Florence potted it up in a large earthenware tub Laura had advised Charlie to buy to house it for the duration of the festive season. When done they placed the pot on an old bath towel and dragged it through the kitchen along the hallway and into the sitting room with help from Charlie who walked behind to make sure it did not topple over.

"Where shall we put it?" Daniel stood upright to get his breath back.

"I think it'd look nice standing near the alcove beside the fireplace," said Charlie.

"Oh yes," enthused Florence, "like the scene on a Christmas card."

Laura shook her head. "Yes it would look lovely there, I agree, but it wouldn't be practical. Better to have it over by the window where the room is a little cooler. We don't want needles everywhere too soon."

Charlie agreed. "Good point, Laura. The window it is then."

After getting the tree into a position agreeable to all, Charlie sat down to watch the transformation and Laura put on Christmas music to help create the right ambience. New fairy lights, baubles in several colours and tinsel bought from the local garden centre were inside a large box along with old decorations which Florence and Daniel remembered from their childhood. Both were touched that their father had kept them after their mother's death even though they had not seen the light of day since then.

"This must be the first Christmas tree this place has seen for years and years," said Florence standing on a stool winding lights over the branches.

"And the first ever to be in here with the building as a house," Charlie reminded them.

"Yes, of course but it's hard to imagine this place was once a pub," Florence jumped down from the stool and stood back to make sure the lights were evenly spaced.

"And before that a coaching inn," said Laura, "I'd love to be able to go back in time and see it as it was then."

"Me too." Florence, happy with the lights returned the stool to its place in the corner.

"So what do you know about this place, Dad?" Daniel asked, "I'm referring to its history, of course."

Charlie picked up a bauble that had fallen from the box and rolled across the floor. "Not a lot. In fact that's something I keep meaning to do. Ring Cissy's grandmother that is and visit her for a chat. She's lived in the village all her life and so did her parents."

"She mentioned some old photos too," Laura added, "So I'm keen to see them."

"Let's go and see her today then. I'd love to hear what she has to say." Daniel spoke with enthusiasm.

Laura frowned. "What all of us! I think that might be a bit much, don't you?"

Charlie picked up his phone. "I'll give Cissy a ring first and see what she thinks. Then I'll ring Joan."

Cissy, who had the day off work, said her grandmother would be thrilled to have a houseful, in fact the more the merrier. She also said she'd give her mother a ring and they would probably be there too because both were equally keen to hear what Granny had to say. After a call to Joan it was agreed that they would all meet at Cuttlefish Cottage at three o'clock when Ruby would have finished her lunchtime stint at the Harbour Lights.

Joan's cottage was semi-detached with whitewashed walls and a small front garden laid to lawns with a flower border around the edges. Either side of the black front door stood terracotta pots containing winter flowering pansies.

Joan welcomed her guests warmly and showed them into her front room where a fire burned in the grate and lights sparkled on a small Christmas tree standing on one of the two window seats. Christmas cards hung from beams on the ceiling and a nativity scene graced the surface of a shelf in an alcove by the fireplace.

"Tea everyone?" she asked as they all sat.

Everyone said yes.

"And I've brought a cake," Laura held up a tin containing a cake she had hurriedly made after the meeting was agreed.

"Ideal," said Joan, "I was going to make one but I tidied up a bit first and vacuumed the floor, then when I went to the pantry I saw the flour bin was empty. I looked at the clock and reasoned if I went out and bought another bag there wouldn't have been enough time to make and bake one anyway. So I didn't bother."

"I would have made some mince pies," said Ruby, "but I was at work when this meeting was arranged and as I didn't finish 'til two-thirty it was impossible. I have brought a packet of chocolate digestives though."

When all had a mug of tea and slices of cake and biscuits were placed on a coffee table so that everyone could help themselves, Joan sat down. "So where shall I begin?" she asked.

"Back to when you were a girl, Mum, and your first visit to the Inn, I suppose."

Joan nodded. "Seems logical to me, Ruby," She picked up a tea plate and a slice of cake, took a bite and then placed the plate on her lap. "Well, I was born in 1957 here in the village. Not this cottage though. When I were a kid we lived in one of the council houses up by the school and I didn't move here until I got married. That was in 1980 and the place was a bit run down but my dear Bill soon got it shipshape. I mustn't go off on a tangent though, must I?"

"No," said Ruby firmly, "We know you're inclined to do that."

"Cheeky, although you're right of course. Your dad always said I had too much of what the cat licks its behind with."

Ruby looked heavenwards.

"Right, well I've known the Inn since my schooldays. The village junior school that is, not the secondary school in town. It was back in 1967 when I first clapped eyes on the place. I was ten years old and new licensees had recently moved in. The reason I went to the Inn was because the landlord had a daughter called Marilyn who was the same age as me. We met when she started our school and we were best friends by break time on the morning of her first day."

"Was that before or after the new road opened?" Ruby asked.

"Not one hundred percent sure but I think it must have been around the same time because that's why the previous owners sold up. I know it was opened in the mid-1960s anyway and I remember my dad saying it'd affect the Old Inn's trade badly. And then as if the new road wasn't bad enough, the breathalyser came into force the very same year Marilyn's parents took over the place. Local people still drank there though and then drove back to Porthgwyns."

"Why did they bother going all the way out to the Inn when they could have gone to the Harbour Lights?" Charlie asked.

Joan chuckled. "Because the landlord back at the Harbour then was a miserable sod and his wife had a face like a fiddle and that's an insult to fiddles. I know my mum and dad didn't like them nor did our neighbours. They had a yappy dog too that chased people up the street, especially kids. His name was Butch."

Laura, a dog lover, smiled. "What breed of dog was Butch?"

"Goodness knows. He was fat, black and white and despite its short legs could run really fast. Faster than me anyway."

"So what happened next?" Charlie was keen to hear more about his new home.

"One of the villagers got breathalysed, that's what. He was well over the limit and got fined. Silly sod. People stopped visiting the Inn after that. They reckoned the coppers were watching the place and said it was too risky and as luck would have it, the miserable licensees at the Harbour Lights left and more sociable folks moved in."

"But isn't there another pub in Porthgwyns other than the Harbour Lights?" Charlie asked. "I'm sure I was told there is."

"That's right there is," said Joan, "but it was damaged by fire in the late fifties. It's a free house and the owner back then had no insurance and so it stood as a ruin for nearly twenty years. It's back up and running now though."

"It's called the Red Lion," Ruby added, "Nice pub actually."

"So what was your friend Marilyn's dad like as a landlord?" Laura asked.

Joan chuckled. "Daft as a brush. He reckoned the place was haunted but I think he made that up to get folks to visit after the breathalyser incident and trade trailed off. He were a cunning so and so. His name was Reggie Williams and his wife was Maggie. As well as Marilyn they had a couple of boys. Roy and Walter they were called and a right pair of little buggers they were. Always up to mischief but then they didn't have Xboxes and stuff like they do now to occupy their idle hands. Not that I think they're a good thing. In fact quite the opposite. I think kids ought to be out more enjoying the fresh air."

"How about the people before the Reggie and Maggie Williams?" Laura asked, "Do you know anything about them?"

"No, I don't but I'm pretty sure the one family had owned the place for generations and it'd been passed down from father to son but I might be wrong."

Charlie was surprised having heard Joan's mention of a ghost. "Any idea who the ghost at the Inn was alleged to be?"

"No, I haven't the foggiest. As I say, I reckon he were a figment of Reggie's imagination. He'd probably read somewhere that a pub with a ghost did good trade and so thought he'd have one. I mean, it's a pretty difficult thing to dispute. I could say this house was haunted and you couldn't prove otherwise."

All eyes automatically glanced around the room just to make sure there was no-one else present. When a bauble fell from the Christmas tree, they all jumped.

Charlie was the first to break the silence: "Well, it seems a bit odd to me that Mickey mentioned a ghost at the Inn. Well in the lane anyway."

Joan chuckled. "Typical of Mickey. God rest his soul. I wouldn't give it another thought though if I were you, Charlie. Mickey was a dreamer and away with the fairies most of the time. Which reminds me, he once said that if someone as talented and educated as Sir Arthur Conan Doyle believed in fairies, then it was good enough for him."

Cissy giggled. "So did he believe in fairies too, Gran?"

"Might have, I don't know but I reckon it's likely he thought if Doyle believed in fairies then there was nothing wrong with him believing in ghosts."

"Maybe but we're still intrigued by the fact he claimed a ghost lurked outside the Inn," said Laura, "He even vowed to have seen it on the cliffs while in a boat out fishing with friends."

"And," continued Charlie, "he reckoned it was most likely the ghost of a highwayman."

Joan chuckled. "Wasn't Dick Turpin, was it?"

"Black Bess must have been a very fast horse if that was the case," said Laura, "Cornwall would have been a long way from home."

"Well, I don't believe in ghosts and so I'm keeping an open mind," said Charlie, "but I don't think Mickey made it up himself because he said he'd been told about it by the chap who sold him Bracken Farm."

"Well there you are then," said Joan, "Because if I remember correctly, Reggie Williams was pally with the old farmer at Bracken Farm, so Reggie would have invented the ghost to boost trade and told his mates to make sure the word got spread around."

Ruby frowned. "But Jack Tripp, the farmer who sold Bracken Farm to the Potts was only in his sixties so he couldn't have been mates with your Reggie, Mum. The dates don't add up."

"You're quite right, Ruby. It would have been Jack's dad, Alf, who was the farmer in Reggie's day so I expect Jack got it from him."

"Is Reggie Williams still alive?" Charlie thought it time to steer the subject away from ghosts.

"Good heavens, no, I should think he's long gone. He'd be well over a hundred by now if he were still alive."

"So how long were Reggie and his family at the Inn?" Laura asked.

"Not long but being a kid it seemed a long time to me. Actually it must have been about five years because they sold up in the early seventies when I was fifteen. Several people owned the Inn over the next few years and the last was Jacob Smythe. Of course I never went there again after Marilyn left. After the Inn was sold I saw a lot more of her though because Reggie and Maggie bought a cottage in the village up by the church just a stone's throw from our place. Nice house it was too."

"So have you kept in touch with your friend Marilyn?" asked Florence.

"Sadly not. After we left school we went our separate ways and then her family left the area. Not sure where they went but I think it might have been somewhere here in Cornwall. She would only have been eighteen or nineteen when they left. I often wonder how she is and what she's doing. I've even tried to find her on social media but not knowing her married name, should she be wed, it's damn near impossible. I've had no luck anyway."

"That's really sad." Florence couldn't imagine losing contact with her close friends.

"So was the Inn always known as the Old Coaching Inn?" Laura asked.

"I think so. Although I remember my gran saying it was just the Coaching Inn when she was a girl back at the beginning of the last century so I suppose they added the 'Old' later. Again it was probably Reggie Williams as did that."

"Well I suppose by the time he took it over it would have been getting a bit old," reasoned Charlie.

"I've just remembered something else. According to my gran there was a time long before she was born when the locals called it the Smugglers Inn."

"Really, I wonder why?" Laura asked.

"No idea. I think Gran was told it by her grandmother so it'd be well over a hundred years ago."

Daniel laughed. "Well there was never any smuggling there then if that's the case."

"Why do you say that so emphatically?" Cissy liked the notion of smuggling.

"It'd be a bit of a giveaway, don't you think?"

"Yes, I suppose it would be."

"You're quite right and I'd like to think the name was started by Reggie," chuckled Joan, "He'd do anything to get folks through the door but it wasn't him because it was long before his time."

"The other day you said you had some old photos," Charlie reminded her.

"That's right I have and I've looked them out." Joan reached beneath her chair and pulled out a tin. "They were taken by Marilyn's mum, Maggie. Reggie bought her a camera one Christmas and she loved it. She took lots of pictures, most are black and white but they're still good. She very kindly gave some copies with me on to my mum, as well as a few others."

After looking at the photographs, Joan and Ruby made another cup of tea for everyone and sliced up what was left of Laura's cake.

"I've just been thinking," said Charlie as Ruby handed him a cup of tea, "Would you like to join us on Christmas Day? You can come over in the evening or even for dinner, either way we'd love your company, wouldn't we folks?"

"Yay, that's a brill idea, Dad." Florence looked across to Cissy who was eagerly nodding her head.

"I think it's a lovely idea too," said Ruby, "What do you say, Mum?"

"Count me in. I'd love to see the old place again and what you've done to it."

"Don't wait 'til evening, come to dinner," urged Florence, "then we can have the whole day together. It'll be fun."

"Well, yes, we'll do that if it's okay," said Ruby, "I know my Steve will be happy about it and he's been saying for years I ought to have a Christmas out of the kitchen. I'll still be happy to help though of course."

"That's settled then. Christmas at Seven Pines for..." Laura counted on her fingers..."eight. Perfect number."

Later, as Joan's visitors were preparing to leave, Mickey Potts' name cropped up yet again.

"So what do you make of the Potts' case?" Laura asked Joan.

"I don't know, really I don't. There has to be a lot that we're all unaware of but for the life of me I've no idea what it might be and so I'm completely baffled. What's more, so are my mates and we've done the subject to death this last week or so."

"Most in the pub think it was an accident," said Ruby, "They reckon Tracey was so angry with Mickey that she wanted to hit him and grabbed the first thing she saw but if that's the case I can't understand why she doesn't confess. I mean if she only meant to hit him then the charge against her would be downgraded to manslaughter and the sentence much less harsh. She might even be granted bail. As it is I've heard she's refusing to say anything at all."

"What does her daughter make of it?" Charlie asked.

"Poor Becky she doesn't know what to think. She thought the world of her dad and is livid with her mum but it makes no more sense to her than it does any of us."

"Does Tracey have a temper?" Laura asked.

Ruby shook her head. "No more than most people. I mean, she's never lost her temper with me. I've never seen her arguing with anyone either. Although actually now I come to think about it she's been quite teasy since she lost her phone."

"Teasy?" Charlie queried.

Ruby smiled. "It's a Cornish expression and means irritable or angry. Mum used it frequently when I was a girl, didn't you, Mum?"

"And I was quite justified too, young lady," Joan turned to Charlie and Laura, "It's taken from the Cornish word *tesek* meaning hot or fiery. You still hear it occasionally but nothing like as much as when I was young. I suppose you can put that down to television, the internet and what have you. Sadly lots of old words and traditions are dying out now."

Chapter Fifteen

Early that evening, Charlie and Laura went to the Harbour Lights; Daniel and Florence were not with them as they had arranged to go to the Red Lion with Cissy, with whom they had struck up a friendship, for a karaoke night.

As usual they took a taxi; as they stepped inside the pub they were greeted by warm air and the sound of Christmas music. "Quiet tonight," said Charlie as he unzipped his jacket and glanced at the empty seats.

"Usually is on weekdays leading up to Christmas unless we have a party on, that is," said Greg, "Having said that it's only just after seven so should pick up a bit later. Might even get a few of the Red Lion's regulars in who don't like karaoke."

There were nine people inside the bar: two lads playing pool in the games area, a party of four by the Christmas tree looking at menus; Tom was sitting in his usual place on a stool at the end of the bar and Landlord Greg and Ruby were serving drinks. Because it was quiet, Charlie and Laura sat on stools at the bar alongside Tom. As Ruby passed a glass of wine to Laura and a pint of bitter to Charlie, the door opened and Vicar Joy walked in.

"Good evening, Reverend. Your usual?" The landlord was clearly surprised to see her.

"Yes, please, Greg." She watched as he poured her a schooner of sherry and then handed over a five pound note.

"You're probably surprised to see me when it's not even quiz night but if the truth be known I sat down a while back to write next Sunday's sermon and found my mind was a complete blank so I thought I'd pop out for a stroll, get some fresh air and enjoy a sherry with company at the same time. You never know it might even give me inspiration."

Tom laughed. "Nothing like alcohol to get the old mind working, Reverend."

"Yes, I always keep a bottle of sherry at home should someone call in but I seldom drink it while alone."

"I'm much the same," said Laura, "I'll drink at home with Charlie while I'm down here but I've not touched a drop at home since my husband went away."

"Went away?" Vicar Joy was puzzled.

"He's in the Army and is away with his regiment until Easter."

"Oh I see. So you've come to visit your brother for a bit of company."

"Yes, and I wanted to see his house too, of course."

"So are you enjoying your stay down here?"

"Very much so and I can see why Charlie loves it."

Greg picked up a small glass, half filled it with lemonade and drank it down in one gulp. "The Rudd brothers said how much they like the area too and I feel quite flattered that they've decided to keep their posh yacht here over the festive period as I should imagine they move in quite glamorous circles."

"Yes, that yacht must have cost a bob or two," said Laura.

"Any idea what they do?" Charlie asked.

Greg shook his head. "No idea and I don't like to ask."

"That reminds me," Vicar Joy lifted her left hand and waved her forefinger. "I went Christmas shopping today and while out I saw the two of them coming out of the police station. I do hope they're not in any sort of trouble as I thought they seemed a nice couple of lads when I bumped into them in the shop the other day."

"Really," said Laura, "How strange."

"Perhaps they're undercover cops pretending to be highfliers and they went to the nick to report their progress into something or other," chuckled Tom.

"Anything's possible I suppose," said Charlie.

"Or they might have gone in to enquire about Tracey Potts," said Ruby, "after all, if you remember, they were asking after her and Mickey when they first arrived. They live next door to old friends of theirs apparently who'd asked them to look the Potts up if they were in this area. I must try and find out why they were at the police station when they're next in."

Vicar Joy took a sip of sherry. "Ah, good, that sort of makes sense. I'd hate them to be in trouble," As she spoke Richard and Edward walked in.

"Talk of the devil." A broad smile crossed Ruby's face.

"Had a good day, lads?" Greg asked.

Richard attempted to smooth down his curls ruffled by the wind. "Yes, thanks we've hired a car for a week or two so we can get out and about now."

"Someone said they saw you coming out of the police station today while they were out shopping," Ruby saw a look of horror appear on the vicar's face and thought it best not to mention her by name.

"Did they?" Edward, fast becoming aware that the pub clientele loved a bit of gossip, smiled.

"It's true, we were there," said Richard, "We wanted to ask about Mrs Potts so we'd be able to pass on the latest news to our neighbours when we go back."

"Bingo," laughed Ruby, "that's just what I said."

Vicar Joy fanned her flushed face with a beer mat.

"Any luck?" Laura asked, "Getting information, I mean."

"Yes thank you and we were able to see her as well," Richard sighed heavily, "I hope they weren't close though. Our neighbours and Mr and Mrs Potts that is, otherwise it's going to be a bit of a shock when we get back and tell them what's happened."

"You've seen Tracey!" Ruby reached for two pint glasses, "How is she?"

Edward shrugged his shoulders. "Hard for us to say really seeing as we'd never clapped eyes on her before today. I mean, we don't know what she was like before all this happened so there's nothing for us to compare her present state with."

"We didn't stay long anyway," said Richard, "After we'd told her how our neighbours were there was nothing else to say. It was all a bit awkward really."

"I can imagine it was," Vicar Joy looked sympathetic, "She wasn't one of my flock but she was always polite and helpful. I hope she's being treated well."

"Humph." Tom watched as Ruby placed two pints of beer on the bar for the brothers.

"Come, come, now, Tom," tutted the vicar, "she's not been proven guilty yet so we must give her the benefit of the doubt."

"Okay point taken but I've heard her fingerprints were on the owl and the recording stuff so she must have been up there, which makes her guilty in my opinion," Tom caught Vicar Joy's eye, "Sorry, Reverend but that's the way I see it."

Charlie tried to keep his beliefs neutral. "What's baffling us is if she's guilty, why did she do it? I mean there would have to be a reason."

"I wonder," mused Laura, "if the answer lies with her missing phone. I mean, this afternoon you, Ruby, said that she was quite...umm...what was that expression again?"

"Teasy," laughed Ruby.

"That's right. I must try and remember that for future reference."

"So what are you trying to say, Laura?" Charlie asked.

116

"Well, I don't really know, but if she was teasy after she lost her phone then perhaps there was something on it she didn't want anyone else to see."

"She said she was cross because she'd lost all her contact details," said Ruby.

Laura frowned. "Yes, and I can understand that but it wouldn't take too long to track her contacts down by other means and then install them in her new phone, would it?"

"Fancy a game of pool, Rich?" Edward noticed the two lads playing had returned their cues to the rack and were putting on their jackets.

"Yeah, why not."

"Maybe Tracey was having an affair," Charlie watched the brothers as they left for the games area.

"No, surely not," Vicar Joy clearly believed in the sanctity of marriage.

Ruby looked thoughtful. "You know you might have a point there, Charlie. You see back in September she started classes at night school to learn Spanish. She thought it'd be handy as she and Mickey were planning a trip to Catalonia next summer. After the first two weeks she seemed more alive and took even more care with her appearance than usual, so perhaps she got friendly with someone else there or even her tutor because she often mentioned his name. I can't remember what it was though but I believe he was actually Spanish."

"Interesting," said Laura, "So perhaps we all ought to keep a look out for the missing phone. Do you know what make it is, Ruby?"

"No idea but it had a candy pink case covered in red high heel shoes."

Tom snorted with laughter. "Sounds just about right. Trace loves her high heels. I don't know how she can walk in them. Ridiculous things."

"Wouldn't be very practical for climbing up Wreckers Hill," said Laura, "it's quite steep."

"That reminds me," said Charlie, "Does anyone know why it's called Wreckers Hill?"

Greg the landlord pointed to an old painting of a sailing ship wrecked on a rugged beach where crowds gathered on the shore. "According to legends, wreckers deliberately decoyed ships along this coast into running ashore. Allegedly, this was done by folks up on the hill waving lights. Then once the ship had run ashore it'd be plundered by more folk waiting on the beach as the picture depicts. Personally, I think it's a load of old nonsense. I mean, surely lights would indicate land and therefore any vessel would keep well away. Having said that, smuggling and wrecking was commonplace down here but I doubt very much that the vessels were wrecked by anything other than bad weather and their own misfortune."

"But if it were true," said Charlie, "then it's possible that ships were wrecked in Quignog Cove."

"I agree and no doubt they were but not deliberately," persisted Greg.

"Quignog," laughed Laura, "I keep meaning to ask what that means. Does anyone know?"

Charlie raised his hand. "I do because I thought exactly the same thing when I first heard it and so I Googled it. Apparently it's an old Cornish word that means ridiculous notion or pipedream. So my theory is the cove was named that because it's a ridiculous notion to try and get down there."

Laura laughed. "Brilliant. I love it."

"You know, I'm so used to the name I've never once queried its meaning. You learn something every day." Tom was clearly impressed.

"I wonder who thought up the names Quignog Cove and Wreckers Hill," pondered Laura.

"Well Wreckers Hill was probably named by the Inn's erstwhile landlord, Reggie Williams," laughed Ruby, "according to Mum he'd do anything for publicity."

118

Greg poured himself a half pint of lager. "I've heard your mother talk about him on several occasions. He sounds like a great character but sadly it couldn't have been him though because it's called Wreckers Hill on that old map over there and that's dated 1852." Greg nodded towards a framed print hanging above the fireplace.

"Well if it was known as that in 1852 the chances are its name goes back a lot longer than that." Laura put down her glass in order to take a closer look. As she slipped from her stool, a man from the party by the Christmas tree approached the bar with a menu and so Ruby went to take their food order. Simultaneously, the door opened and in walked Jeffrey Lemon, more commonly known as Jiffy, with an attractive younger woman.

"One of the perks of being a celeb I suppose," whispered Charlie to Tom, "the ability to attract glamour, that is."

Tom chuckled. "You're right but in this case she's his daughter from his first marriage. She comes down from time to time to see her old dad. Looks like she's on her own though as she usually has a chap with her."

"A chap?"

"Yes, poncey bloke. You know the sort. Full of himself. I think he's an actor but I've never seen him in anything. Not that I watch stuff like that. I prefer the pub to the telly."

Jiffy's daughter sat down at a table and removed her scarf while Jiffy went to the bar for drinks. As he returned a bank card to his wallet, Charlie caught his eye. The erstwhile drummer placed their drinks on the table, took his daughter's arm and nodded in the direction of Charlie. "Now, this my love is the young man who pipped me to the post in the auction for the Old Coaching Inn. Not that I bear a grudge."

"I should think not, Dad. At your age you should be enjoying life and not taking on building projects."

"Ouch!"

"Sorry, I keep forgetting you're a bit touchy about age."

"Apology accepted but it was never my intention to do any physical work to the Inn. I'd just have overseen it, that's all."

Laura, distracted by the latest arrivals left the map and returned to her seat.

"Anyway, I drove by the other day," continued Jiffy, "and I have to admit the place is looking superb."

Charlie beamed. "Thank you."

"My pleasure."

"So are you going to introduce us to this lovely young lady?" Charlie put down his glass.

"Of course. Charlie allow me to introduce you to my only daughter, Elderflower. And Elderflower, allow me to introduce you to Charlie umm…umm…"

"Everton, and this is my sister, Laura who is down for Christmas." The three rose from their seats and shook hands in turn.

"Elderflower, that's a beautiful name," said Laura.

Elderflower scowled. "Yuck! Do you really think so? I think it's horrible."

"Well you could always use your middle name," Jiffy took a sip of his gin and orange.

"What! Cactus? That's even worse."

Charlie smothered a smile. "Well I think you'll find lots of people dislike their names."

"Maybe, but can you imagine growing up with a name like Elderflower Cactus Lemon and have a father known as Jiffy?"

"I would have thought it fun," Charlie felt impish.

"So what is your mother called?" Laura asked.

"Was; sadly Mother is no longer with us."

"Oh, I'm sorry to hear that."

"Her name was Amelia," said Jiffy.

"Yes, it was but you called her Honeysuckle."

"It was her favourite flower. She loved its scent."

"I know," Elderflower squeezed her father's hand, "and she loved you for it."

"So are you down for Christmas, Elderflower?" Laura estimated Jiffy's daughter to be a similar age to her brother.

The new arrivals pulled up stools and sat at the bar. "Yes, Dad rang me last night and suggested I come down. I jumped at the idea, I've recently split up with my partner you see so I've rather indulged myself in self-pity."

"Oh, I'm so sorry to hear that," Laura was really delighted and hoped her brother didn't sense the excitement she felt.

Jiffy shook his head. "Don't be. The guy was a narcissist and she's best rid of him."

"That's a bit harsh, Dad and maybe you're right but I still miss him. And his chocolates. He always bought me chocolates. In fact if I'm honest, I probably miss them more than him."

"Oh dear," sighed Jiffy, "whatever happened to the romance we sang about in the sixties?"

Chapter Sixteen

Three days before Christmas, Tash and Jerry, a married couple in their early thirties, arrived in Porthgwyns to stay in a holiday cottage down by the harbour. After they had unpacked their luggage and other items from their van they went for a walk around the village to explore and get their bearings. On their way back they called in at the Harbour Lights for a drink and a late lunch. Greg was working and he greeted them warmly as they sat down on two of the bar stools and studied the menu.

"Do you know anywhere in the village where we can hire a boat?" Jerry asked, after they had ordered food and Greg had sent the order through to the kitchen, "We're staying at Fuchsia Cottage."

"Or even someone to take us out," Tash added.

"Would that be for a fishing trip?"

Jerry shook his head. "No diving."

"I see, well you can do either," Greg nodded towards a notice board. "A few of our locals have adverts on there and I can vouch for all of them. Not sure if they'll all be available this time of the year as some of them take their boats out of the water in the winter to do them up but there's no harm in asking."

"Excellent," Tash crossed to the notice board and made notes of the names and phone numbers while Jerry paid for their drinks.

"So what makes you want to dive this time of the year?"

"We're hoping to locate some shipwrecks. We've had a look on the internet and there are lots along the Cornish coast. We've got one or two lined up and the chances are we'll never find them but there's no harm in trying."

"No, I suppose not but isn't it a bit too cold this time of the year?"

Tash tucked the paper with the notes she'd made in the back pocket of her jeans and sat back down beside her husband. "Well actually the difference between summer and winter sea temperature is only a few degrees and we'll be wearing wet suits so we'll be fine."

"Well I never. You learn something new every day. I've never been diving. Well I can't even swim but I must confess I do like to watch films on YouTube taken underwater. Must be quite thrilling down there."

"Oh, it is," enthused Tash, "we've only ever swum in the sea around the British Isles but one day we hope to go to the Mediterranean and explore warmer waters."

"Anywhere in particular?"

"Corsica. That won't be for wrecks though it'll be for the marine life."

As she spoke, Grace came out from the kitchen with bowls of homemade soup and so the couple vacated the barstools and sat down at a table in the corner.

That same afternoon, Laura was in her room putting away laundry. As she closed the door of her wardrobe she heard the sound of horse's hooves. Curious as to whom it might be she crossed to the window and peeped out. In the lane two horses and their riders had stopped by the spot where Mickey Potts had died. It was not possible to establish the identity of the riders for they wore riding helmets, trousers and dark hacking jackets. Laura watched as one of the pair dismounted and approached the stump of the fallen tree before stepping back and taking several pictures, Laura assumed on a phone. Inspired by the idea, she reached for her own phone and took a picture of each rider. She then zoomed into the pictures to see if she recognised either of them. To her surprise she saw the person who had dismounted was Elderflower Lemon. The other, a female, was unknown to her but for some reason her attractive face seemed familiar. As she tried to recall why, she remembered the leaflet picked up at the hotel in Porthgwyns for the riding stables at Treverry Cross. She looked in the drawer of her bedside cabinet where she had placed the leaflet. The image on her phone was a match for the proprietor of the stables. Pleased by her discovery she ran downstairs to tell Charlie.

In the evening, tired after walking for several hours through the country lanes that morning with Ben, Charlie and Laura sat by the fire enjoying glasses of red wine. Florence and Daniel were both out having gone to the Harbour Lights for Quiz Night. As they sat writing a list of food items needed for Christmas dinner, the lights went out. "Bugger," Charlie stood and went into the kitchen to see if the trip had gone off. It hadn't. He returned with candles which he lit and placed around the room. "Looks like a power cut. If it's not back in an hour I'll ring the helpline and see what the problem is."

"Might be wind damage somewhere. I can hear it in whistling in the chimney," Laura placed the pen and notepad on which the shopping list was written on the floor and then tucked her feet in the chair.

"Yes, you could be right." Charlie removed the cork from a fresh bottle of wine to let it breathe.

"I rather like the room in candlelight," said Laura dreamily, "It's very relaxing even if the shadows are a bit eerie. I can almost imagine it as it would have been in days gone by, and the smell of the Christmas tree is divine."

"Okay but don't rub it in, I've already admitted you were right. An artificial tree would have looked out of place although you have to admit some are very realistic these days."

Laura took a sip of wine. "They are but they don't have the lovely smell. Anyway, having an artificial tree was never discussed. If I remember correctly you were in favour of nothing at all."

"No, we didn't discuss it, but when you insisted we have a tree I thought an artificial one would be okay, I just didn't dare suggest it, that's all." Charlie sat down, leaned back in his favourite armchair and quickly changed the subject. "All that's missing now is the calming steady tick of a grandfather clock."

Laura sat up. "Oh, yes, I like that idea. You must get one, Charlie, when we go into town for the food shopping. We'll pop into the antiques shop there and hope they have something appropriate."

"Is there an antiques shop in town? I can't say that I've ever noticed."

"Yes, there is. It's a couple of doors away from my bank. I noticed it the other day when I drew out some cash."

"I see," Charlie half closed his eyes, "we'll definitely pop in there then because I can imagine the right clock in here standing against the bit of wall between the door and the radiator. That, along with the log fire and candles would make the room even more romantic than it is now."

Laura laughed. "You think the room is romantic now then?"

"Yes, don't you?"

"Absolutely but it would be even more so if you were here with someone other than your big sister."

Charlie's eyes rolled. "Are you going to start nagging again?"

"I'm not nagging, I'm just speaking the truth and that's because I have your well-being in mind as did Mickey, God rest his soul."

"Yes, I know you are and he was too but I've yet to meet that someone and to be honest I'm not even looking. In fact I quite like living on my own and doing my own thing."

125

"Now maybe but I think after a while you'll find the novelty will wear off and you will crave companionship. I get lonely at times with hubby being away despite the fact I have neighbours who are also very good friends."

"Maybe I will get lonely eventually. Who knows?"

"Meanwhile we've yet to meet Crazy Chris. Every time I see a female come into the pub who fits Mickey's description I listen to see if anyone calls her Chris but no luck so far."

"What! How would you recognise someone from Mickey's description? All he said was she's about my age, got a nice face, good figure and had never been wed as far as he knew, so not much to go on."

"And she collects compasses."

"Oh that's a great help. Anyway, why would I want to hook up with someone who is crazy?"

"Good point, so how about Elderflower? She's pretty, footloose and fancy free now and I can just imagine her sitting in here by the fire listening to the clock you've yet to get ticking in the candlelight."

Charlie laughed. "Oh, come off it, Laura, she's way out of my league. I could never fit in with celeb types, I'm much too down to earth and remember her last bloke was an actor and a poncey one at that according to Tom."

"Celeb types are only people and deep down they're just like you and I. Anyway, just because her dad was a pop star doesn't mean she falls into that category. I thought her very unpretentious."

"Well, whatever, there's no mileage there so don't let her presence in Cornwall raise your hopes."

"Perhaps the reason she was up here earlier on horseback was because she was hoping to see you," Laura persisted.

"Yeah, yeah and pigs might fly."

The power came back on within the hour and so Charlie had no need to try and find out the reason. He and Laura were just thinking of retiring to bed when Daniel and Florence arrived back by taxi slightly inebriated: jubilant having won first prize at the Quiz night.

In the early hours, Dan, who had consumed several pints of lager while at the Harbour Lights followed by three Jagerbombs downed quickly to celebrate their win, woke with a very dry mouth and because his room was not en suite he had to go to the main bathroom for water. As he approached the wash basin he remembered he'd taken the glass from there downstairs that morning for washing and so there was nothing to put water in. As he cursed, he heard a loud thump from the rooms below. Assuming someone was down there he went to join them and get a glass of water at the same time. He crept down the stairs so as not to wake other family members sleeping; however, when he reached the kitchen the lights were off and there was no-one there. He looked in the sitting room; it too was dark except for the slight glow from the dying embers of the fire. Daniel shuddered, the room seemed eerily quiet for Ben had gone with Laura to her room. Thinking he must have been hearing things, he returned to the kitchen, took a glass from the cupboard, filled it with water and went back to his room.

Chapter Seventeen

On the morning of Christmas Eve, Laura and Florence were busy in the kitchen at Seven Pines; Laura was making mince pies and Florence was putting finishing touches to the icing on the brandy soaked Christmas cake made by Laura back in October. As Laura put the last tray of mince pies in the oven, Cissy arrived in her yellow VW Beetle.

"Hmm, something smells good," Cissy closed the door, removed her coat and hung it on the back of a chair.

"Mince pies. Fancy one?" Laura sieved icing sugar over the pies on a cooling rack.

"Yes please. Homemade ones are tons better than bought ones."

"I agree. Coffee to go with it?" Laura reached for the kettle.

"Yes please."

"All done now." Florence stood back to examine her handiwork.

"That's really pretty," said Cissy, admiringly, "Simple but very effective."

"I always think that. Latticework is easy if you have a steady hand."

"I really ought to get into baking and stuff. At least that's what Mum says." Cissy pulled out a chair and sat down at the table.

"Same with me."

"But you've made a Christmas cake."

Florence shook her head. "No, Auntie Laura made it. I've just added the almond paste and iced it."

"If it had been left to me to finish, I'd have smothered it in royal icing and made it stand up in peaks like snow," said Laura, "I've never been any good at artistic stuff."

"Ah, but it's what the cake tastes like that matters," said Florence, "and your cakes are to die for, Auntie."

"Thank you."

"So, what brings you here this morning, Cissy?" Florence asked, "Not that I'm not pleased to see you."

"I came over to see if you fancy going for a walk. It's a lovely morning and I thought it'd be nice to go along the coastal path back to Porthgwyns. If we do we won't have to walk both ways because Mum said she'll run us back here and then I can pick up my car."

Florence washed icing from her hands. "I'd like that as I could do with a bit of exercise."

"Same with me. Mum bought a tin of toffees the other day and Dad and me have nearly pigged the lot."

Laura made coffee and placed mugs and mince pies on the table for the girls, she then carried a tray of refreshments into the sitting room for Charlie who was piling logs in the fireplace and Daniel who was using his laptop to reply to an email from a friend.

The girls left the house just before midday. To access the coastal path they walked partway down the lane and climbed over a gate; crossing the corner of a small field, they clambered over a drystone wall and then jumped down onto a patch of grass. The sun was shining and its rays produced very little warmth but the coastal path looked much the same as it would on a summer's day. Yellow flowers bloomed on the prickly stems of gorse and tufts of grass flourished either side of the well-worn track; the only sign of winter were the fern-like leaves of bracken, no longer green but a reddish brown.

As the girls looked down to the sea they saw a small boat close to the shore. They watched with interest as one of the two people on board jumped over the side wearing a wetsuit and swam towards the beach on Quignog Cove.

"I recognise that boat so they must be the people Gran told me about," said Cissy, "They're staying at Fuchsia Cottage in Porthgwyns and have hired Bill Harvey's boat for a fortnight. Gran reckons they're bonkers because they're divers and are looking for wrecks. She said no one with any sense would go into the sea in winter."

"Really? Well I don't think they'll find a wreck in Quignog Cove. Not that close to the shore anyway."

"Well I suppose they're just exploring the beach. I should imagine it looks quite interesting from a boat."

Much further along the coast as they approached Porthgwyns they saw Edward and Richard's yacht moored in its usual spot half a mile away from the harbour.

"Hey, they're still here," Cissy's voice was tinged with excitement.

"Well they did say they'd stay for Christmas," said Florence.

"I know but I thought they might change their minds. After all Porthgwyns isn't the most exciting of places."

"Don't you think so? I must admit I love it and the surrounding area too. I can see why Dad's smitten."

"Maybe but I can assure you that the novelty of village life by the sea does wear a bit thin after a while and the winter can be pretty dead. Especially January and February. Having said that, when the sun shines in summer it's the best place in the world."

Florence stopped walking and turned to gaze at the yacht. "How I'd love to be wealthy enough to own a boat like that. Still, I can but dream and you never know - they might invite us on-board to have a nose round before they finally sail away into waters new."

"I very much doubt it," Cissy stood by Florence's side. "I do wonder how they made their money though. The brothers, that is. I mean they don't appear to be in a hurry to get back and I've never heard them mention work. Having said that, if they're staying here for a while I suppose they might have finished whatever until the New Year."

"It's probably inherited wealth and so they don't need to work," reasoned Florence, "Let's sit down for a while."

"Or they won the Lottery like your dad." Cissy sat down beside Florence on a flat rock.

"Yes, even that's possible." Florence touched the locket she wore around her neck in which was a picture of her late mother. "Mum would have loved it here because she and her parents had lots of holidays in Cornwall when she was young. It's such a shame: she and Dad often talked of coming to Cornwall for a break but they never did and now they never will although Mum's ashes are at the house and that's partly why Dad decided to move down here. That and the fact his grandmother was born in the county and then moved away up-country when she married his granddad."

"Really. Any idea where your dad's grandma lived and where she was born?"

"Born and bred in Lostwithiel I think, or was it Liskeard. It might even have been Launceston. Not sure but I should know as I've been looking into family history and stuff but don't tell Dad as I want it to be a surprise."

Cissy smiled. "I won't and I take it that wherever it was it begins with an L. So it might even have been Looe."

"Looe. Yes of course, that's it. Apparently Dad's grandmother's dad was a fisherman there. I never knew him of course and nor did Dad because he died long before he was born."

"So you have a little Cornish blood?"

"Yes, I suppose I do. I'd never really thought about that."

Cissy looked up to the sky. "Looks to me like it might snow."

"Oh, I do hope so. I know they've had some up-country but your mum said it doesn't often snow down here and if it does it doesn't stay long."

"No, it doesn't and for that reason we're usually unprepared. It'd be nice if it did though, especially as it's nearly Christmas."

Inside the house of Bracken Farm, Ruby helped Tracey and Mickey's daughter, Becky, pack up her parents' things in order to store them in the loft. She and her boyfriend had arrived from Plymouth the previous day and intended to live in the house so they could help the farmhands run the business until they knew the outcome of Tracey's trial. Becky liked the idea of a spell in the country and her fisherman boyfriend was happy to take his boat out of the water for a while and help out too. Meanwhile, Sam Nixon, Mickey's right hand man with years of experience had agreed to take charge in the running of the farm for the foreseeable future.

"I'm sorry to hear your mum was refused bail," said Ruby, as they entered Tracey's bedroom which Becky and her boyfriend intended to use.

"Yeah, so was I but I'm not surprised. Poor Mum, she's not helped her situation at all by being so uncooperative. She won't even tell me what happened let alone the police. When I see her she chats as though everything is quite normal. It's weird."

"You've been to see her then. I'm glad about that."

Becky shrugged her shoulders. "Yes. I didn't really want to but my conscience got the better of me. I mean, I'll never forgive her but she is my mum and the only one I'll ever have. I miss Dad terribly but what's done is done and me being bitter and unwilling to see her won't change things."

"You're a wise young lady, Becky. Your dad would be proud."

"Yes, thank you. I just wish Mum was wise. She lives in a dream-world, you know. Goodness knows why but she's always had a thing about owning a health farm. Daft really because she's no business woman. Poor Dad, they hadn't been living here long when she went exploring, drove up Wreckers Hill and came across the Old Coaching Inn. When she came back she told Dad what a smashing place it was and really that was the end of it. Then about a year ago she started going on about it again saying she wanted to buy it and turn it into her dream health farm. Dad made enquiries as to who owned it and learned that it belonged to a Jacob Smythe. He wouldn't sell though. Word has it that he was an awkward so and so."

"So she had to wait 'til Jacob died," said Ruby.

Becky nodded. "Yes, and he died in early spring this year. When Mum heard he'd gone and the Inn was to be auctioned she was ecstatic and nothing else mattered but getting that place. Dad tried to talk her out of it saying they probably wouldn't be able to get planning permission for change of use anyway but she was adamant it was what she wanted and she was determined to get it."

"Oh dear, she used to go on about it to me. Your poor dad though, it must have been very difficult for him."

"Yes, but Dad adored her and so went along with the idea. He arranged a loan from the bank but of course there was a limit to how much he could borrow. Mum didn't understand that though: she had no idea about money. She was gutted when Charlie Everton got the place and just couldn't see why Dad had stopped bidding."

"I know deep down he was troubled by it. He even tried to shrug it off."

"Yes. Still as I say what's done is done and we can't turn back the clock can we, Ruby?"

"Sadly not."

While Becky emptied the drawers of her mother's dressing table and placed the contents in a cardboard box,

Ruby emptied the wardrobe. Clothes she neatly folded and packed in a suitcase and shoes, stacked in a two foot high pile, she placed in a plastic storage container. As Ruby reached to pull out a pair of sheepskin boots, the last item of footwear at the bottom of the pile, she saw they were standing on a cardboard box. Assuming it was yet more shoes she pulled the box out and opened the lid. To her surprise inside was an old heavy book.

"Well I never. Look at this, Becky. A Bible."

"No! Surely not? Mother was an atheist." Becky looked over Ruby's shoulder as she opened up the book. The name Catherine Freathy was neatly written in copperplate writing on the first page.

"Who on earth was Catherine Freathy?" Ruby asked.

"Search me. It's not a family name as far as I know so Mum probably bought it in a junk shop or something like that."

"Or an auction even," suggested Ruby, "she was very fond of them and it's where lots of this furniture came from. In fact being a Bible it most likely came from the auction they had at the vicarage a year or so ago. I know your mum went to that and so did lots of other folk from the village. One of the things she bought was an old trunk to put her surplus shoes in and it's in the cupboard under the stairs. I would have gone to it as well but I had to work that day because we had a birthday lunch party at the pub."

"There's the answer then. I expect it was in a job lot of odds and sods and she stuck it in the wardrobe because it seemed a shame to throw it away. It was probably even in the trunk you just mentioned."

"Most likely. So, what shall we do with it?"

"You have it, Ruby. Mum won't be needing it although right now it might do her good to read something like that."

"Are you sure?"

"Yes, you have it and do whatever you want with it."

As planned, Ruby collected Cissy and Florence from the harbour following their walk and drove them back to Seven Pines where Cissy picked up her car. When they returned home, Cissy saw the Bible in its box lying on the kitchen table. As Ruby washed her hands before making sandwiches for them both, she explained how she had found it in the bottom of Tracey's wardrobe hidden beneath copious numbers of shoes.

"Really! I wouldn't have thought the Bible was Tracey's reading material."

"That's just what Becky and I said."

Cissy chuckled. "Perhaps she was a closet religious fanatic. Closet...do you get it?"

Ruby dried her hands on a towel. "Hmm, mildly amusing."

Cissy sat down at the table, lifted the Bible from its box and opened up the book. "Catherine Freathy. I don't know any Freathys. Do you, Mum?"

Ruby shook her head. "No, and Becky's pretty sure it's not a family name of theirs. It's not a name I've ever come across before and I've lived in the area all my life. Your gran might know though, I'll ask her tomorrow when we go to the Old Inn for Christmas dinner."

Slowly Cissy flicked through a few pages. "It's very ornate and looks really old. There are illustrations too."

"Yes, I had a quick look at it."

"So what will you do with it?"

"I think we'd better hang on to it as it could be worth a bob or two to the right person."

"Might be worth showing it to Dan and Flo's Aunt Laura," said Cissy, "she's into history and stuff like that. She collects old books too."

"Really! I didn't know that, but what a good idea. We'll definitely ask her opinion then."

"If I remember I'll mention it tonight because Flo said they're all going to the pub. Should be a good atmosphere being Christmas Eve." Cissy carefully closed the Bible and returned it to its box.

"Absolutely and I'm really excited to have the night off. I'll be able to enjoy it even more than usual this year." Ruby took a sliced wholemeal loaf from the bread bin.

"I didn't know you had the night off. How come? I mean. It's bound to be busy."

"Sorry, didn't I tell you? It's because Greg's brother and his wife are here. They arrived last night and they've offered to work on the bar. Greg jumped at the suggestion because he knows I've done Christmas Eve for the last six years and reckons I deserve a break. That's why I have tomorrow lunchtime off. Being Christmas Day there's no food of course so Grace will be on the bar too. Four should manage easily and they're only open for a couple of hours anyway from twelve 'til two."

"Excellent. If you're not working tonight you'll be able to go with Dad."

"Yes, and keep an eye on what he drinks especially if Tom's in which he's bound to be."

Cissy chuckled. "Can you imagine Vicar Joy's face if Dad turned up drunk to ring the bells?"

"I'd rather not think about it, but then I've known the good lady herself to indulge in a glass or two of sherry, and on Christmas Eve last year she had a permanent grin on her face during the midnight service."

When Charlie and his family arrived in Porthgwyns shortly before half past six they saw a great number of people gathered down by the harbour where a local brass band played Christmas carols beneath the coloured lights. Enthralled by the setting they wandered down to join the crowd and soak up the atmosphere. When the band stopped playing at half past seven, they and many others made their way to the Harbour Lights and within minutes the place was packed out with standing room only. Christmas music rang out from the speakers around the bar and to add to the decorations already in place, Greg's sister-in-law, a florist, had made a garland which was draped from the beams across the top of the bar.

Laura, Charlie, Florence and Daniel who were some of the first to arrive after the band finished were lucky enough to get seats but shortly after, Florence and Daniel vacated theirs and offered them to late arrivals, Jiffy and Elderflower. The siblings then went to join Cissy and the two Rudd brothers who had made friends with divers, Tash and Jerry.

At half eleven, several people got up to leave.

"Where's everyone going?" Charlie asked Jiffy.

"Church for the midnight service."

"Of course," he looked at his watch, "What time does the pub shut?"

"Half past twelve," said Jiffy, "At least that's what it's been since I've known the place."

Charlie looked at Laura. "Shall we go to the service and give Vicar Joy a bit of support? I rather fancy belting out a few carols."

Laura looked at her half empty glass. "Might be a good idea. I think we've both had more than enough to drink and we have dinner for eight to cook tomorrow, but what about Flo and Dan?"

Charlie finished his drink and stood up. "We'll see if they want to join us." He turned to Jiffy and Elderflower. "How about you two? Care to come along as well."

Jiffy shook his head. "Thanks but we've a taxi booked for half twelve so we wouldn't be out in time and I'd hate to have to creep out half way through. Having said that, it's not really my thing anyway."

"Fair enough."

"Were it not for the taxi I'd love to join you," said Elderflower, "but it's too late to change things now."

Laura quickly finished her drink. "We're not reliant on a taxi tonight, thank goodness. Dan said he wouldn't drink so he's our driver."

"But knowing my boy I bet he'll make up for it tomorrow," added Charlie.

Florence and Daniel agreed the midnight service was a good idea. Cissy was going anyway as also were Tash and Jerry. The brothers, however, said they wanted to get back to the yacht as it'd been a long day.

"What are the lads doing for Christmas dinner?" Laura asked as the party made their way the short distance from the pub to the church.

"They're entertaining us," said Tash, excitedly, "so we'll be dining on the yacht. We were going to have dinner for just the two of us but on hearing us say that, the brothers who would also be on their own, suggested we join them. We're dead chuffed about it. The lads are providing food and we're taking booze and crackers."

"There will be lots of boat talk then," laughed Charlie.

"Yep, that and diving. Ed and Rich have done a bit of diving too, you see. Not on wrecks though, more just for the fun of it and no doubt in warmer waters than here."

"Sounds thrilling," said Daniel, "I should imagine life under the waves is pretty fascinating."

"It is," said Tash, "I love it."

"The church bells are fascinating too," said Florence, "especially on a cold winter's Christmas Eve night. I find them very comforting."

"Who rings the bells?" Charlie asked, "Anyone we know?"

"Dad," said Cissy, "and he seems to be doing okay despite the fact Tom was trying to get him onto whisky in the pub. He does it every year thinking if dad messed up it'd be a laugh."

The service taken by Vicar Joy was a happy affair. Lots of carols, lots of smiles and a huge dose of *bonhomie*. When the service finished, the congregation made its way towards the door where they all shook hands with the vicar who wished them a happy Christmas. As they stepped out onto the gravel path, Florence and Cissy, beaming with festive cheer, squeaked with excitement, for in the golden light glowing from the old church porch lamp, snowflakes gently floated down from the heavens.

Chapter Eighteen

To the delight of everyone at Seven Pines, the snow settled overnight and on Christmas morning they awoke to find a white world. It was only a thin layer but nevertheless looked very much in keeping with the season as it sparkled over the landscape in the sun's watery rays.

Rather than opening presents they had bought for each other in the morning, the family decided to leave them until after dinner and open them along with their guests whose gifts from the family were also beneath the tree. To pass the times, they listened to Christmas music, ate chocolates and prepared vegetables. Laura watered the poinsettia and removed two fading leaves; she then moved the bowl of hyacinths from the kitchen window sill onto the coffee table in the sitting room so that everyone could enjoy their scent. Later, while Laura and Charlie were in the kitchen cooking, Daniel and Florence laid up the table in the dining room. To add a festive touch, Florence placed two table decorations made the previous day using holly and ivy from the hedgerow in the lane.

At midday, Cissy along with her parents, Ruby and Steve, and her grandmother, Joan arrived at Seven Pines; the ladies bearing flowers, wrapped gifts and chocolates and Steve clutching a case of canned beer and a bottle of malt whisky. After greetings and hugs the guests were shown into the sitting room and offered drinks.

"I wouldn't have recognise the place." Joan glanced around the room as she warmed her hands by the fire. "This must have been the main bar but it looks nothing like I remember it. Mind you, I only ever came in here once, when the pub was closed of course. Children weren't welcome inside licenced premises back in those days so I usually went no further than the kitchen."

"Well when you're ready I'll escort you around," Charlie was eager to show the transformation his house had undergone.

Joan placed her glass of wine on a shelf in the alcove. "Well there's no time like the present, young man and I have to admit I'm dying for a nose round."

"Me too," said Ruby.

"Come on then I'll take you both on a grand tour."

"Coming, Steve?" Ruby asked.

"Yes, why not."

As they returned to the sitting room following the tour, a grandfather clock struck one and Charlie automatically looked at his watch. "Still keeping good time, Laura."

Laura gave her brother's comment the thumbs up.

"We only bought the clock yesterday," said Charlie, "That's why we're keeping track of the time."

"It's a beauty," Steve approached it to take a closer look, "May I ask where you got it from?"

"Of course, it was in the antiques shop in town near the bank."

"Oh I know where you mean. They're very obliging in there."

"They certainly are," said Laura, "as Charlie said he only bought it yesterday and they insisted on delivering it straight away free of charge. We had intended, should they have had one, to bring it back in the car but they said it really needed to remain upright. We were very impressed by the service especially with it being Christmas Eve."

During dinner, Ruby told of the Bible found in Tracey's wardrobe.

"Oh damn, I meant to mention it last night but with all the noise in the pub it slipped my mind," admitted Cissy.

"It sounds fascinating and I'd love to have a look at it," said Laura, "History is my passion."

"So Cissy said. You collect old books too, I hear." Ruby passed the dish of sprouts to her husband who had asked for more.

"Yes, I have quite a library at home. Book shelves run floor to ceiling on three walls in the room I call my office."

"What sort of books do you collect?" Steve spooned sprouts onto his plate and then passed the dish to Daniel.

"Anything that takes my eye really."

"First editions?"

"Yes, when I can get hold of them."

"Well I'm sure you'll love Tracey's Bible," said Ruby, "It's got to be twelve inches by eight and a couple of inches deep. It looks quite fancy too and has an ornate cover."

"And illustrations," added Cissy, "with sheets of tissue paper to protect them.

"Sounds extremely interesting. I'd love to see it so drop it in sometime or shall I pop round to you?"

"I'll drop it in tomorrow afternoon when I've finished work. Be about four if that's alright."

"Ideal. We might be going out in the evening but we'll still be here at four."

"I wonder why Tracey kept the Bible in the bottom of her wardrobe," said Laura.

"Goodness only knows but we reckon she probably bought it at an auction and stuck it in there because she didn't know what else to do with it. After all according to Becky her mother was an atheist."

"So why buy it?" Florence asked.

"Mum reckons it was in a job lot," said Cissy.

"I see. Makes sense, I suppose."

Laura seeing everyone had finished their main course stood at the end of the table so empty plates could be passed along. "Talking of auctions, that's where Charlie's clock came from. The one at the vicarage apparently."

142

"Really! I thought you said it came from the antiques shop." Ruby realising her party hat was missing picked it up from the floor.

Charlie placed his plate on top of Joan's and passed them along the row. "It did and that's because someone from the antiques shop bought it at the auction. I'm told it wasn't working at the time and so there was very little interest. As it is they have a chap on hand who does clock repairs and he got it going."

Ruby nodded. "Now you come to mention it I recall someone saying something about a grandfather clock that didn't work."

"Probably me," said Joan, "I remember seeing it but didn't take a great deal of notice because it would have been far too big for my place and as you say it wasn't working anyway."

"Has anyone figured out this Tracey person's motive for killing her husband yet?" Daniel asked.

Ruby sighed. "No, Dan and, according to Becky who is Tracey's daughter, her mum refuses to talk about it so we're all in the dark still."

"Perhaps it's because she's innocent then," reasoned Laura.

"Surely all the more reason for her to talk then," Joan winked as Charlie sitting next to her topped up her wine glass.

"She can't be innocent anyway," said Ruby, "according to gossip doing the rounds in the pub the evidence against her is pretty solid."

"Totally agree but for all the wracking of brains amongst village folk, no-one has been able to come up with a believable motive despite the fact they all say she's guilty." Steve leaned back and loosened the buttons of his festive waistcoat.

"Oh well, I suppose the prosecution will drum something up." Laura picked up the dirty plates. Charlie seeing the door was closed leapt to his feet and opened it for her, he then followed her out with serving dishes.

Cissy tired of hearing about Tracey Potts decided to change the subject. "It's really nice to be here knowing my workmates will be going flat out."

"Are there many booked into the hotel for Christmas dinner?" Florence asked.

"One hundred and twenty and it'll be done in two sittings."

"Really! So how come they let you have the lunchtime off?" Daniel picked up the tiny spinning top he'd found inside his cracker and sent it flying across the tablecloth.

"Because I worked last year. I have to work tomorrow though and that'll be quite busy too and then probably on New Year's Eve as well. They try to work it so we all have some time off over the festive period."

"And you had yesterday off," Ruby reminded her.

After pudding the ladies cleared the table, loaded up the dishwasher and made coffee. They all then returned to the sitting room where Charlie made up the fire.

"Are you alright, Flo?" Laura asked, "You look a little pale."

"Yes, I just feel a bit chilly."

"Chilly, but it's lovely and warm in here," Laura had removed her cardigan.

"Yes, I'm sure it is but I feel a bit shivery. I think I'll pop to my room and get a warmer top."

"You probably drank too much last night," teased Daniel, "You and Cissy were certainly knocking back the lager."

After she had pulled on a thick jumper over her sparkly vest top, Florence left her room. As she passed the landing window she saw a Land Rover driving slowly along the lane. She paused to watch as it stopped by the lower gates. The driver then wound down his window, stretched out his arm and tapped the side of the door while gazing at the house. Florence leapt back so she would not be seen. The driver then closed his window and slowly drove away. Back in the dining room she mentioned it to the others.

"Probably someone who saw the place back in its state of disrepair who was interested to see what it looks like now," reasoned Charlie.

"Yeah, I suppose so. It just seems a bit odd. You know, most people are indoors on Christmas Day."

"Most but not all," said Laura, "Lots of people visit family and friends so that's probably where he was going."

"And a lot of people have to work as well," said Charlie, "Doctors, nurses, restaurateurs, police, television companies and loads of others."

The day continued with games, chat, laughter, food and drink.

At eleven o'clock Ruby glanced at her watch. "As much as I don't want to leave this cosy room I think it's time we made a move. You have to work tomorrow Cissy and so do I."

During the afternoon most of the snow had melted and with the fall in temperature after dark the resulting slush had frozen hard.

"Do be careful driving, Cissy. It looks treacherous out there and the lane won't have been gritted." Charlie was concerned.

"Don't worry, I'll be fine and drive really slow." Cissy unlocked the car.

"She's a good driver," said Ruby, "and is always careful."

"She is that and we really appreciate her offer to do the driving so we could have a drink," Steve slurred.

"Well I wouldn't have been able to offer to drive anyway," chuckled Joan, "I've never learnt so never driven. I've got me old bike though and that's good enough for me."

"Not on a night like this though," Steve gave his mother-in-law a hug. "Be fun seeing you wobbling off down the icy road though especially after the amount you've had to drink."

The temperature on Boxing Day morning was below freezing and a thin layer of fresh snow had fallen during the night. Feeling sorry for the birds, Laura defrosted peas, chopped up an apple and placed all on a tray along with some nuts. As she put the tray outside on top of the snow, Charlie poured boiling water into the bird bath to melt the solid block of ice. He then fetched his garden broom and swept a pathway from the kitchen door to the log shed. After sprinkling the cleared area with salt he brought in a basket full of wood and lit the fire. Feeling lethargic the family decided to save their energy and have a lazy day.

From her home in Porthgwyns, Ruby went to work at the Harbour Lights and was there from midday until half past three. When she finished she drove to Seven Pines with the Bible as pre-arranged with Laura.

"You obviously got back alright last night," said Laura, as Ruby stepped into the warm kitchen and wiped her feet on the doormat.

"Yes, thank you and thank you again for such a lovely day. We all really enjoyed it."

"We enjoyed it too and it pleases me a lot to know that Charlie has some good friends down here." Laura closed the door, "So was the pub busy this lunchtime?"

"Yes, Boxing lunchtime is always a busy one. I think people are glad to get out for a while and get some fresh air. It won't be so busy tonight though as lots of people visit family and friends for a second bash," Ruby handed the box to Laura, "and as promised, here's the Bible."

Laura placed the box on the kitchen table and removed the lid. "My goodness, it's even better than I'd imagined."

With care she lifted out the Bible, placed it on the table top and opened it to the first page.

"Catherine Freathy," she read, "Beautiful writing too. In my experience all educated people did copperplate writing once upon a time. Such a shame the art is dying out." Laura turned over a few of the delicate pages and then closed it up, "Would you mind if I kept it for a day or two. The thing is I'd love to have a proper look now but I really haven't the time to do it justice. We've decided that we will go out this evening, you see, and I'll need to get ready soon."

"Of course, keep it as long as you like."

"Thank you, I'll put it in my room for safe keeping and I promise it'll have my undivided attention tomorrow."

"Lovely, and we all look forward to hearing what you come up with."

Laura glanced up at the wall clock. "Would you like a cup of tea?"

"No thanks. I'd like to get home before it's dark. I could do with some new tyres, you see, so don't want to risk driving when it drops below freezing again."

"Don't blame you and this hill is particularly dicey."

Ruby picked up her gloves from the table top. "So are you going somewhere nice tonight?"

"I hope so. There's a band touring the West Country at the moment and they're playing at a pub in Truro. I've Googled them and reviews are very good, in fact most people are raving about them. We thought about going when we first heard about it but the weather turning wintery put us off. It's not too bad now so we've decided to risk it even though more snow is forecast."

"Yes, but I don't suppose it'll come to much down here. I know the band you mean though and I've heard that they are very good. In fact, Greg and Grace are hoping to book them to play at the Harbour Lights when they do another tour in the summer. They reckon it'll go down well with the visitors and the locals too."

"We'll let you know our thoughts then when we next see you but I should imagine they are good. Elderflower and Jiffy were raving about them in the pub on Christmas Eve. They've seen them on several occasions. In fact Jiffy said were it not for the fact that he and Elderflower are going to stay with friends in St Ives for Christmas and Boxing Day then they would have gone to see them as well."

Ruby glanced at the window. "Well you take care and if I were you I'd pop Wellington boots and blankets in the boot just to be on the safe side."

Laura nodded. "That thought had crossed my mind. The last thing we want is to get stranded but then if it snows, and is anything like we had on Christmas Eve, it won't last long."

"True, and what little fell last night didn't settle on the roads that were gritted. Anyway, I'll have my fingers crossed for you," Ruby turned towards the door, "I hope you all have a fantastic time, Laura and I'll think about you while I'm pulling pints at the Harbour tonight."

"Thank you and thanks for bringing the Bible over too. Looking at it will be the highlight of my day tomorrow."

It was intended that the whole family go to see the band but as darkness fell Florence said she wasn't feeling too well. Her head ached and she felt very tired.

Charlie looked concerned. "Oh dear, I hope you're not coming down with something nasty."

"I don't think I am although I felt a bit shivery yesterday and didn't sleep too well last night. I don't know why but I'm sure I'll be fine after a good night's rest."

"Well I think it might be better if we all stayed at home then. I don't like the idea of you here on your own."

"Dad, don't be silly. I'll be fine."

"Are you sure?"

"Yes and don't forget Ben will be with me."

"Yes, of course. Okay, well you stay then, but keep warm and have an early night."

"I shall. In fact I'll probably go to bed soon after you've gone and watch a film or something on the television in my room."

"Good, and make sure you lock up after we've gone. Leave the gates open though so we can drive straight in when we get back. I have keys to both doors and I promise we'll creep in like mice and not disturb you."

Reasoning that some of the country lanes they would need to travel along to reach the main road might not have been gritted, they left early for Truro just after six. Daniel volunteered to drive saying he was happy to forgo an alcoholic drink as he'd had one too many on Christmas Day.

Florence waved to them as they drove away, then she locked the back door, made herself cheese on toast and sat by the fire to eat it while half-heartedly watching the local news. The weather forecast followed; more snow was predicted. Florence shuddered at the prospect and put another log on the fire. The theme tune of a popular chat show followed the weather. She watched it for a while and then looked to see if there were any films to her liking. To her delight there was a mild horror one on a little later which sounded promising and so at half past eight she made herself a mug of drinking chocolate and with a hot water bottle tucked beneath her arm went to bed leaving the lower hall lights on and Ben sleeping on the rug by the fire. In her room she plugged her phone into its charger, drew the curtains, climbed into bed and using the remote control switched on her television set.

Inside the Truro pub, the highly rated band lived up to expectations and played to a full house. At half past nine they took a twenty minute break to enable them to rest and refill their glasses. During the break a party of people

149

arrived, their hats and heads covered in snowflakes. On hearing them tell friends they were late because it was snowing heavily, Charlie and Laura went outside to see for themselves while Daniel chatted to members of the band. To their amazement the pavements were several inches deep with snow and there was no traffic on the road.

Charlie folded his arms to keep warm and watched as the snow fell heavily in the circle of light beneath a streetlamp. "We'll never get home, Laura. It would be madness to try."

"But we must try because we can't sleep in the car."

"In that case perhaps we ought to leave now before it gets any worse and forgo the second half of the show."

Laura tutted. "I suppose that makes sense but what a shame."

Desolately, Charlie turned to go back indoors and report the situation to Daniel.

"No, just a minute, Charlie, look." Laura grabbed his arm and pointed to a hotel further down the road. "How about we book rooms for the night? That's if they have any left."

Charlie's face lit up. "Sounds like a brilliant idea. Let's go and see what Dan thinks as he's the driver."

After looking from the window and seeing the snow, Daniel agreed that to stay made sense and so Charlie and Laura gingerly crossed the road; to their relief they were able to book the last room. It was a twin room but the hotel proprietors said under the circumstances they would allow three to occupy it and would provide bedding so that the third person could make up a bed on the floor. Relieved to have made their decision, Charlie then phoned Florence to tell her not to expect them back before lunch at the earliest the following day.

"Is it snowing at your place?" Laura asked Charlie as he switched off his phone.

"Yes. Florence didn't even realise 'til I called though because she was in bed but she got out and opened her window and said it already looks quite deep. It's windy there too and so drifting."

As Charlie and Laura stepped back inside the pub and stamped their feet to remove snow stuck to their shoes, the music began again and within minutes the snow was temporarily forgotten, the drinks flowed and a good time was had by all.

To the dismay of Florence the film put her on edge. She knew it was a mild horror but didn't expect to witness a terrified young woman walking around the dark corridor of a house during a storm, a knife in her hand having heard strange noises. Had she been with friends they'd have laughed but in her current situation Florence felt more like crying. The circumstances did not improve and as the scene progressed Florence slipped further and further beneath the bedclothes. Unable to take the tension any more, she reached for the remote control and switched the television off. As the screen went blank she heard a loud thud; Ben barked and then whined. Florence sat up in alarm and listened. Had the thud come from outside or was it somewhere inside the house? Because it coincided with the television going off it was impossible to be sure. Knowing she would not be able to sleep unless she knew the source of the noise she slipped out of her warm bed, crossed to the window and pulled back the curtains to see if there were any obvious reasons outside. She opened the window and in the beam of light from her room saw the upper gateway was partly blocked by drifting snow and so assumed the lower gateway would be likewise. She sighed, branches of trees and shrubs, laden with frozen crystals looked beautiful in the glow of her bedroom light but because of the mysterious thud she was unable to fully appreciate its beauty. With a shiver she closed the window, drew the curtains together and crossed the room for her dressing gown; as she reached up and removed it from the hook on the back of her door, the light went out. With heart thumping she quietly opened the bedroom door and peeped out onto the landing. The hall light downstairs was also out. Florence suppressed the urge to cry. She needed to investigate a strange noise; was very much afraid and the power was off. As she slipped her arms onto the sleeves of her dressing gown and tied its sash, she heard the mutterings of muffled voices. Shaking with fear, she tip-toed back into her room, felt for her phone and pulled it from its charger. With fingers trembling she switched on its torch and in case someone should ring, turned down the volume. With a little more confidence she stepped back out onto the landing and shone the light on the hall clock above the window; the time was twenty-five minutes past ten and so she knew it was too early for the family to have returned home and they were staying in Truro anyway.

Quietly she walked towards the top of the stairs. There was no sign of life but it was obvious that someone was there. Knowing the front and back doors were locked and the windows were all closed she assumed that whoever was there must have broken in. Not wanting the light on her phone to be seen she turned it off and slipped the device into the pocket of her dressing gown. Holding the banister rail tightly she then quietly descended the stairs, pausing every few seconds to listen, eager to establish where the voices were coming from. As she reached the bottom and stepped onto the rug, she realised the voices had stopped. Had whoever was there gone? She hoped so. Unsure which way to go she crept slowly along the dark hallway feeling the walls as she went. On reaching the sitting room door she found that it was ajar. She paused; without doubt she had closed it when she had gone to bed because Laura had asked her to do so in order to prevent Ben from wandering around the house. She gasped. Where was Ben? Why wasn't he barking? In desperate need of answers she edged further along the passage. As she approached the kitchen she saw the door was slightly open and inside lights were flashing. A sudden cold draught caused her dressing gown to flap around the legs of her pyjamas and she realised the back door must be open. But how? She had locked it. Florence stood rigid; too afraid to move. Why was someone in the kitchen? Where was Ben? What should she do? Hide. She must hide and hope that whoever was there would go away. As she took a step backwards towards the cupboard beneath the stairs, her eyes fixed on the kitchen door, she felt sudden warmth on the back of her neck and heard the steady sound of breathing. Someone was behind her. The grandfather clock struck half past ten and everything went black.

Chapter Nineteen

The snow continued to fall gently throughout the night and finally stopped just before dawn. Beams of light from the rising sun intensified the brightness of the white world and residents of Porthgwyns and beyond gazed from their windows in awe at the spectacle before their eyes.

Inside their Truro hotel room, Charlie, Laura and Daniel having slept well, drank tea and eagerly watched the morning news and especially the weather forecast. The local news bulletin informed them that gritters and snow ploughs had been out all night and most main roads were clear, however, people were advised not to travel unless it was absolutely necessary. Feeling it was imperative they attempt the journey back to Seven Pines, they left Truro just before eleven after Charlie rang Florence's number to assure her they were fine; because she didn't answer he assumed she was either asleep or in the shower.

The journey home was hair-raising; the pace was very slow and at times they hardly moved, hence they all heaved a sigh of relief when they drove through the lower gates of Seven Pines just before one o'clock. Delighted to be back all gathered in the warm kitchen eager for a hot drink and a bacon sandwich.

"Gosh, it's good to be home," Laura kicked off her damp shoes and reached for her slippers left beside the Aga.

Daniel unzipped his jacket. "Likewise, that drive was bonkers. At times I thought we'd never get back but I didn't like to say so."

"I thought exactly the same," Charlie reached for the kettle, "Tea or coffee, folks?"

"Whatever you're having," said Laura. Daniel said likewise and took three mugs from the cupboard.

"Has someone lost an earring?" Charlie picked up a small gold cross lying in front of the dishwasher.

Laura took bacon from the fridge and placed it in the frying pan. "Not mine."

"Must belong to Florence then." Charlie dropped it into a pot on the Welsh dresser, switched on the kettle and then bent forward to stroke Ben's head. "Are you alright, old boy? You seem a bit tottery today."

Ben held up his paw for Charlie to shake.

"I thought that," Daniel spooned coffee granules into the mugs and then sat down, "he seems a right old sleepy head and he didn't even stir when we first walked in."

"Must be the sea air," said Laura, "I feel sleepy too."

"Hmm, that bacon smells good," Charlie made the coffee and placed the steaming mugs on the table. He glanced around. "Where's Flo. I've just realised she's not here."

"Good point," said Laura, "perhaps she's still feeling a bit under the weather and isn't up yet. Keep an eye on the bacon and I'll pop up and see."

"No need, I'll go. I'll enjoy kicking her out of bed." Daniel took a sip of coffee and then left the room.

"Oh, to have that much energy," said Laura, as they heard him running up the stairs two at a time.

Daniel knocked on Florence's door. There was no reply. It was ajar so he pushed it open and looked inside. The duvet on her bed was pulled back so he assumed she was in the en suite bathroom. But as he glanced towards it he saw the door was slightly open. He peeped inside. Florence was not there. Thinking he must have missed her he went back downstairs.

"Oh, she's not here either." Daniel scratched his head. "That's odd because she's not in her room."

"Probably in the shower," said Charlie.

"No, she's not. I looked."

Charlie's face dropped. "Perhaps she's lying ill in the house somewhere. Remember she wasn't feeling too good last night."

They all left the kitchen and searched the house. Florence was nowhere to be found.

They returned to the kitchen and Daniel sat back down heavily on the chair he'd recently vacated. "Where can she be?"

"A walk maybe," suggested Laura, "It's a lovely bright day so she might have gone out to take pictures of the snow. As we were driving home I thought I'd do the same when we got back."

Charlie glanced from the window. "Possible, I suppose. Everywhere certainly looks stunning."

Daniel took his phone from the pocket of his jeans. "I'll give her a ring." The phone rang and rang but there was no answer.

"Perhaps she didn't take her phone with her," suggested Laura.

Charlie shook her head. "I doubt it, she takes it everywhere and if she's out taking pictures she'd need it anyway."

"I'll go and see if it's in her room." Daniel went to check but returned empty-handed. "There's no sign of her phone and it's not on charge. What's more her curtains are still drawn and her bed's not made. Flo would never go out and leave her bed unmade."

"You're right," agreed Laura, "she said the other day that unmade beds is one of her pet hates."

Charlie picked up his own phone. "I'm calling the police."

"You can't, not yet, Dad. They'll say to leave it a while in case she turns up."

"Okay, I'll wait 'til teatime but not a minute longer. Meanwhile I'm going out to look for her."

"Have a bacon sandwich first. You've not eaten since breakfast and it's bitterly cold out there."

"Okay." Charlie sat down and Laura placed the sandwiches on the table.

"When you go, Dad, I'll go with you and Auntie Laura can wait here in case Flo comes back."

By four o'clock the light was starting to fade. Daniel and Charlie's search had been fruitless; knowing it would soon be dark, Charlie rang the police. Ten minutes later two police officers who were in the area, arrived: a tall man, and a young woman who looked not much older than Florence. After taking seats around the kitchen table, Charlie, Laura and Daniel told them everything they could.

"I've just realised something," said Charlie, "When we got home the back door was unlocked but I know for a fact that Florence would have locked it even if she'd only gone out for ten minutes. She's very security conscious." The male police officer leaned back in his chair and steepled his fingers. "Now bearing in mind the atrocious weather, do you think it's possible that she went out last night and like you couldn't get home?"

Charlie sighed. "Well, it's possible of course but I think it's highly unlikely. You see, she was going to go with us to Truro but wasn't feeling well and that's why she was here on her own."

"No way she went out," said Daniel, "I mean she doesn't have a car and is hardly likely to walk when the nearest village is five miles away."

"Maybe she made the excuse not to go with you so that she could then go off with someone else and that someone picked her up here. I know what youngsters are like."

Charlie laughed. "Officer, she's twenty not twelve. If she wanted to go somewhere else no-one would have tried to stop her. Besides I know she was home around nine thirty last night because I rang her. What's more at the time she

157

said she was in bed watching television and I could hear it in the background."

"Another thing worth remembering is she doesn't really know anyone down here anyway," Daniel added, "this is the first time she's been to Cornwall and she only arrived a week or so ago."

"She gets on well with Cissy," said Charlie, "but we know for a fact that Cissy was working last night at the Porthgwyns Hotel."

The male police officer sighed. "I see. So have you checked to see which of her clothes are missing so that we can have some idea what she might be wearing?"

Charlie scratched his head. "That's a tricky one, because she's away from home now I'm not very familiar with her wardrobe. Not that I'm much good at remembering women's clothes anyway."

"I know what she was wearing yesterday. I'll go and see if those things are missing." Laura left the room and went upstairs.

"Well, we'll put out an alert and add her to our missing persons Facebook page," The male officer glanced around the kitchen, "Do you have a recent picture of her?"

"Very recent," Charlie picked up his phone. "I took this on Christmas Eve."

"Ideal. Forward it to my phone then, please," the officer gave Charlie his number.

Laura returned to the kitchen. "The clothes she wore yesterday are on the chair in her room but the clock beside her bed is flashing so it looks like there might have been another power cut last night."

"Really," said Charlie, "Can you remember what time was flashing, Laura?"

"Five-thirty. Why?"

Charlie looked at the kitchen clock and then did a quick calculation in his head. "It's four-thirty now. So the power must have come back on either at eleven last night or eleven this morning and my guess is it would have been eleven last night."

"How do you know that?" Laura asked.

"Because the clock reverts to twelve when the power returns and adds the time from there. It then keeps flashing 'til someone puts it right."

"So it might have been a power cut that got her out of bed," reasoned Daniel.

The colour drained from Charlie's face. "Yes. It also means that if the power came back on at eleven last night then she wasn't in her room to reset the clock and I know she would never have left it because the continuous flashing is really annoying."

"Are you prone to power cuts out here?" asked the young female officer.

"Maybe. The power went off the other night but it came back on after fifty minutes or so. On both occasions it was quite windy so there might be a loose connection somewhere or something like that. I'll ring the electricity helpline later to see if they can help at all."

"Hmm, so we have a time she might have gone missing. Not a lot to go on then but at least we have that and a recent picture so that's something," the male officer nodded approvingly as his phone received the picture from Charlie. He stood up. "If you think of anything else please don't hesitate to call."

"There is one more thing," said Laura, "the earring, Charlie. Might that be of some significance?"

"I don't see how?"

"Earring?" The male officer queried.

"Yes, I found it on the floor in here this morning. It doesn't belong to Laura but it might be Florence's."

"May I see it?"

"Of course." Charlie tipped it onto the table from the pot on the dresser.

"Do you mind if I take this with me?"

"Of course not, but why?"

"It's just routine." He produced a small plastic bag, picked the earring up with a handkerchief and dropped it inside.

"Do you think then there might have been intruders in here last night?" Laura asked.

"At this stage nothing can be ruled out."

"That's daft," said Charlie, "nothing's missing."

"Flo is," said Daniel.

Charlie gasped. "Surely you're not suggesting she's been kidnapped?"

"Until we know more we have to keep our options open, Mr Everton. I'm sorry."

Laura gasped. "Perhaps someone knows you won the Lottery, Charlie and they'll be after a ransom."

Both officers raised their eyebrows.

"But if someone had been in here Ben would have barked," reasoned Daniel.

All eyes looked at Ben who wagged his tail on hearing his name.

Laura knelt to stroke her dog. "Yes, but he's not his normal bouncy self today and so he might have been sedated."

"Any sign of a break in?" the young female officer asked.

"We've not looked," admitted Charlie, "but there are no broken windows or anything like that and the doors have not been forced open."

"Perhaps someone has a key," said Daniel.

"No-one has a key except me," Charlie spoke with confidence.

"You might think that," Laura said, "but anyone could have got a copy made while the place was being renovated."

Charlie placed his elbows on the table and rubbed his brow with his fingertips. "You're right, Laura. All sorts of people had access and some of them I only saw occasionally as they were sub-contracted by the builders I'd employed."

"Okay, well we'll get back to the station and get these details circulated," said the male officer, "Meanwhile if you think of anything else please let us know."

As the police officers stepped out from the back door, Charlie pointed out indentations in the snow. "Might there be tyre tracks under there? It looks very uneven and none of us park this close to the house so if there are tracks they'll not have been made by us."

The male officer cast his eyes around the courtyard. "I'll get someone round to check it out. It certainly looks like there could be tracks of some kind under there and if that's the case there might even be footprints too."

Laura shuddered. "I've just remembered what Flo said on Christmas day about a Land Rover stopping outside and looking at the house."

"Could be something or nothing," said Charlie, "but as none of us saw it, it won't be of any help. We don't even know what colour is was."

"No, we don't but I've a sneaky feeling that someone might have been watching the house to see when we went out. Otherwise how would they have known we were out last night?"

Charlie nodded. "Could be, Laura. Either that or they heard us saying we were thinking of going to Truro to see the band."

"Ah, so where were you when you discussed going out?" The male police officer noticed his colleague was shivering and so gave her the keys to the car.

"Thank you," She gingerly walked across the snow and slipped into the passenger seat.

"We were at the Harbour Lights," said Charlie, "We only mulled over the idea briefly though because we knew there was snow forecast and thought it might not be possible. Laura and I were talking to Jiffy Lemon and his daughter Elderflower at the time."

"Ah, yes, our local celebrity. I know he's been away for a couple of days though because he mentioned it when I saw him last week. He sounded a bit nervous and I know he doesn't like leaving his home because it's so isolated. There was a burglary at his place last year, you see and he lost a lot of valuable paintings."

"Oh dear, poor Jiffy," said Charlie, "No wonder he was jittery about going away."

"Doesn't he have a burglar alarm then?" Laura thought it strange.

"He does, but whoever broke in deactivated it."

"Professionals then," said Daniel.

"Yes, looks like it. Anyway, you chatting to him about going out last night might be a lead so any idea who might have overheard you talking?"

Charlie groaned. "Just about anyone. It was Christmas Eve and the place was packed."

Chapter Twenty

Shortly after the police left, Cissy arrived. Having worked the breakfast and lunchtime shifts at the hotel she had the evening off and was keen to hear details of the Truro trip.

"Hi, how did last night go?" She cheerfully asked as Laura opened the door to her. Her mood changed when she saw the glum looks on their faces, "What's wrong?"

"Flo's missing," said Daniel.

"Missing? But how, I don't understand."

"We had to stay in Truro last night because of the weather," said Charlie, "And when we got back at lunchtime today she wasn't here."

Cissy was confused. "Wasn't here? Didn't she go with you then?"

Daniel shook his head. "No, she wasn't feeling very well and so decided to stay home in the warm and watch television instead."

"Yes, now you come to mention it she said on Christmas Day that she thought she'd caught something but didn't want to say anything to you and spoil the day. Although she couldn't hide the fact she felt shivery."

"Come and sit down, Cissy," Charlie pulled out a chair for her and they all sat down around the table.

"When was the last time you heard from her?" Daniel asked.

"Yesterday morning. She sent me a message saying *Happy Boxing Day.*"

"And she's not messaged you or anything since?"

"No, and I suppose she wouldn't have because she knew I was working all day yesterday with the hotel being fully booked and she knew I was doing breakfast and lunchtime today. On Christmas Day we left it that I'd pop over today after work and we'd probably go to the Red Lion. They have a local band on there, you see. They're not very good but they always liven the place up."

"Yes, she did say something about that now you come to mention it." Laura nervously twisted a strand of hair.

"So what do you think might have happened to her?" Cissy asked.

Charlie shook his head, "We don't know, but it's possible she might have been kidnapped."

"Kidnapped! But why and by whom?"

"Again we don't know," said Daniel, "but we're pretty sure someone was in here last night."

"So are there any clues? You know, footsteps in the snow, things missing and stuff like that."

Charlie nodded towards the back door. "It looks like there might be tyre tracks but they've been covered with fresh snow. The police are going to investigate and there might be footprints there too."

"Another strange thing is, Charlie found an earring on the kitchen floor," said Laura, "It wasn't mine so it might have been Florence's. The police have taken it anyway."

"What was it like?"

"A cross," said Charlie, "a small gold cross."

Daniel agitatedly drummed his fingers on the table top. "What can we do? There must be something. I mean, we can't just sit here. She might be lying injured somewhere. We need to go out searching again."

Laura glanced towards the window where the stable block, its roof covered in several inches of snow, was just visible in the light from the kitchen. She knew that anyone outside overnight could not have survived the freezing temperature especially if in an exposed area.

"But where do we look? We've no idea where she might be, the weather's hideous and there's more snow forecast," Charlie's voice trembled with emotion.

Daniel stood up. "I'm going to the Harbour Lights to ask if anyone has seen her there. Is anyone coming with me?"

Cissy sprang to her feet. "I will, Dan. Mum's working so she might be able to help too."

"I would," said Charlie, "but I feel someone must stay here in case she returns home or God forbid we get a call asking for ransom money."

Laura patted her brother's arm. "I agree and so I'll stay too and keep you company."

"Before you go, Dan, print off this picture of Flo so you can show it to people in the pub. The printer's in my bedroom on a desk behind the door." Charlie handed Daniel his phone where his daughter's face smiled up from the screen.

Inside the pub, Daniel and Cissy eagerly asked if anyone had seen Florence. A few remembered seeing her on Christmas Eve but no-one had seen her since then. Feeling deflated, Daniel asked Landlord Greg for permission to pin the picture of his sister printed from Charlie's phone on the pub's notice board.

"Of course, Dan and if there's anything we can do to help please let us know."

Having heard the news from her daughter, Ruby working behind the bar, was very concerned. "I know it's a bit of a long shot, Dan, but have you looked in the Old Inn's cellar? There was talk years ago of there being a tunnel from the Inn to Quignog Cove. Mum told us about it when we were kids but she reckoned it was just a rumour because Reggie Williams searched the place from top to toe when he had the decorators in and she and Marilyn helped by tapping on walls and so forth. I'm just thinking if it does exist she might have found it and got trapped down there.

Having said that, if Reggie and the rest of his clan couldn't find it, it's highly unlikely Flo would come across it by chance."

"Thanks, Ruby. We're keeping our options open so it's certainly worth looking into. I'll give Dad a ring."

Charlie was still sitting at the kitchen table agitatedly drumming his fingers against the stripped pine surface when his phone rang. Hoping for good news he answered instantly.

"A tunnel," despite his anxiety, Charlie had to smile, "I doubt there is one but we'll go and have a look. I need something to occupy my mind anyway. Thank Ruby for suggesting it and I'll ring you back if we find it. Actually, Dan, I'll ring you back anyway to see if there's any news at your end."

Charlie repeated his conversation with Daniel to Laura.

"Well, I'm game if you are, Charlie but I'm going to put a scarf or something over my head because there are rather a lot of spiders' webs on those beams."

Charlie stood up. "I'd put something warm on too because it'll be pretty chilly down there."

"We must both take our phones as well in case anyone rings."

"Good idea although we might not get a signal underground."

Despite both thinking the notion of a tunnel was silly they went down with coats on and heads covered determined to have a thorough search.

"It doesn't look to me as though anyone has been down here," said Charlie, as they reached the bottom of the stone steps, "It looks just the same as when you and I came down here."

"I agree and to be honest I can't see a young woman who's feeling unwell deciding to explore by herself when alone in the house on a cold, snowy night. I certainly wouldn't have done so at her age. In fact I wouldn't have done at any age. Not even now."

"I'm inclined to agree and if you remember when she and Dan arrived she took one look down the steps, shuddered and said 'I wouldn't go down there for all the tea in China'."

Laura smiled. "But then she added she would were it all cleaned up."

Charlie looked above his head where a few electricity cables ran along the beams. "It's just a thought, but we know the electricity must have gone off last night and according to my calculations it came back on around eleven o'clock. We don't know what time it went off but it couldn't have been before half nine otherwise Flo would have mentioned it when I rang her to say we were staying in Truro. So it's possible Flo could have come down here looking for the trip switch. I mean she's a bright girl and so might have thought she'd be able to fix it."

"But the trip wasn't the problem the other night when it went off, was it? You checked and the power came back on, on its own."

"Yes, but Flo was out with Dan then so she wouldn't know that and I don't think we mentioned it to them afterwards. There would have been no point."

"Okay, it's a thought but the dust down here looks pretty undisturbed to me so I think we're on a wild goose chase. What's more, if she was looking for a means to get the power back on I'm sure she'd have looked in the kitchen first or under the stairs. I mean no-one would have their meters, trip switch and so forth in a cellar, would they?"

"No, I suppose not. I think the meter readers might moan if they did."

"Exactly. What's more how would that fit in with her being stuck down a tunnel? I mean she'd hardly just stumble on it, and I doubt it exists anyway."

Charlie's shoulders slumped. "Yes, I suppose you're right and I was just grasping at straws."

Laura gave him a quick hug. "I know you are. Come on, it's too cold down here to hang around. Let's do a thorough search and then get back in the warm in case anyone rings on the landline."

"So where do we start?"

"Well if we're looking for a tunnel we need to look for a secret entrance. You know, a moving stone, a trap door or something like that."

"A bit like Indiana Jones," Charlie half-smiled. "If Florence were not missing I'd be able to enjoy this but as it is I think it's quite futile because as you say clearly no-one has been down here."

Nevertheless, they tapped on all of the walls. Pushed tea chests, barrels and old furniture around looking for a trap door.

"It might be worth keeping an eye out for an iron ring or something like that, Charlie. I'm thinking of a means of opening a door or whatever."

They thoroughly searched from one end of the cellar to the other but it was all in vain.

Charlie sneezed. "I think I've had enough. The dust down here is awful, what's more my feet are like blocks of ice."

"Mine too."

"Let's go back up then."

Laura readily agreed. "One day when Florence is safely back home we'll all come down and tackle this lot."

"If she ever comes back home." Charlie's voice trembled with emotion. Laura put her arm round her brother. "We'll find her, Charlie. We'll find her, I promise."

Inside the Harbour Lights, Daniel rushed to the door every time someone new walked into the pub. Eager to know if they had seen his sister, he either showed the picture of Florence he had on his phone or pointed to the printout on the notice board but to his dismay, no-one had seen her. Tired and deflated he finally sat down.

"You look as though you could do with a drink, mate," Jerry, having just arrived with Tash was saddened to hear the distressing news, "Please let me get you one."

"Thanks. I think perhaps it might help calm me. I'll have a pint of Doom Bar if that's okay."

"Right, coming up."

"While Jerry went to the bar, Tash sat down at the table and eagerly questioned Daniel about his sister's disappearance. Simultaneously, Jiffy arrived with Elderflower.

Daniel's eyes flashed when he saw the latest arrivals. He leapt to his feet and approached them before they had time to close the door. "I don't suppose you've seen my sister at all today have you?"

"Flo?" Elderflower stamped her feet on the doormat to loosen snow stuck to her boots.

"Yes, Flo."

"Sorry, no. We haven't seen her since Christmas Eve. We were away on Christmas Day and Boxing Day and only got back this afternoon."

"Why? Is she missing?" Jiffy closed the door quickly to keep out the ice cold draught.

"Yes, she is and we're sick with worry."

"Good heavens, I should imagine you are," Jiffy took Elderflower's arm and they followed a subdued Daniel over to the table where Cissy and Tash were sitting. As Daniel sat, Jerry returned with his pint, then he helped Cissy push two tables together so they could all sit in a group.

"So what appears to have happened?" Jiffy sat, all thoughts of drinks having gone from his head.

Daniel took several sips of his beer hoping it might help steady his nerves, then he explained the situation in detail. Elderflower watched Jerry and Tash who both hung onto every word throughout the lengthy explanation. Jiffy expressed his concern and cast a questioning look at his daughter.

"So is anything missing from your dad's place, Dan?" Jerry asked, "Was anything out of place when you got back? Did it look just as you'd left it? Were doors open that you'd left closed for instance?"

"Nothing appears to be missing or out of place. As for doors, when we went to Truro, Flo was there so she could have opened or closed any."

"Yes of course. What about footprints in the snow then?"

As Daniel was about to respond to Jerry, Richard and Edward walked in rubbing their hands to warm them.

"Two pints of Guinness please, Ruby," said Richard, cheerfully, "The snow looks great but it's freezing out there."

"Certainly is," Edward made for the fireplace, stood with his back to it and removed his glasses to wipe away the newly formed condensation on the lenses, "There are even bits of ice floating in the harbour. We had to go carefully in case they punctured the inflatable even though we're pretty sure it's a lot tougher than that."

While the Guinness settled, Ruby asked the brothers if they had seen Florence.

"Florence! What as in Dan's sister?" Richard cast a look at the party round the two tables.

Everyone nodded.

"No, we've not seen her since Christmas Eve. In fact today's the first time we've been ashore since then." Edward left the fireplace and pulled up a chair to join the party, "So what's this all about?"

"Flo's missing," said Elderflower, "No-one has seen her since last night."

"What!"

Cissy explained the situation to the brothers.

"But that's crazy," said Edward, "I really don't know what to say."

Daniel looked at his phone. "Damn. No word from Dad so it doesn't look like they've found a tunnel. It's over half an hour now since I rang him."

"A tunnel?" spluttered Tash. She cast a quick look at Jerry who seemed equally surprised.

"Tunnel!" Jiffy arched his eyebrows.

Daniel told them about Ruby's suggestion.

"I've just heard about your sister, Dan. How long's she been gone?" Tom, having just arrived took a sip of beer and stood by the group.

Daniel explained again.

"Oh no, that's horrible. Your poor dad. So are the police taking her disappearance seriously?"

"Yes, because they think she's been kidnapped and they're expecting Dad to get a call asking for a huge payment."

"Really!" Edward seemed surprised.

Tom sat on the edge of an empty table. "Sounds feasible though. I mean, your dad's Lottery win is common knowledge now so anyone could be behind it."

"Yeah, but what they wouldn't know is that there's not a lot left after what he's spent on the house and so forth," said Daniel, "It wasn't a super big silly win, you see. Just three and a half million."

"Yeah but shady characters do daft things just for a few grand," said Jerry.

"Well, I think it's horrible," said Richard, "it seems some people have no moral scruples."

"So are the police actually looking for her?" Tom asked, "Or are they waiting to get a call first?"

"I believe they're looking because they're pretty sure she's in the vicinity somewhere."

"Well let's keep our fingers crossed," sighed Tom, "but the coppers can do wonders these days and if Flo has her phone with her they might be able to track it down."

"I do hope so," said Cissy.

"Yeah, yeah, that'd be great but what a miserable note for us to leave on," Edward rested his hand on Daniel's shoulder, "We're really sorry mate. Aren't we Rich?"

Richard looked confused. "Yeah, yeah, we are."

"You're leaving," Daniel looked puzzled, "but I thought…"

"…yes, yes, we've been invited to a party in London. We just popped in for a last drink and to say goodbye." Edward gabbled his words.

"But I thought you were going to stay to see in the New Year with us." Cissy was clearly disappointed.

"We were but as I say, change of plan now, Ciss." As Edward spoke, Richard pushed back a strand of hair from across his confused, flushed face and Daniel's jaw dropped when he saw Richard wore an earring identical to the one found on the kitchen floor. Cissy saw it too and knowing the lone earring was a small gold cross, sensed the reason for the startled look on Daniel's face. Desperate to know if Richard wore a pair, she jumped up and jokingly flicked his dark curls. "I wish I had hair like you, Rich. My hair's as straight as pump water." She struggled to keep the jollity in her voice for Richard's exposed ear lacked a small gold cross.

"I'm flattered." His laugh was false.

Edward saw the alarmed look between Cissy and Daniel. Elderflower saw it too. Jerry was nowhere to be seen. Tash looked shocked.

"Drink up, Rich, we need to get going."

"Yeah, yeah, coming, Ed."

"Wouldn't it be better to wait until morning?" Daniel was desperate to stall them.

172

"No, no we want to get away tonight." Richard quickly downed his pint.

"Yeah, lovely to have met you all. Perhaps see you again one day. Meanwhile, all the best for next year." Edward turned and slammed his empty glass down on the bar. Before they were out of the door, Elderflower had dashed to the Ladies for privacy and was on the phone to the police. But they already knew. Jerry had beaten her to it.

Chapter Twenty One

Florence woke up to find she was lying on the heavily carpeted floor of a dimly lit room, its only source of light the glow from a tropical fish tank. Her hands and ankles were bound; she felt light-headed and slightly nauseous. With effort she rolled onto her back and managed to sit up. Her mouth was dry and her throat burned; as events of the previous evening came back she realised she had been drugged. She recalled feeling warm breath on her neck, the clock in the sitting room chiming the half hour and then someone's hand smothering her face. After that, nothing. Casting her eyes around she tried to figure out where she was. The sound of the sea and a gentle rocking motion told her that she was inside a boat. A luxury boat. A yacht. Her heart sank. Surely it was not the *Golden Sunset*. For if it was then the two brothers, Richard and Edward Rudd were who she had disturbed the previous evening. Holding her breath she strained to listen but could hear no voices. Was she alone on the yacht? Her ankles were bound and her hands were tied behind her back but that was not a problem. Florence was petite, an amateur gymnast and she had long arms; with ease she passed her hands beneath her bottom and under her legs until they were in front of her. She then untied the rope that bound her ankles. Once on her feet she looked around for something to free her wrists. In the semi-darkness she spotted light reflected on the side of a glass bottle. She crossed the room and heaved a sigh of relief. On a counter amongst numerous bottles of alcohol sat a chopping board and on its surface alongside lemons, limes, and a jar of cherries lay a knife with a serrated edge.

Carefully she lifted the knife and laboriously sawed at the rope until finally it snapped. With hands free she rubbed her wrists and then tried the door. It was locked. She crossed to the windows, pulled back the curtains and tapped on the glass. It was clearly thick and strengthened; she doubted it would break easily. At the far end of the room was a small passage. She walked towards it and saw another door. It was a bathroom. She switched on the light; a wall clock said the time was half past seven. Her stomach rumbled as she realised she had been asleep for over twenty hours. Feeling light-headed and giddy she steadied herself by gripping a towel rail and looked towards the ceiling where a small window was partly open. She climbed onto the toilet seat and pushed it wide open. She was too low to see out but could hear the sea splashing on the side of the yacht. She returned to the lounge and again listened at the door for the sound of voices. Satisfied that she was alone on the boat she looked for something on which to stand to enable her to see out of the small window. Nothing looked suitable and then she noticed the rope that had bound her ankles and wrists. She tied the severed ends together until she had one long piece. She then carefully made loops on either end, one small, the other large enough to take her foot. With heart thumping she returned to the bathroom and threw the rope up until the small loop caught on a hook. She then placed her foot in the lower loop and eased her way up until she was able to look from the window. It was dark outside but a string of lights illuminated the deck below. Sensing freedom she squeezed her slim body through the open window and dropped down onto the icy wooden deck.

The yacht was still anchored off the village of Porthgwyns. Desperate to get back on dry land, Florence ran around the deck looking for a punt, motor boat or anything that might enable her to reach the harbour. Her heart sank when she realised that as neither Richard nor Edward appeared to be on the yacht then they must already have taken their boat ashore. Her feet were cold; she had no shoes. She cast her eyes around looking for any item of footwear. To her relief she spotted two pairs of Wellington boots beneath an awning. Alongside them, part covered by a huge tarpaulin, were a deflated inflatable boat, a foot pump, a rope ladder and air bottles; above hung two wetsuits. With a feeling of hope she looked at the boots. One pair was size ten the others size seven. Florence's feet were size four. Appreciating the smaller pair were better than nothing, she slipped her foot into the right boot and her toes touched something soft. She looked inside and to her delight found a pair of long, thick socks. Eagerly she pulled them on over the legs of her pyjama trousers and then slipped her socked feet into the boots. Feeling a little more comfortable, she looked at the foot pump and tried to figure out a way of attaching it to the inflatable boat. Suddenly the hairs on the back of her neck stood up. She sensed danger. Jumping back she cast her eyes towards Porthgwyns. A small boat in the distance was leaving the harbour and heading in her direction. It had to be the brothers. Florence dropped the foot pump and ran towards the stern of the yacht. There was only one way she could escape. With trembling hands she climbed the railings and then stopped; she was an excellent swimmer but common sense told her she would not survive in the icy water; her dressing gown would be a hindrance and the boots would pull her down. Furthermore, to reach the shore she would have to pass the approaching boat. Panic stricken she found a place to hide to give herself time to think; she shivered as the piercing sound of the motor on the brothers' boat drew closer and closer penetrating the stillness of the cold, dark, frosty night.

When Richard and Edward climbed back on board they were shocked to find Florence had escaped. Guessing she must have attempted to reach the shore they looked over the side of the yacht towards the harbour.

"She'd never survive if she attempted to swim," said Edward, "it's got to be nearly a mile so. I think it best if we let nature take care of her. I mean, we didn't pass her so she's probably already succumbed to the cold."

"But ought we not go back out and try and find her. I don't want her death on my conscience."

"Are you mad? We need to get out of here. The look on the face of Dan when Ciss tugged at your hair tells me they've put two and two together."

"What?"

Edward looked at his brother and yanked back his hair. "You've lost an earring, you fool. It must be at the Inn. They know it was us who broke in."

"I guessed they'd realised that I but didn't know I'd lost an earring."

As Richard spoke they heard a noise from the stern of the yacht. He lowered the arm he had raised to touch his earlobe, "What was that?"

"Shush, I don't know. Perhaps she's still on board."

The stillness of the night was suddenly broken by a roaring sound. The brothers ran to the stern of the yacht and watched in disbelief as the inflatable motor boat they had just arrived in pulled away from the ladder.

"After her," shouted Edward, "Looks like she's heading back along the coast to Quignog Cove."

Richard started the engine and turned the yacht eastwards while Edward went below deck for his rifle.

Inside the sitting room at Seven Pines, Charlie was on the phone talking to Daniel who had rung to tell him the latest news. "The police are everywhere," said Dan, "and the coastguard. They're all in pursuit of the yacht which seems to be heading your way."

"What about Flo?"

"We assume she's on the boat."

"Okay, we'll nip out there and see if we can see anything. Meanwhile keep us updated."

"Will do. Bye, Dad."

"Bye Dan."

As the call ended, Charlie and Laura heard a series of loud bangs.

"Is that fireworks or a car back firing?" Laura asked.

Charlie's face turned white. "Neither; I think it might be gunfire." He explained the call from Daniel as they ran outside and into the lane.

As Florence approached the beach of Quignog Cove she knocked out the engine and ran the small boat aground. Without looking back, she gathered up the hem of her dressing gown, jumped into the water and waded onto the beach hoping to find a way to climb up the side of the cliffs. It was too dark to see and she could hear the yacht getting closer. As she stumbled in the overlarge boots across loose shingle, the beach was suddenly flooded in light; shots rang out and ricocheted off the surrounding rocks. Realising the beam of light was from the yacht, she ran towards the cliff base and with the aid of the floodlights ran into the opening of a small cave and crouched behind the first rock she came across.

From the cliff top, Charlie and Laura saw the yacht floating off shore, its spotlight focused on the beach at Quignog Cove. As they strained their eyes trying to see what the brothers were searching for in the beam of light, they heard the sound of motors. Two boats with flashing lights approached the yacht at high speed commanding the vessel to stop and the brothers to surrender their weapon. The response was more gunfire this time aimed at the authorities. As the shots rang out a whirring sound could be heard in the distance. Charlie looked to the east and saw a helicopter approaching with searchlights sweeping across the waves below.

Inside the cave, Florence shivered, fearful of her next move. Water dripped through gaps in the granite above her head and she could hear the muffled rumble of engines. Unsure from which vessel the noises came, anxiety struck, until she realised the brothers had no time to inflate their other boat and so had no means of reaching dry land; reassured she felt herself relax. To get her breath back she sat down on the rough wet floor of the cave shivering: her teeth chattering. As her hand knocked against her dressing gown she remembered the phone in her pocket. She withdrew it quickly, desperate to ring her father but to her dismay saw she had no signal. The phone, however, did have the torch and so with the aid of its light she stood and walked deeper into the cave hoping with each step to reach an area large enough to seek refuge until she felt confident it would be safe to leave and attempt to climb the side of the cliffs. In less than three minutes she was faced with a dead, narrow end and no place to hide, she cried out with frustration. Knowing she could neither hide nor go any further, her only option was to retrace her steps but as she turned, the light of her torch reflected on a piece of glass. She knelt down: lying on the dry shingle was a pair of spectacles. She picked them up; they were broken and looked as though someone had stepped on them. She touched the earth beneath her feet; it was dry which told her that where the spectacles had fallen would be well beyond the high water mark, meaning they must have been dropped by someone in whose footsteps she was following. Feeling a sudden pang of excitement she studied the rocks where she thought the cave ended and to her delight saw a gap to the left in the shadows more than big enough for her to slip through. Hoping it would provide somewhere for her to hide, she dropped the broken glasses into the pocket of her dressing gown and stepped through the gap. To her surprise it was not a dead end but the entrance to a tunnel. She flashed her torch around; in front of her stretched a long narrow passage, less than three feet in width and roughly six feet in height. Excitedly she made her way along it hoping it would lead her to safety; her enthusiasm increased dramatically as she recalled Cissy's granny saying at one time the erstwhile Inn was known as the Smuggler's Inn. If that were the case and there had been smuggling in the area then the passage must lead to Seven Pines. However, after a few yards her euphoria faded along with the light from her phone. Florence cursed and wished she had had the time to fully charge it the night before.

With nothing to light her way, she returned the phone to her pocket and stumbled on touching the rough, uneven walls to aid her along. The angle of her feet told her that she was going up-hill and over sporadic steps. After a while the height of the tunnel rapidly decreased and when she was almost bent double, she came to a dead end and was forced to stop. Hopeful of a way out she felt around for evidence of an exit and to her delight found above her head a wooden panel. She ran both hands across it looking for a bolt or a catch. She found neither and so gently pushed against it. It moved and was hinged on one side. When fully opened she was able to stand up straight and look around. The area surrounding the trap door was in complete darkness and so she carefully heaved herself up through the gap and onto a cold surface. Assuming she was in the Seven Pines cellar she then made her way across the floor careful to avoid the clutter she knew was stored there. When her foot crushed a small object she stooped and picked it up. After shaking it and brushing her fingers over its smooth surface she concluded it was a box of matches. Hoping they might work and light her way, she pulled one from the crushed box, struck it, and to her surprise found she was in a small square room. The room was windowless and empty but marks on the dusty floor indicated things had once stood there. As she looked around wondering where she was she heard muffled but familiar voices.

Having watched with excitement whilst the police and coastguard boarded the *Golden Sunset* helped by the searchlights from the hovering helicopter, and seeing two figures wearing diving equipment board the yacht and surprise the brothers while they were distracted, Charlie and Laura, shivering with cold, plodded their way through the snow and returned indoors to await a call from Daniel with the latest news. Inside the sitting room, Charlie put a match to the fire while Laura poured them each a glass of wine to steady their nerves. As they sat impatiently biting their nails waiting for Charlie's phone on the arm of his chair to light up, they heard banging on the back of the shelving in the alcove beside the fireplace. Both jumped in surprise.

"Dad, Auntie Laura," they heard a muffled voice call.

Charlie sprang to his feet. "Flo, Flo, where are you?"

"I don't know. Where are you?"

"We're in the sitting room. Your voice is coming from behind the bookcase."

Charlie felt around the shelves. "There must be a catch here somewhere, Laura."

As Charlie felt around the upper shelves, Laura got down on her hands and knees and felt around the lower area where the shelves were two feet deep. She squealed with delight when in the top right hand corner beneath the bottom shelf she located a small lever tucked between the granite stones on the outer wall of the fireplace. She pulled it and to the surprise of all, the whole unit moved to one side behind the adjoining wall. When Charlie saw his daughter in her dirty, damp dressing gown, with hair tangled and wearing a pair of enormous Wellington boots he didn't know whether to laugh or cry.

181

Chapter Twenty Two

The next day, Tash and Jerry called bright and early to see how Florence was. They found her in the sitting room with the rest of the family, curled up in a chair writing in her diary having been checked over by a doctor and given the all clear. After Laura had made mugs of coffee for everyone, Florence told the visitors of her escape.

"Poor you, you must have been terrified." Tash sounded older; her voice changed from the giggly person they had got to know.

"So where is this secret hidey-hole?" Jerry asked.

Laura sprang to her feet and demonstrated how the catch worked. Jerry, followed by Tash eagerly went inside the empty room.

"Amazing isn't it but goodness only knows how this fits in with Richard and Edward," said Charlie, "I mean it looks as though they must have got in this way on Boxing night, but why?"

Florence stood in the doorway. "We've discussed it and can only assume they had something hidden in here. When I came downstairs that night the sitting room door was ajar and there were lights flashing in the kitchen. We assume they cleared out whatever from this room and took it out through the kitchen to a vehicle parked outside the back door. I didn't hear a vehicle arrive I must admit but Dad tells me the police found tyre marks beneath freshly fallen snow."

"And there was no sign of a break-in," said Daniel, as they all returned to their seats leaving the secret room entrance open, "that's why we're sure they must have got into the house by way of the tunnel. What's more, a few days ago in the early hours when I was in the bathroom upstairs I heard a thud down here. I was coming down for a glass of water anyway and expected to find one of the family still up but when I got down here it was in darkness and there was no-one around, not even Ben because he was in Auntie Laura's room. So I reckon they were in the secret room then making sure the stuff or whatever was still there. Something like that."

"Ben?" Jerry queried.

"My dog," Laura, pointed to her Golden Labrador stretched out on the hearth rug.

"I see," chuckled Jerry, "I thought for a minute we'd missed one of you."

"Anyway, we'll know more when we hear from the police," said Charlie, "they and forensics were all over the place last night but they didn't tell us much."

"At least we know the brothers have been arrested," said Laura, "Ruby rang this morning to say it's the talk of the village."

Jerry laughed. "I'll say it is. When we left the cottage this morning the tongues of a group of people down by the harbour were well and truly wagging. The weather for now has taken a back seat."

"We reckon they must have had smuggled or stolen goods stored there," said Daniel, "because I don't know whether you noticed but there are scrape marks on the dusty floor. We've no idea what it could have been though or how long the stuff had been there."

"We'll just have to wait and see," said Charlie, "because it's not right to speculate although it might even be that they had valuables hidden there taken illicitly from a wreck or something like that. Flo said they had wetsuits, air bottles and what have you so they might be divers of some sort."

Laura turned to Tash and Jerry. "You're interesting in diving, aren't you? If they were involved with artefacts

183

taken from shipwrecks do you know how things stand as regards the law?"

"It's actually quite straightforward," said Jerry, "Wreck material found in UK waters must be reported to the Maritime and Coastguard Agency's Receiver of Wrecks within twenty-eight days in order to give the rightful owners a chance to claim it. If no-one claims the goods within a year, they become the property of the Crown and the person who has found the goods receives a salvage award based on the value of the find."

"Wow! I'm impressed by your knowledge," admitted Charlie, "very impressed."

Jerry laughed. "Well, I have to confess that it's the sort of thing I should know. I work for the Maritime and Coastguard Agency, you see."

"Ah, so you know your stuff."

"Yes, and actually I can answer a lot of your questions but not until you've been brought up to date by the police."

As he spoke they heard a car pull up outside.

Charlie put down his empty mug and crossed to the window. "Talk of the devil," He left the room and went to the front door to let the officers in. To his surprise when the officers entered the sitting room, Jerry and Tash rose and they all shook hands. As an explanation unfolded the family learned that the couple were not married but were work colleagues and both were employed by the Maritime and Coastguard Agency. They were in Cornwall because someone reported seeing the *Golden Sunset* anchored off Porthgwyns which had triggered a memory of the same yacht being further along the coast the previous September when illegal activity on wrecks was suspected and several burglaries had taken place in the area.

"So you were really here to keep an eye on Richard and Edward," Charlie was flabbergasted.

"Yes, the plan was to get friendly with them and glean as much about them as possible. It worked really well and we were delighted when they invited us to have Christmas dinner with them on their yacht," said Tash, "They even took us on a tour of the boat after which we agreed that we thought it unlikely any illegal stuff was stashed on-board. We still needed to watch them though because we were convinced they were up to no good. For instance we asked about their occupations and they skillfully changed the subject without making it look as though they had."

Daniel frowned. "So how did they manage to give you the slip on Boxing night then and come out here?"

"Ah, well that's a bit embarrassing," admitted Jerry, "You see, as we left their yacht on Christmas night, they said they'd most likely not go to the pub the next day as they thought they'd lay off the alcohol for forty-eight hours. We could see their yacht from Fuchsia Cottage and alongside its steps the inflatable boat with an outboard motor which they used to get ashore. On Boxing night both yacht and inflatable were there together so at nine we went to the Harbour Lights for a drink but at the same time kept popping outside to make sure the inflatable was still there meaning of course that the brothers were still on-board. What we didn't know was that under the awning they had another inflatable which must have been hidden beneath the tarpaulin we saw on the deck during our tour of the vessel. We assume they used that to get to Quignog Cove, nip up the tunnel and let their mates in."

"And they'd have used the rope ladder I saw to get down to it," said Florence.

"And who are their mates?" Daniel asked.

Detective Inspector Reynolds shook his head. "Sadly we don't know yet and so can only speculate. The brothers refuse to say anything at all but we're hoping we'll be able to prove they were here on Boxing night when we get back the DNA results on the earring found in your kitchen. We know it's identical to the one Richard Rudd wore but that doesn't prove it was his and sadly it wasn't possible to get

185

fingerprints from it. On the other hand the spectacles found in the tunnel did have Edward's prints on them but then again that doesn't prove he was in your house."

"Might it have just been the two of them?" asked Charlie.

"We very much doubt it. The tyre tracks found under the snow don't match up with the vehicle the brothers have hired down here so we're pretty sure they have accomplices."

"I wonder how they knew we'd gone to Truro," said Daniel, "I know we mentioned it in the pub on Christmas Eve, I even said I'd drive as my car is pretty durable when it comes to hazardous driving conditions but we only said we might go because we couldn't be too sure how bad the weather might get."

"Drones," said the DI, "We found a couple of drones on the yacht and so assume they used them to see if any of your vehicles were missing. In fact we're pretty sure they've used them on other occasions too to check whether or not people were at home. Less suspicious than driving by, especially in isolated spots where CCTV is installed."

"I can't keep up with all these new-fangled gadgets," said Laura, "Give me a dose of history any day."

Florence looked towards the open door of the secret room. "It's just a thought, but if Richard and Edward got into the house through the tunnel then there must be a catch, lever or something on the other side of the bookcase as well as this side."

Police Sergeant Sally Truman stood up. "There is, come and see."

All eagerly followed the officer into the secret room where she lifted a cracked floor tile in the corner. Beneath was a small lever. She pulled it and the bookcase slid back into place.

Chapter Twenty Three

The following day, as things slowly returned to normal, Laura entered the sitting room where the family along with Cissy and Ruby eagerly awaited her appraisal of the Bible. For earlier in the day Laura had telephoned Ruby to tell her she had found something of great interest tucked inside the back pages. Eager to hear what that something was, Ruby said she would be round in the afternoon sometime after she finished work at three and she would bring Cissy with her.

After entering the sitting room, Laura placed the Bible on the sideboard. "Sorry to have kept you all waiting but the reason I rang you this morning, Ruby was because of papers I'd found which I must say make very interesting reading."

"Papers. So were they inside the Bible?" Ruby asked.

"Yes. There are three sheets and they were carefully placed on different pages towards the back. To make it easier to read I've copied out the text and printed it," She pulled two folded sheets of paper from her pocket, "The originals are back in the Bible. I'll show them to you later."

"So who wrote the papers?" Charlie asked, "Was it Catherine whatever she was called?"

"Catherine Freathy, yes. Now shall I read it to you or would one of you like to do it?" Laura sat down on the hearth rug and crossed her legs.

"You read it, please," said Ruby, "I think my hands would be shaking too much."

"Okay. Well, as I've just said it was written by Catherine Freathy and would you believe it is dated 1827?"

"But that's nearly two hundred years ago," gasped Charlie.

Laura smiled. "Yes, and that's why I've made a copy. The original was difficult to read in parts as some words have faded but with a lot of concentration and the use of a good magnifying glass I've managed to do it."

"Okay, so what does Catherine have to say?" Ruby was on the edge of her chair.

"It's a sort of diary," said Laura, "but it's all written on the same day."

"We're all ears," Charlie folded his arms and leaned back in his favourite chair.

Laura cleared her throat and then read from the first sheet of paper in her hand.

Tomorrow, June 18th 1827 I am to be wed but before I leave my home here at the Vicarage in Porthgwyns I shall for my own gratification write down events that have thus far shaped my life. Events that I can share with no-one especially my parents and my husband to be.

I was born in the year of our Lord eighteen hundred and one, ten minutes after my dear brother, William, to our father the Reverend George Freathy and our mother Isabella. We were brought up here at the Vicarage and educated by a private tutor, hence we did not mix with children of our age other than when we attended church, but I did not mind for the birds and all God's creatures were my friends and my passion, my hobby, was pressing the wild flowers that bloomed in the meadows and hedgerows. Each day after our tuition I would walk and drink in the beauty of nature, while my brother studied hard so that he might enter the church and follow in the footsteps of our father.

When I was nineteen and out walking one day a sudden storm arose from nowhere. A passing coach containing an elderly gentleman and his wife, picked me up to save me from the rain and we took shelter inside the Coaching Inn that overlooked Quignog Cove.

When the rain cleared I thanked the couple for their hospitality and then made my way back to the Vicarage but not before I had been introduced to the landlord of the inn, Septimus Villiers who said that I would be most welcome to call again should I ever need to seek refuge from the rain. After our meeting I could not get Septimus out of my mind and so I went to the inn on pretence of needing to rest purely so that I might see him again. From that day on we became friends and eventually lovers. But of course no-one knew save a few of his closest friends and I did not dare tell my brother.

Those days were some of the happiest of my life. Septimus and I would meet in secret and slip to the beach at Quignog Cove. We were never seen because we had access by means of a tunnel which Septimus told me had been used by smugglers back when the inn was first built. Quignog Cove is picturesque, beautiful and serene and because it is tucked beneath the cliffs much of the beach cannot be seen from the road above and the watchful prying eyes of passers-by.

Sadly, as Chaucer wrote: all good things must come to an end. For one day I learned that many inhabitants of Porthgwyns were still in this modern day involved with the illicit act of smuggling along the Cornish coast. I disapproved strongly of the sin but kept my council until on one occasion when a ship was wrecked off Quignog Cove in a storm. Porthgwynians eager to salvage what they could begged Septimus for access to the beach through the tunnel and he agreed. Sadly none of the crew survived the tempest for conditions were horrendous but much of the cargo was saved and dragged into the caves away from the tumultuous waves.

Septimus was not involved with the looting but to save the necks of people he knew and loved he let them store their takings in his secret hiding place – a hidden room with access from a sliding panel in the alcove by the main fireplace. Opened by a lever beneath the bottom shelf, the secret room was the means of accessing the tunnel.

Septimus, my Septimus was a good man at heart and I persuaded him to ask his friends to not keep all for themselves but to put some of the takings to good use and to help those less fortunate than ourselves. And Septimus being Septimus agreed.

A few days later, the authorities cognizant of the situation raided the inn and fearing for his life and the lives of his friends, Septimus attempted to flee on his beloved horse. But no sooner had he reached the lane than a shot was fired. He fell from his horse and while wounded attempted to climb down the side of the cliff and onto the beach so that he might hide in the caves. In his haste he slipped and fell to his death.

Afterwards the place was searched but no contraband was found. For to save their necks and the reputation of their landlord, those who knew where the entrance to the secret room lay, chose not to speak. Another who knew, was me, and likewise I would never tell.

Following his demise, the contraband was taken away in small quantities until none was left. The inn was then sold by Septimus's sister to Henry James Pengelly. Henry and I were acquainted through the church but he knew nothing of the inn's involvement with smuggling.

It is to Henry that I am to be wed tomorrow. To him I shall be a good and dutiful wife but my heart forever shall be with Septimus Villiers. A man who history may judge harshly, a villain, even though the authorities found no evidence to label him thus. He was a good man who to my dying day I shall remember as a tender soul with a heart of gold.

"Villiers," whispered Ruby, "Catherine Freathy was crazy about a chap called Septimus Villiers. What a delicious name. I can almost imagine him here at the Inn pouring pints of ale."

Laura smiled. "I think I can go along with that, Ruby. I should imagine he was dashingly handsome too."

"Freathy," muttered Florence, "How weird."

"Why weird?" Cissy asked.

"Well, it's just that I wonder if Catherine is any relation to us. What do you think, Dad?"

Charlie frowned. "Why on earth would she be a relation to us, Flo? Dad was obviously an Everton and Mum was a Nicholls."

"Yes, but your mother's mother was a Freathy."

Charlie gasped. "Was she? I never knew Mum's parents because they both died years before Laura and I were born. I just know that Mum's maiden name was Nicholls."

"So what makes you think Mum's mum was a Freathy, Flo?" Laura asked.

"One of the girls at university is doing her family history and she offered to look into ours. I've not mentioned it before because I wanted to find out more before I did and then surprise you. Anyway, I gave her your full names and dates of birth and she took it from there."

"And she found out Mum's mum, our grandmother, was a Freathy. That's interesting. I mean, it's hardly a common name."

"Exactly. Anyway, your grandmother, my great grandmother's name was Nancy Freathy. She was in born in 1907 and married George Nicholls in 1932."

"Any idea who her parents were or what they did?" Charlie was intrigued.

"I can't remember their names but her father was a Looe fisherman. I left it with my friend to find out more so I'm afraid that's all I know 'til we go back to university in January."

"Well, that's more than we ever knew," laughed Charlie, "so well done, Flo."

"We knew Grandma was Cornish though, didn't we, Charlie? But just not who she was or whereabouts she lived."

"Yes, and that's one of the reasons I chose to live down here. It was my intention to one day find out more about her but it looks like our Flo is beating me to it."

Florence beamed with pride.

"So do you know anything about our father's parents?" Laura asked.

"Not yet. I'm doing your mum's side first. All the names and dates take a lot of remembering."

"So where did you say you thought Tracey got the Bible from, Ruby?" Charlie was intrigued.

"We can only assume an auction or something like that. And now Laura has found papers saying Catherine was the vicar's daughter and lived at the vicarage in Porthgwyns, it's quite likely that it came from the auction held there a year or so back because Tracey definitely went to it."

"But why was it still at the vicarage after all these years?" Florence asked, "I mean surely she would have taken it with her when she married Henry Pengelly."

"Not if she didn't want her new husband to see what was in it," reasoned Ruby.

"It's a good point though," said Laura, "I wonder if the auctioneers know anything about it."

"Well I know the person to ask," Ruby lifted her handbag from the floor and pulled out her phone, "my mother."

Everyone sat quietly while Ruby spoke to Joan. After five minutes she hung up.

"We're in luck and Mum's going to ring me back. She said the auction was carried out by Gerald Jackson & Son which is ideal because Mum's known Gerald all her life. They were at school together. He's coming up for

192

retirement now but she said he was definitely at the auction because he gave her a lift home in his van with the bike she bought. Both tyres were punctured, you see so she couldn't ride it."

Florence made tea for everyone while they waited for Joan to ring back.

"I wonder where Catherine, Henry Pengelly and Septimus Villiers are buried," mused Charlie, as his daughter handed him a mug of tea, "it can't be far away if they all lived locally."

"Porthgwyns I suppose," reasoned Daniel, "I've not seen any other churches around here and Catherine's dad was the vicar there so it stands to reason she at least would be there."

"Can we drive over there and see if we can find them?" Florence sat down by the fire with her mug of tea.

"I suppose so, but why?" Daniel asked, "I mean it's freezing out there and the graves will be covered with snow."

Florence smiled. "Because I want to see their graves. I don't expect for one minute we are related to Catherine but it'll still be nice to have a look and as for the snow it might not completely obliterate the inscriptions but if it does we'll just have to brush it off."

"Good idea," Laura agreed. "We'll do that when we've heard from Ruby's mum."

As Laura cleared away the empty mugs, Ruby's phone rang. Laura not wanting to make a noise, sat back down.

"Well, well," Ruby dropped her phone back inside her bag, "The Bible was sold at the auction and Gerald remembers it was Tracey who bought it. It wasn't sold on its own though: it was in a job lot along with books of pressed flowers and a few old pictures. They were all sold along with the trunk they were found in. The trunk was in the vicarage loft along with all sorts of stuff that looked like it'd been there forever. Which makes sense to me now because I know Tracey got a trunk at the auction but she told me there was nothing in it but tat. She bought it because she liked the look of it and wanted it to keep some shoes in because they wouldn't all fit in her wardrobe."

"Philistine," muttered Laura, "I bet she destroyed the pressed flower books."

"Maybe," agreed Charlie, "but at least she kept the Bible."

Ruby and Cissy who had to work that evening left soon after. The family then donned boots, coats, scarfs and gloves in order to visit the churchyard. Having twice before been to the church for the midnight service and Mickey's funeral they were familiar with its location. Laura drove and after parking in a layby opposite, the family walked beneath a lichgate and followed footprints in the snow to the back of the church, beneath which they assumed was a path. Behind the building were row upon row of gravestones.

"Can anyone remember when Catherine Freathy was born?" Charlie asked.

"Eighteen hundred and one," said Laura, "That sticks in my mind because it was one hundred years before Queen Victoria died."

"Right, so we'll assume Septimus Villiers was older than her and was born in the late seventeen hundreds." Charlie cast his eyes over the graveyard.

"It shouldn't be too difficult to find him," said Laura, "After all we know he was killed before Catherine married Henry James Pengelly in 1827 and so all we need to do is look at graves in the eighteen twenties."

"Of course. Silly me."

"We also need to look out for Freathys," said Florence.

"Well that shouldn't be too difficult either," said Charlie, "If Catherine's father was the local vicar I should imagine his grave is quite elaborate."

They found the stone box grave of the Reverend Harvey George Freathy and his wife Isabella alongside the main entrance to the church. The inscription, however, did not help their search and so they made their way along the path towards more humble graves.

The churchyard seemed quite desolate. There were very few flowers but holly wreaths were just visible on some of the newer graves peeping through the snow. The most recent was the final resting place for Mickey Potts where a wreath of holly, conifer and ivy entwined with artificial red roses lay on top of the snow covering wreaths laid on the day of the funeral. Attached to it was a card which said, *Where there is love there is happiness...RIP, Dad, Love you always, Becky. xxxxxxx*

It was Daniel who found the grave of Septimus Villiers and although it was neglected, it gave the impression that he had been much loved by his family. It stood in the middle of a row; a perfect square filled with snow, encased with white granite. A matching urn lay on its side and looked as though it had seen no flowers for many years. The inscription on the tombstone indicated that Septimus Villiers who died in 1825 aged 29 lay alongside his wife, Beth who died in 1817 aged 23.

"Well, I never. Catherine made no mention of his wife, Beth," said Daniel.

"Well if she died in 1817 it's likely that she didn't know her," reasoned Florence, "She would only have been sixteen then and from what we've read it seems she led a sheltered life."

Charles chuckled. "Until she was nineteen and met Septimus. That must have been a bit of a culture shock."

"When we next see Vicar Joy we must ask her if the church has a record of past vicars. Because I'd like to see it if it does," said Laura, "and learn more about the Freathys."

Daniel pulled up the hood of his jacket. "It's really chilly here. We've found what we were looking for so can we go now?"

"No, no just a few minutes more, Dan because I want to find Catherine." Florence hurried along the row brushing snow from headstones. Eager to get back in the warm everyone joined the search.

It was Laura who found her. "Oh no, poor, Catherine."

The rest of the family gathered to read the inscription on Catherine's gravestone.

In everloving memory of Catherine Pengelly, beloved
wife of Henry James Pengelly.
Dearly loved daughter of Reverend Harvey George
Freathy and his wife Isabella
Taken from us on December 29th 1829 aged 28.
Also Isabella Rose Pengelly, daughter of Catherine and
Henry
who passed away on January 3rd aged five days.
Asleep with the angels
Rest in Peace.

"So Catherine must have died during childbirth and her poor daughter followed on five days later," whispered Laura, "Life was cruel back then."

"And it would also explain why her Bible was in the vicarage attic," said Charlie, "Her grieving parents must have put it up there for safe keeping following her death."

As they made their way back to the car in silence, Florence noticed that her brother was frowning. "You alright, Dan?"

"Yes, yes, I'm fine, Flo. It's just that…well, seeing all the graves, I wonder if there's any connection between all this. You know, the stuff allegedly stored at Dad's place, the Bible, Mickey's murder, the Rudd brothers and the fact

Tracey may well have read Catherine's papers and so have known about the secret passage."

Tracey Potts lay back on the bed in her cell and stared at the cracks in the ceiling lamenting the mess her life had become. "If only I could turn back the wretched clock," she said to Raymond, the old bear she had owned since childhood who was with her for company, "It was madness to have killed Mickey. Madness. And the worst thing is, I didn't mean to do it. I hit him on the head certainly and he toppled over but I didn't expect him to die on me. I assumed he'd get up, get in his car, come home and then we'd have a tiff in the morning. You must believe me, Ray because I know you liked him. And then the silly tree fell down on top of him. I mean, how cruel was that?" She sat up and put Raymond on her lap. "I promise you it really was an accident and it wouldn't have happened at all if he hadn't followed me that night and he wouldn't have known I'd gone out if I'd not tripped over the gormless cat in the kitchen and knocked into the saucepan rack. I mean, why did he have to follow me? I suppose he might have thought I'd slipped out in the middle of the night because I was having an affair. As if I would. There are no decent blokes in this neck of the woods. Perhaps he thought I was sleep walking and was concerned for my welfare...oh dear. Anyway, whatever, it doesn't matter now but I wish he'd have stayed in bed instead of creeping out and catching me trying to scare the living daylights out of that Charlie sodding Everton and his soppy sister.

It seemed a good idea at the time and Mickey played right into my court when he started going on about the Inn's ghost when we were in the pub, and when Charlie thingy said about poltergeists that really was the icing on the cake. I'd have had such fun with that and I know for sure that he'd agree to sell eventually. I mean, after I'd put *all* the plans I had up my sleeve into action he and his sister would have been quivering wrecks. Mind you it was a bit cold sitting there spying on the place waiting for all the lights to go out. And I had to wait 'til they were in bed because if I'd played the tapes before that they might have come out and caught me red-handed and I'd have looked a right ninny then, wouldn't I? Of course had stupid Mickey won the stupid auction in the first place then there wouldn't have been any need for me to do anything, would there?" Tracey growled, "And to think he lost simply because neither of us knew the ghastly man had won a packet of dosh in the Lottery and so had money to burn. Some people have all the luck." She chuckled, "Mind you, it was gratifying when the ghastly man's fingerprints were found on the owl and for a while I really thought they'd nick him. The scarf was a bit of luck too. It was still in my pocket from when I picked it up after whatever she's called left it in the café. You see, my intention was to give it back to her when I saw her. You know, I thought my kindness might make her feel guilty. As it is, it must have slipped from my pocket when I left Mickey lying amongst the conifer needles and went back to my car in a huff. Not that it being there did me any good, the jacket saw to that. When I heard Mickey was dead my first thoughts were I must burn it in the garden and then bury the ashes but after the police had gone I realised I couldn't risk smoke being seen and there was a chance the coppers might come back anyway. Then the next thing I knew Becky had arrived because she left Plymouth as soon as she was told of Mickey's death. There's no justice in this life, Raymond." She waved her fingers angrily and accidently knocked the bear onto the floor.

"I'm sorry, sweetheart," She picked him up and sat him on her pillow. "Of course, had I not met sodding Richard and his sodding brother in the sodding supermarket last September then none of this would have happened, but after so many years I really was pleased to see them both and it seemed a good idea to go for a coffee." She turned to look at the bear. "You remember Richard, don't you, Ray? My boyfriend from many moons ago. You know, the one with the dreamy eyes and the gorgeous brown curls. He liked you and I'm sure you liked him. I must admit I was a bit shocked when he told me how they made a living but then they always did sail close to the wind when it came to the law." She tutted, "But fancy them raiding ship wrecks and not declaring it as well as doing a bit of burglary. I mean, what naughty boys. No wonder the pair of them own a sodding great yacht." She stroked Raymond's head affectionately. "I shouldn't have got involved though, should I? It was a silly thing to have done but I've always liked a bit of an adventure and when I told them I knew the perfect place to hide the stuff they'd nicked they were dead impressed. You see, I'd read what Catherine thingy wrote about a secret hidey hole at the Old Inn. I knew where it was and how to get to it. What's more, I knew it still worked because I'd had a poke round. Rich and Ed were really grateful because some busybody had told the police, coastguard or whatever that he suspected divers were looting one of the shipwrecks further down the coast. That made the authorities keep a lookout so we agreed the stuff had to be stashed away and pretty quick. It all went really well and when I messaged them a few months later to say the old boy who owned the Inn, Jacob, Josiah, Joseph or whatever he was called had popped his clogs and that Mickey and me were going to buy it when it came up for sale, they said I was a star."

She sat up straight on the bed. "If only I'd not lost my phone with their contact numbers stored on it. They knew I lived at Bracken Farm because I told them but I had no idea where they lived, you see, and needed to let them know we'd lost the auction and the stuff must be removed before that damn Everton man took possession of the place." She suddenly threw back her head and laughed hysterically. "What am I going on about, Ray? I'm starting to believe my own lies. I didn't lose my phone at all, did I? I had it in my hands during the auction ready to message my pal at the hairdressers because she said to let her know how it went. And then when I realised Mickey had lost it, I was so mad I stormed out of the hotel, chucked the phone against a wall and when it fell to the ground, I jumped on it several times and then dropped it down a drain. What an Idiot! I couldn't tell Mickey though, could I? So I was doubly mad. Mad because we couldn't have the Inn and mad because I no longer had my phone. And what did Mickey do when I pretended I'd lost it? He bought me another, even better, but was I grateful? No. Poor Mickey."

Tracey rose from the bed and paced the small room. "God, I feel old. Hardly surprising though, is it? What a nightmare. What would you have done, Raymond? I mean, I couldn't remove the stuff myself, could I? There was loads of it. I had nowhere to hide it and could hardly have stored it under my bed. It wouldn't have fitted anyway and if it had Ruby would have found it. Bah, Ruby! Best not let me express my opinion of her. It was a nightmare, Ray, because no-one knew about it apart from me and the brothers. I have to confess I did at one point think of telling Mickey, but I knew it wouldn't go down very well. Silly sod was too law abiding and would no doubt have turned the three of us in. And I was right, because when I told him in a rage after he'd caught me outside the Inn that's exactly what he said he'd do. Turn us in. That's why I grabbed the owl and hit him. What a fool. What a pair of fools. Me and Mickey." She sat down on the bed. "And now they're both here in Cornwall. The brothers, that is. Remember, they came here to see me the other day. How embarrassing was that! They were clearly disgusted to learn from the folks in the pub that I was a murderer. Would you believe they went in there pretending to be the neighbours of old friends of ours? Daft really because they don't even live together. I don't know where they do live but I know it's not in the same house so they couldn't have the same neighbours, could they? Oh dear, Richard seemed so disappointed with me. I mean, I know they're dishonest but they'd never stoop to murder."

She stood and looked up to the tiny high window where snowflakes brushed against the glass. "It's snowing again. I love the snow, it's so pretty and the trees near the farm must look gorgeous now." She picked up the bear and raised him above her head so that he might see out of the window. "I wonder how they got on. Rich and Ed, that is. Did they manage to get the stuff out? I know they had a couple of friends with a Land Rover coming down to take it away by road because they thought it might be unsafe by sea. Did they manage it? I expect we'll hear one day. But looking back on it, I wish I'd never gone to the vicarage auction and found the wretched Bible in the chest with old flower books. Had I not, I'd still be living at Bracken Farm, Mickey would still be alive and well and everything would be tickety-boo."

Chapter Twenty Four

In the evening the Everton family went to the Harbour Lights where the main topic of conversation was still the arrest of the brothers; Florence having recovered from her ordeal was treated like a celebrity. Everyone wanted to shake her hand and wish her well. She was also bought far more pints of lager than she would even consider drinking on a crazy night out with her university friends. However, the drinks did not go to waste for Daniel was more than happy to help his sister out.

While Daniel and Florence chatted to Tash and Jerry, Jiffy and Elderflower arrived and after buying drinks joined Charlie and Laura at their table by the fire.

"How is everything?" Jiffy unwound a very long scarf from around his neck and draped it over the back of his chair.

Charlie smiled. "We're sort of getting our heads round it all now. There are still lots of unanswered questions of course but hopefully over time we'll get some answers."

"That's good to hear and I have a confession to make," said Elderflower.

"*We* have a confession to make," corrected her father.

"Alright then, we."

"Oh no. Don't tell us you both work for the Maritime and Coastguard Agency as well."

Elderflower laughed. "Well actually it is something along those lines. You see my stay here wasn't so much because I needed to get away following the breakup with my partner. That happened months ago anyway and if the truth be known I'm happier without him. No, the reason was Dad asked me to come down. You see, years before I made a career change. I was a police officer."

"Never," gasped Charlie, "you don't look a bit like a copper."

"I never really felt like one either and career wise I'd never have gone far. In fact I was pretty hopeless despite my initial enthusiasm."

"Was it hard work?"

"Gosh, yes and that was the problem. Like many I watched a lot of television and thought it looked glamorous but I can assure you it's not."

Laura nodded. "It's not something I could ever have done especially in this day and age with terror threats and so forth."

"So why did you want Elderflower to come to Cornwall, Jif?" Charlie asked.

"Well I suppose you've heard most of it by now anyway. The thing is though, last September I had some paintings and other valuables stolen while I was out. I called the police and they did a thorough search of my place but were unable to find any useful clues. Now my house is further along the coast in an isolated spot on top of the cliffs with far reaching views of the sea and when I came here the other night and saw the *Golden Sunset* moored off the village, it triggered a memory. You see, at the time my paintings were stolen I recall a yacht being anchored further along the coast and when either Richard or Edward said they had been this way last year I had a feeling they might have had something to do with the theft. And so on hearing they'd decided to stay around for Christmas, I asked Elderflower to come down to see what she thought and she's been keeping an eye on them."

"Ah," said Charlie, "so it was you Jiffy who notified the police and coastguard of your suspicions. The police told us someone had but didn't say who."

Elderflower nodded. "Yes, Dad got the ball rolling and I tried to keep an eye on the brothers. Of course I didn't realise at the time that Jerry and Tash were doing the same and when I heard they were meeting on Christmas Day I even thought they were all in it together. It wasn't until I saw how quickly Jerry reacted to the earring incident that the penny dropped."

Jiffy chuckled. "Believe it or not we even thought you might be involved, Charlie, because we were pretty certain the Old Inn played a part somehow. We'd heard tales of the Inn being involved in smuggling way back and reckoned if that were the case then there must be a hidey-hole somewhere within the building."

Charlie chuckled. "Well you were right to a point because we were involved but not in the way you suspected."

"So have you got the paintings and stuff back?" Laura asked.

Jiffy shook his head. "Not yet but if the brothers were behind the theft then I suppose as long as there's life there's hope."

"We have every reason to believe they were involved though," Elderflower added, "so we have our fingers crossed for their safe return."

"But only if the brothers come clean, tell the police who their accomplices are and where they've hidden the stuff now."

Charlie looked over to his daughter who was laughing with Tash, Jerry and her brother. "Poor Flo, she's really annoyed with herself for not being able to describe any of them. She heard muffled voices but didn't see anybody. The last thing she remembers before blacking out is sensing someone standing behind her."

"The brothers were definitely involved though," said Laura, "despite denying it and refusing to answer questions. Daft really when she woke up on their boat."

"We did have some good news this morning though," said Charlie, "Detective Inspector Reynolds rang to say that the earring found in our kitchen has Richard's DNA on it."

"Good, so hopefully they'll be able to charge them now," Jiffy was clearly delighted.

"They have been charged," acknowledged Charlie, "so I suppose it's just a case of building up a case against them now."

"I wonder how they got Flo from your place to the yacht without being seen," mused Elderflower.

"The police assume she was carried through the tunnel," said Charlie, "and then taken by sea in the inflatable boat the brothers must have used to get to Quignog Cove."

"So let's see if I've got this right. The police think the brothers accessed your house, Charlie, through the tunnel and then let their mates with the Land Rover in through the kitchen door. Then when their mates had driven off with whatever was at your place, the brothers with Flo went back the same way they had arrived to their yacht."

"Spot on," said Laura.

"Just as well Flo's petite then," giggled Elderflower, "they'd have struggled had she been a big lump like me and could well have suffered serious injury had they needed to drag her."

"You're not a big lump," said Charlie, "Your size is perfect to me."

"Oh, thank you. That's made my day."

Laura thrilled by her brother's response turned to Elderflower. "So what made you leave the police force?"

"I was useless. I mean I liked the people I worked with but it was so stressful and I felt they'd be better off without me. That's when I started eating too much chocolate."

Jiffy, who was as slim as a reed, tutted.

"So what are you doing now?" Charlie asked, "Following in your dad's footsteps in a band?"

"What! No way. I like a quiet life. I'm into genealogy now and have been for the last seven years. I love delving into people's past. Lots of families have skeletons in their closets and so all sorts of unexpected things crop up. I've also discovered we have roots down here."

"Really, do tell," Laura was fascinated.

"Well, our ancestors at one time owned an old coaching inn but not your one on Wreckers Hill, Charlie. Our one was over on the north coast somewhere but sadly it no longer exists as it was demolished fifty years ago."

"No way. Is that why you wanted to buy mine, Jiffy? So you could sense how your ancestors might have lived."

"Sort of, but you beat me to it, Charlie and I'm glad you did. You see, I just wanted to turn your place back into how it would have been. A sort of museum piece which would have been a dreadful waste. When I saw how keen you were I pulled out and I know it was the right thing to have done. The place deserves to be lived in. Deserves to hear the sound of laughter. It'd be nice if you had a horse though so the sound of hooves on the cobbles could ring out again."

"Well, I have thought about it but sadly I know nothing about them so it'd be daft."

"We found out something about Charlie's erstwhile Inn today," said Laura, "Apparently the other day Becky Potts, and Ruby who works here were going through Tracey's things at Bracken Farm and they found an old Bible in the bottom of a wardrobe which had originally belonged to a Catherine Freathy. Inside were a few sheets of paper dated 1827 saying how she was going to marry a Henry James Pengelly, landlord of the Old Coaching Inn on Wreckers Hill. We wonder if by any chance we're descendants of Catherine's family. Not Catherine herself of course because she died two years after her marriage and we have reason to believe in childbirth, hence she had no children and if she had they would have been Pengellys anyway."

"But that's amazing," laughed Elderflower, "It'd be uncanny if you were related though."

"But that's not all," said Charlie, "It appears the landlord before the Pengellys was a bit of a rogue and so what really intrigued us is that Catherine had a dalliance with him. Before she married Henry Pengelly of course."

"Really," chuckled Elderflower, "So who was this rogue?"

"Septimus Villiers," said Charlie, "He was killed in 1825 and apparently he was into smuggling and what not."

"No he wasn't," hissed Laura, "according to Catherine he let the Inn's tunnel be used to access and hide the stuff when a ship was wrecked off Quignog Cove. It was a one-off occurrence and he wasn't involved with the plundering and looting."

"You're quite right. I stand corrected."

Elderflower frowned. "Villiers...no way. Now that is weird."

"Why?" Laura was puzzled.

"Because earlier this year Tracey Potts asked me to do family trees for her and Mickey. I've nearly finished Tracey's but have yet to start Mickey's. One thing that stands out though is that Tracey told me that Mickey's mother was a Villiers. I must check this Septimus chappie out when I get home."

"If you let me have your email address I'll send you a copy of what Catherine had written," Laura said, "because it's fascinating and will help with dates and so forth."

"Wonderful, yes please do." Elderflower wrote down her email address on the back of a beer mat.

At the far end of the bar, Florence and Daniel were still chatting with Tash and Jerry; the main topic of conversation as elsewhere in the pub was the yacht and the Rudd brothers.

"So what'll happen if they both continue to protest their innocence?" Daniel asked, "I mean is there enough evidence for them to be charged and it go to trial?"

"Yes and they have been charged," Jerry said, "and there's no question as to whether or not they'll be convicted. I mean, shooting at the authorities is a heinous crime in itself without even taking everything else into consideration."

Tash nodded her agreement. "Absolutely, Jerry, but as regards the thefts, the earring and spectacles are pretty damming evidence so they should be able to nail them for that too."

Florence finished her drink and placed the empty glass on the end of the bar. "Not to mention they shot at me as I escaped. I mean, if they hadn't known I was on their boat in the first place they'd have had no reason to have done that, would they?"

"Pity the stuff they nicked wasn't on the boat though, Flo," said Daniel, "Because had it been there would be no question about their guilt."

Florence glanced out of the window towards the harbour wall and the spot beyond where the brothers' yacht had been moored. "I don't think there's any question, Dan, but I just wish they'd confess or at least come up with a reasonable explanation.

Chapter Twenty Five

Richard Rudd sat in the interview room waiting to be questioned once again by DI Ian Reynolds and Police Sergeant Sally Truman. He was not alone; by the door stood a police constable who was keeping watch until the officers arrived.

Richard was tired. He was sleeping badly; his head ached and he was undecided how to respond to the forthcoming interrogation. In previous meetings he'd answered some of the questions but denied all knowledge of breaking into the Inn, pillaging ancient shipwrecks, burglary and kidnapping. He knew though that he was skating on thin ice. Florence Everton was free. The fact she had been on their yacht was irrefutable and to make matters worse they had not only fired at her as she made her escape but they had fired at the authorities too. The only thing he felt confident about was that they had no reason to associate Edward and himself with Tracey Potts and he hoped to keep it that way. For as disgusted as he was with her for taking the life of her husband, she had done it for them and for that he felt extremely guilty.

He quietly cursed. If only he could meet up with his brother to ask what he intended to say or indeed what he had already said. He knew that was not possible though. He also knew his brother was a survivor and would not go down without a fight.

Edward Rudd sat inside his cell drumming his nail-bitten fingers on the side of his firm thigh cursing his younger brother, for had they done as he had wanted after they had sedated Florence Everton the police would have had no reason to suspect they were in any way involved with her disappearance. Admittedly Richard's earring had been found inside the Inn's kitchen but they could have fobbed that off. They could have claimed he had lost it, that it must have become attached to an item of clothing belonging to a member of the Everton family when they had mixed as a group inside the Harbour Lights and no-one could have proved otherwise. As things stood they were in a mess. The fact that Florence had woken on their boat trussed like a chicken was impossible for them to explain away, hence Edward had refused to comment on that fact and he hoped Richard had had the sense to do likewise. Somehow he doubted it though. Richard was weak and would probably crack if the going got tough. On the other hand, Edward knew that his brother still had a soft spot for Tracey Potts and so it was likely Richard would be very reluctant to make her situation any worse than it already was.

One thing of which Edward was confident was that their accomplices, Buzz and Jacko had made it back to Plymouth on Boxing night, for Buzz had messaged him from his burner phone with belated Christmas greetings, a coded way of saying all is well and we're back safe and sound. The Land Rover being sought by the police would no doubt be securely locked away in one of the barns belonging to the farmhouse the pair had rented for the festive season where they would lay low until they believed the coast to be clear. Of course, had Edward had his way, with them Buzz and Jacko would have taken the sedated body of Florence and dumped her somewhere on Bodmin Moor where she would have succumbed to the freezing conditions long before she had the chance to wake up and seek help. But no, Richard would not have it. He insisted they take her back to the boat while they considered what to do with her. A silly move that had most likely cost them their freedom.

Edward thought back to his childhood. Richard had always been his mother's favourite. "Look after your little brother. Don't bully him." Bah! And all because of his angelic face, his dreamy eyes and curly brown hair. Life was so unfair because he, Edward, had straight mousy brown hair, weak eyes and the need to wear spectacles from the age of eleven. In later years though they had become good friends, partners in crime and with Mother gone, there was no-one around to judge him. But sometimes he heard her voice and last night he had dreamed of her. She had called him an 'unprincipled contemptible person' and begged him to do the right thing. Right thing! What, confess? Not bloody likely. But then a memory came back. A distant memory. A memory long forgotten. It was shortly after Richard and Tracey started dating and they were in a pub with numerous friends celebrating Tracey's birthday. Towards the end of the evening he overheard one of the girls say to Tracey that she had the better looking of the two brothers. But Tracey had disagreed. Said she didn't think there was anything to choose between them when it came to looks and that Edward had a lovely smile, perfect posture and beautiful hands.

"Beautiful hands." As her words came back Edward looked down at his bitten nails and felt a massive pang of guilt. He had been prepared to do anything to get himself out of the mess he was in. Lie, cheat, blame everyone else. Everyone but himself. Anything but take responsibility for his own actions. His own devious, corrupt actions. He thought of Tracey charged with the murder of her husband, Mickey. Tracey who had helped them hide their stolen goods and who refused to talk no doubt to protect Richard and himself. His mother's words came back to him loud and clear. He stood up. "You're right, Mum," he shouted, "I am an unprincipled contemptible person and I'll confess. I will, I promise. I'll tell them the truth. That it was me, Edward Rudd, who murdered Mickey Potts."

211

Chapter Twenty Six

Inside the sitting room at Seven Pines, the family were gathered around the fire debating whether or not to wear fancy dress for New Year's Eve at the Harbour Lights. The theme was twentieth century film characters. Laura and Florence were in favour; Charlie thought he might be persuaded but Daniel said definitely not. As Florence teased Dan and said that he had the perfect physique for the Terminator they heard a car pull up outside the kitchen. Laura went to see who it was and to her surprise found Ruby closing the door of her Micra.

"I've just had the most extraordinary phone call," said Ruby before Laura had a chance to greet her, "And just had to come and tell you."

"I'm fascinated. Come in."

Laura led Ruby into the sitting room and took her coat.

"Ruby, this is a surprise," Charlie stood and pecked their visitor on the cheek.

"Ruby has something exciting to tell us," said Laura, "at least I get the impression it's exciting."

"More like earth shattering," Ruby sat down on the sofa beside Florence. All eyes were on her.

"So who rang you?" asked Laura.

"Becky Potts. You know Tracey and Mickey's daughter."

They all nodded.

"And...?" Laura was feeling impatient.

"The charge against Tracey has been downgraded from murder to assault, a charge to which she has confessed. She didn't do it, you see. Certainly she hit him with the owl and knocked him over but that wasn't the blow that killed him." Ruby paused to get her breath back.

"I knew it," said Laura, "I always thought her innocent."

"So was the tree the cause of death after all then?" Charlie asked.

"Oh no, he was murdered, not by Tracey, but by Edward Rudd."

"But Edward and Richard didn't get here 'til after Mickey was killed," Charlie shook his head. "I'm confused."

"Okay, I'll try and explain but you must understand that my account will be part what Tracey has told Becky - Becky went to visit her today - and part what Tracey has been told by the police. Tracey of course being the widow of the victim is entitled to updates in the investigation. The police also wanted her to verify declarations made by Edward in his written confession."

"Meaning we must allow you a little poetic licence," laughed Laura.

"Probably a bit more than a little."

"Enhance the facts as much as you like, Ruby," Charlie, bright eyed and intrigued, sat up straight in his chair and crossed his legs.

"Right, well it all started in September last year when Tracey bumped, quite by chance, into the brothers while out shopping. They were all surprised to see each other because many years before Tracey and Richard had been an 'item'. But that was a long time ago and neither Richard nor Edward even knew that Tracey was living in Cornwall. They didn't even know she was married. Anyway, the three of them went for a coffee together and apparently the brothers told Tracey of their illicit style of life. She was fascinated and when they told her they thought the police might be onto them and they really needed somewhere to hide their stolen goods, she suggested they store it here in the secret room."

Laura gasped, "Which she knew about because of Catherine's Bible."

"Precisely. I mean, she knew no-one came up here much and because the place had been left to decay since 1977 it was likely to stay that way until Jacob Smythe died. Tracey knew that because Mickey had made enquiries as to who owned it because he was interested in buying it for Tracey's health farm. Needless to say when word got out that he'd died Tracey was over the moon saying they'd be buying it when it came up for sale."

"And then I came along and put the cat amongst the pigeons," Charlie almost felt guilty.

"You did rather. No wonder Tracey was in a flap. She needed to let the brothers know the stuff had to be got out before the sale was completed but couldn't because she'd lost her phone with their contact numbers on. Actually, she hadn't lost it, she'd broken it, but that's another story. Anyway, as I've already said, she had no way of getting in touch with them and couldn't find out because she had no idea where they lived."

"Did neither do social media then?" Florence asked.

Ruby shook her head. "Apparently not."

"Okay, I'm with you so far," said Charlie, "but where does Edward killing Mickey fit into this?"

"Well according to Becky, Tracey reckons Edward was the brains behind the whole thing because he's money orientated and always has been, which means he's continually looking out for the means to make a few bob. Anyway, one day he was walking by a charity shop and he saw something or other in the window for ten pounds which he knew was worth far more than that so he went in and bought it. I can't remember what Becky said it was but whatever it was breakable and so the shop assistant wrapped it up in newspaper. When Edward got home he unwrapped whatever he'd bought and was about to dispose of the paper when something caught his eye. It was an

214

article about a local man who had won the Lottery and had bought an old inn in Cornwall where he was planning to make a new life for himself."

Charlie felt his face flush. "Me."

"Yes you. And Edward realised it was the very inn in which their goods were hidden. As soon as he'd read it he rang Tracey but got no reply which is hardly surprising because she'd 'lost' her phone by then."

Laura frowned. "But if Edward read about Charlie in a local paper he must have been in Buckinghamshire but the brothers said they live in Oxfordshire."

"You're right. I forgot that bit. Edward was there to meet an old girlfriend or something like that."

"Okay, so when Edward couldn't get hold of Tracey I assume he came down here to find her," said Laura.

"Yes, we believe Richard was away on holiday at the time so Edward came down to try and sort it out himself. But of course he couldn't go and knock on the door at Bracken Farm because that would mean telling Mickey who he was and why he was there. Anyway, one night after he'd been watching the farmhouse and seen the lights go out, he knew there was no chance of seeing Tracey and so he drove out here. He'd already been several times before according to the police because he wanted to find out how many were living here and what sort of routine you had."

"I knew it. I said we were being watched, didn't I, Charlie?"

"Yes, you did."

"So what happened next?" Daniel asked.

"Well the night in question was the night of the storm and while Edward was lurking around outside wondering if it'd be possible to get in here and take the stuff without you knowing, he heard a car stop further down the road so he hid behind a bush and watched to see who it was. He must have been very surprised to see it was Tracey and she was carrying recording equipment which she put down under the conifers..."

"...What!" interrupted Charlie, "so it was Tracey trying to scare us and not Mickey at all."

"Yes, it was."

"Well that makes sense," reasoned Laura, "because we always got the impression Mickey didn't want the bother of a health farm anyway."

"I can go along with that," agreed Ruby, "deep-down he always thought it a crackpot idea."

"So what happened next?" Florence was on the edge the sofa.

"Well, I assume Edward was intrigued as to what Tracey intended to do with the equipment. I know I would have been. Anyway, whatever, he watched to see what she did next and would you believe she went up to your back door and took down the holly wreath. I suppose Edward wondered why but he never did find out because both suddenly heard another car further down the road. It stopped and then Mickey appeared on the scene. He asked Tracey what she was doing and they had a blazing row but kept their voices low so as not to alert you. I know that because Tracey told Becky that was the case. However, it was not that low because Edward could hear and he heard her tell Mickey about the stuff stashed in the Inn and how she needed you gone, Charlie, so she could access it. Mickey was livid and called her an idiot. He then told her he was going to tell the police and turned to walk away. In a rage Tracey ran to the gatepost grabbed one of the owls and smashed Mickey on the back of his head. As he toppled over she ran off down the road fuming. Edward would have heard her car drive away and we assume he then went over to see how Mickey was. For having heard what had been said he obviously realised he was in a very tricky position. I mean, Mickey knew about the stolen goods and if he were to report it as he had threatened to do, he and Richard would be in deep trouble. I don't know what happened next but Edward has confessed and so we can only assume he picked up the owl and hit Mickey on the head until he stopped moving. Becky said the wreath Tracey must have dropped was found on Mickey's chest. I like to think Edward felt really bad over what he'd done and for that reason laid the wreath there. A way to ameliorate perhaps. A way to say he was sorry."

"Good gracious me, I suppose he then went home and had to act as though nothing had happened," said Laura.

"And when he arrived back here with Richard he had to fake shock when they heard of Mickey's death," tutted Charlie.

"Exactly," said Ruby, "but funnily enough even if he'd not confessed they might still have nailed him because it turns out the cigarette packet you found here, Charlie, had Edward's DNA on it. They hadn't bothered checking it before because they believed Tracey was guilty."

"Poor Mickey. So he wasn't trying to scare us at all," said Laura, "So sad."

"And had he not followed Tracey out here that night he'd still be alive," Charlie felt yet another pang of guilt.

The following morning the sun shone brightly, the temperature rose above freezing and the snow slowly began to thaw. Melting ice dripped from the gutters, railings and the branches of trees and shrubs and for the first time in several days Charlie did not need to defrost the bird bath.

In the afternoon a car pulled up on the cobbled area at Seven Pines. From it stepped Elderflower and Jiffy. As they approached the back door, Elderflower waved a sheet of A2 paper.

Seeing through the kitchen window that the two were all smiles, Laura rushed to the door to let them in. "You've found something out about the Villiers? I can tell by the expression on your faces."

217

"I most certainly have. Take a look at this," After wiping her feet on the doormat, Elderflower placed the paper on the kitchen table and unbuttoned her coat.

Laura, who was familiar with family trees studied the paper and then gasped. She sat down. "I don't believe it. Mickey Potts was a descendant of Septimus Villiers. I must call the others."

Florence and Daniel were upstairs chatting to a mutual friend on Skype and Charlie was in the sitting room lighting the fire. On hearing Laura call them from the hallway, all three entered the kitchen keen to hear the latest news.

"We rushed straight over with it because I'm going home later today," said Elderflower as Charles kissed her cheek while keeping his sooty hands behind his back.

"Oh, that's a shame," Laura sat back down at the table, "We shall miss you although of course I'll be going home myself in a few days' time. It's a pity you won't be here to see in the New Year though."

"I agree," said Charlie, "it is a shame and I shall really miss you. You've been good company this last couple of weeks." Charlie was surprised by the huge pang of disappointment he felt.

"Oh, thank you, that's very sweet of you both. It was my intention to stay to see in the New Year but before I came down here a very dear friend of mine said that should I wish to return early she was hosting a dinner party on New Year's Eve and she'd love it if I could be there. So I've decided to go home for that, but fear not for I shall soon be back and then I can spend every New Year's Eve at the Harbour Lights. You see, I've decided to sell up and move down here. Dad's house is enormous so there's plenty of room for little old me."

"And I couldn't be happier," acknowledged Jiffy, "It means I can stay put and won't have to go up-country to visit."

"You're not keen on travel then?" Charlie asked.

"Nope, I did enough of it when I was young. I've never liked driving and so now I'm happy to stay in Cornwall for the rest of my days and tend my garden. In fact I'd be quite happy to never cross the Tamar again."

"But what about your genealogy business?" Laura asked Elderflower.

"I can do that from here. I work from home anyway and Dad has the perfect room in his house to be my office."

After washing his sooty hands, Charlie tried to make sense of the family tree but after several minutes had to confess it was mumbo jumbo to him. "So if Mickey is related to Septimus then Septimus must have had children. I can't see where it says that."

Laura pointed to the tree. "Look, he and Beth had one son, John, born in 1817. It's the year Beth died so it's likely the poor soul died in childbirth as did Catherine. John was brought up by a sister who was probably the one who sold the Inn to Henry James Pengelly after Septimus died."

"So when Catherine Freathy met Septimus he was not only a widower but he had a son who was being brought up by his sister," said Florence, "Poor man. I should like to think that Catherine brought a bit of joy into his life."

"I'm sure she did," Elderflower pulled another sheet of paper from her bag, "I mean she must have been a nice person because her twin brother, William, was your ancestor."

"What! Are you sure?" Laura gasped.

"Without doubt. I was up into the early hours checking it out and William Freathy of Porthgwyns, Catherine's twin brother, was your great, great, great, great, great grandfather, Laura. Yours too of course, Charlie. What's more William went on to become a vicar like his father, as Catherine said, and his church is not too far from here. It's at Little Treverry."

"Little Treverry," said Charlie, "but that's out near Bracken Farm."

"Bracken Farm is at Treverry Cross," Laura reminded him, "but according to Cissy they're no distance from each other."

Elderflower nodded. "That's right. I've checked it out and it's only a small village. Just a church, a school and a few houses. It did have a pub but that closed twelve years ago and is now a house."

Chapter Twenty Seven

Early in the New Year all traces of snow had vanished. The bare apple trees looked lifeless in the orchard and all was quiet inside Seven Pines. For Laura had gone home, having vowed to return in the summer with her husband to help clear out the cellar. Daniel likewise was gone in order to prepare for his return to the school where he taught music and Florence was back at university. Before she went home, Laura, moved by the untimely deaths of Catherine and her five day old daughter, put flowers on their grave. They were after all distant relations and she wanted to keep their memories alive.

Two days after the last of his family had gone, Charlie in need of company ordered a taxi to Porthgwyns so he might visit the Harbour Lights. It was early evening and the pub was quiet but to his delight he was welcomed by a familiar face; Jiffy was celebrating the return of his paintings and other stolen goods.

"I'm really pleased for you," Charlie took a seat on a stool beside Jiffy at the bar, "So when did you get your things back?"

"This morning although I already knew they were found because the police rang a few days ago to tell me but they needed to hang on to them while they sorted everything out. It was quite a stash they found at the farmhouse in Plymouth so the Rudd brothers had been very busy boys."

"So did they get the two blokes who drove the stuff away?"

"Oh yes. I'm told they were watching TV when the police raided the place. They were arrested, the property searched and the goods found. DI Reynolds is delighted with the outcome and so is his boss."

"And you too no doubt."

"I couldn't be happier but at the same time I wish poor Mickey Potts was still here. He was a good bloke and Elderflower used to get on really well with Tracey. I think Tracey liked her because she thought she lived a glamourous lifestyle."

Ruby behind the bar heard what was said. "You know Tracey's out on bail."

"Is she? I'm really pleased to hear that," Jiffy's enthusiasm was genuine. Charlie's was likewise.

"In fact I saw her today when I went to the farm. Poor soul, she's a changed person. She's lost loads of weight and looks much older than her forty-five years. She told me she's turned a new leaf and when she's served her sentence, however long it might be, she intends to knuckle down and help on the farm. She said it's the only way she can make it up to Mickey."

"When does her case come up?" Charlie asked.

"Not sure but I hope it won't be too long because she needs to get it over and done with so she can move on."

"So what charges will she face?" Jiffy asked.

"Assault and aiding and abetting criminal activity. Something like that."

As the days grew longer, the weather warmed up and bulbs Charlie had planted in the back garden were in bloom. Daffodils nodded beneath the apple trees in the orchard, tulips, primroses and forget-me-nots bloomed in the trough where horses once drank and along the lane, bluebells, red campion and cow parsley flowered on the grass verges just as they had when Charlie walked up Wreckers Hill that very first time. The field beyond the orchard had been cleared and Ruby's brother Laurence, was in the throes of creating a wild flower meadow.

One sunny afternoon as Charlie sat outside thinking how grateful he was to have discovered the Inn, his thoughts turned to his late wife, Rachel. For several years her ashes had been confined indoors, yet she was someone who loved to feel the sun on her face and the wind in her hair. Charlie stood up; it was time to set her free. He went into the sitting room, picked up the urn and then scattered her ashes over the grass in the orchard. Knowing it was a dream of hers one day to have a swing dangling from the branch of an apple tree, he made up his mind to organise the installation of one in her memory.

As he replaced the lid on the empty urn her dying words came back to him 'Promise me you'll find someone else, Charlie because I can't bear to think of you alone for the rest of your life'. With her words ringing in his ears he returned indoors and rang Tom to ask about a swing.

Chapter Twenty Eight

In early June as Charlie sat in the back garden on the swing beneath a cloudless blue sky wondering if he should make elderflower champagne from the abundance of flowers everywhere as his mother had done when he was young, he heard a car drive slowly down the lane. Thinking it might be the postman with a parcel he was expecting, he walked around the house to see. The lower gates were open and a convertible car, its roof down, had driven in and was being parked on the cobblestones. The driver was Elderflower.

"Yay! You're back."

She switched off the engine. "Yes, I got completion on my house sale two days ago and arrived back here yesterday. So everything up-country is done and dusted now and Cornwall is my home."

He leaned forward, kissed her cheek and opened her car door. "Well, it's lovely to see you again and well...welcome home."

"Thank you. It's lovely to be back especially this time of year. A bit different to when I left."

"Hugely different. So what brings you to see me?"

"I have something for you," She stepped from the car, reached to the back seat and withdrew a large rectangular package encased in cardboard and tied with string, "It belongs to Dad but he insists you have it."

"Really! What is it?"

"Open it and you'll see." Elderflower removed the silk headscarf she wore to prevent her long hair tangling and dropped it onto the driver's seat of her car, "I sure you'll like it."

Charlie untied the string and removed the packaging. Inside was the portrait of two young people dressed in early nineteenth century clothing who looked very much alike. "Who are they? I feel I should know."

"Twins, Catherine and William Freathy. The date on the back is 1817 so they would have been sixteen when it was painted."

"What? No way! So this chap is my great, great, great, great, great grandfather who went on to become the vicar at Little Treverry?"

"Yes, and with him is his twin sister Catherine who was landlady here after she married Henry Pengelly. Albeit for only a short while."

"But how come your father has it? I'm confused."

"Would you believe the auction at the vicarage in Porthgwyns?"

Charlie laughed. "What, the famous auction where the antiques shop bought my grandfather clock, Tracey Potts bought the Bible and Ruby's mum bought her bike?"

"The very one. Dad said there were some smashing things there."

"So why was the stuff auctioned? I've been meaning to ask Ruby for some time. I mean, if the last vicar retired why didn't he take his belongings with him?"

"Because he died and left all he owned to the church to be sold in aid of the roof which I'm told is in need of extensive repair work."

"Oh, I see, and when the auctioneers cleared the place out they found the trunk containing the Bible in the attic."

"Yes."

"How about this painting then. I mean it couldn't have belonged to the last vicar so was that in the loft too?"

"No, it was hanging on the study wall along with other paintings and more recently photographs of Porthgwyns vicars and their families over the years."

"So the pictures were permanent fixtures like the kitchen sink."

"Yes, that's one way of putting it, I suppose. Your grandfather clock belonged to the church too along with a few pieces of very old furniture but everything was auctioned not only because funds were desperately needed but because the vicarage itself was to be sold and therefore needed to be emptied."

Charlie chuckled. "I see and the clock was probably a permanent fixture to make sure the clergymen were never late for services."

"Could well be. I hadn't thought of that."

Charlie looked down at the painting. "So if your dad bought this at the auction he hasn't had it for very long."

"No and for a while it was lost. It was amongst the things stolen from his place, you see. Which is weird because it means for some time it was back here, albeit hidden, inside what was for two years Catherine's former home."

"And none of us knew it was here," Charlie tried to read the signature, "So who painted it? I can't read the name."

"A local chap called Leonard Richardson. He painted lots of people from the area back in the early eighteen hundreds and they are held in high esteem. I've no idea who else he painted or where the paintings are now but Dad might know because he's into art and stuff like that."

"Well, it's beautiful and I'm lost for words," he kissed her cheek, "Thank you so much and please thank your dad too. I must buy him a pint when we're next in the pub. Meanwhile, I shall give it pride of place in my sitting room. In fact come on in and we'll decide where to hang it right now."

After much deliberation they finally hung the painting on the wall opposite one of the windows reasoning that by doing so it would enable Catherine to see out into the cobbled courtyard as she would have done two hundred years before. As they stepped back to admire their handiwork, the grandfather clock struck midday. Both listened in silence until the last chime faded.

"Weird to think that Catherine would have heard that clock ticking and heard its chimes when it stood at the vicarage," said Elderflower, "and now it's here along with her picture in a room she would have worked in as the wife of Henry Pengelly."

"And also where she would have met Septimus Villiers for the first time. I must take a photo of the picture and send it to Laura. She'll be fascinated."

"And while you do that I'll be very presumptuous and make us both coffee."

When the picture was sent and the coffee made they went back out into the garden.

"So what are you doing with yourself now the family are no longer here?"

"Oh, this and that. A bit of gardening. A bit of DIY."

"Do you ever get bored?"

"Sometimes, yes. It can get a bit lonely up here especially if it's wet."

"I think you ought to do bed and breakfast. It's a lovely spot. The air feels fresh and clean. Ideal for those who want to get away from it all."

"It's a nice idea and I have contemplated it often but I'm not sure that I want people walking around my home."

"Well, they'd not be in all the rooms and you needn't be open all the year round. If you want time off just say there are no vacancies. It's so easy these days as it can all be done on-line."

"That's true but do you really think people would like to stay here? I mean, there's a lovely beach just a stone's throw away but access to it is near impossible. I certainly wouldn't attempt to climb down the side of the cliff. It's far too steep and dangerous."

Elderflower folded her arms. "Yes, I firmly believe people would want to stay here and as for the beach, well

227

you have your own private access to that, Charlie. The tunnel."

"The tunnel! But surely no-one would want to go down there."

"Why not. Flo walked along it in the dark on a bitterly cold night after being drugged and she said the going was quite easy. Have you been along it yet?"

"Well, no, actually I haven't. Not all the way along that is. I went a few yards but it was December at the time and with snow on the ground the idea didn't appeal. Daniel went exploring though and was very impressed. In fact he said when he comes down during the summer holiday he'll bring his surf board."

"Good old Dan," Elderflower jumped up and then pulled Charlie to his feet. "Come on. Find a torch and we'll go and suss it out. I'm in the mood for adventure."

As they stepped into the tunnel Elderflower noted the time on her phone.

"Four minutes and thirty two seconds," she said as they reached the other end, "that's all it took us to get from the house to the beach. I think that's pretty good going."

"Is that all? I must admit I'm very impressed. Some parts looked a bit dodgy but if I'm going to have people walk along it I'll get it checked by a structural engineer to make sure it's safe."

"Yes, and it might be a good idea to install lighting of some sort."

"Good thinking. Save messing around with torches and so forth."

Charlie stepped onto the sand, walked down to the water's edge and looked back towards the cliffs. "The beach looks bigger down here than it does from up above. Not that you can see it very well unless on the cliff path."

"It's a lovely spot. Secluded too. I think it would appeal to lots of holidaymakers. I know it would me." Elderflower sat down on the sand and hugged her knees.

"And the house has history too," Charlie waved his arms, "Up there on the cliffs Mickey's great, great, great, great, great grandfather Septimus Villiers was killed while on horseback trying to escape arrest."

"And not far from the spot where poor Mickey also died."

"That's really sad and I know you'll think me bonkers but Becky asked if it'd be alright to occasionally put flowers on the spot where he died. Of course I said yes and to make it easier I've gouged out a hole in the tree stump and placed an old vase in it so it doesn't topple over and we've agreed to take it in turns to leave flowers. I'm really pleased because I had thought of going to Porthgwyns and putting them on his grave in the churchyard but I don't think his spirit is there. I reckon it's here with his ancestor, Septimus Villiers," Charlie laughed, "That's silly though because I don't really believe in ghosts. Never have and never shall although I must admit when I think about Mickey I feel sort of peaceful, as though he's around. Which I wish he was."

"I believe in ghosts."

"But it's all in the mind surely."

"Maybe, but I think this place is magical, enchanting, special," as Charlie sat down beside her, she took his hands in hers and squeezed them tightly. "I believe in fate too. I mean, it was on this beach that Septimus Villiers and Catherine Freathy met in secret and here we are brought together through their history on their beach all these years later."

Charlie's eyes sparkled. "Mickey said he hoped I'd find a nice lass down here to keep me company – his words, not mine – perhaps you are she."

"You are she! What sort of language is that, Charlie Everton?"

"I've no idea where that came from. It must be the influence of ghosts from the past," Charlie frowned, "It's just a thought, but you're not by any chance known as Crazy Chris are you?"

"Who?"

"Crazy Chris. Mickey said she might be a good partner for me. I've never met her or heard anyone other than Mickey mention her but apparently she collects compasses. Ones that tell you which way to go, not mathematical ones."

Elderflower threw back her head and laughed. "That'll be Christabel Bray. She's not crazy at all except when it comes to horses. I know her quite well and we often go out together for a ride when I'm visiting Dad. She owns and runs the stables with her partner at Treverry Cross and I know there was always a lot of banter between her and Mickey and she was really upset when he died."

"So who is her partner? Anyone I know?"

"Probably not as neither are really pub goers. Her partner is also her fiancée and they got engaged last week. Dilly Prescott she's called and a nicer couple of ladies you could not wish to meet."

"Dilly. Fiancée. Oh, I see. Silly Mickey. He made a bit of a bloomer there then."

"Yes, he did, I'll tell Chris next time I see her. That'll make her laugh," Elderflower sprang to her feet and pulled Charlie up from the sand, "Come on, let's go back to the house and make plans for your bed and breakfast business. If we get it up and running now you could have your first guests before the summer is out."

"Okay, but will you help me run it? I'll buy you chocolates. Please say yes."

"There's nothing I'd enjoy more, Charlie. And I mean being with you. Not eating chocolates."

As they walked hand in hand, chattering and laughing towards the caves, a sudden gust of wind ruffled the flowers on the old tree stump. The label left by Becky fluttered in the wind until it broke free; it then floated down onto the beach and settled on the sand in front of Charlie. A large smile crossed his face as he picked it up and saw the message. It simply quoted Mickey's favourite phrase: *Where there is love, there is happiness.*

THE END

Printed in Great Britain
by Amazon